BENT

HEAVƎNS

ALSO BY DANIEL KRAUS

The Monster Variations

Rotters

Scowler

Trollhunters (with Guillermo del Toro)

*The Death and Life of Zebulon Finch, Volume One:
At the Edge of Empire*

*The Death and Life of Zebulon Finch, Volume Two:
Empire Decayed*

The Shape of Water (with Guillermo del Toro)

Blood Sugar

BENT
HEAVENS

DANIEL KRAUS

Henry Holt and Company

New York

Henry Holt and Company, *Publishers since 1866*
Henry Holt® is a registered trademark of Macmillan Publishing Group, LLC
120 Broadway, New York, NY 10271 • fiercereads.com

Poems and excerpts from *Resurrection Update*, including those used for all section titles, are
printed with the permission of James Galvin.

Library of Congress Cataloging-in-Publication Data
Names: Kraus, Daniel, 1975– author.
Title: Bent heavens / Daniel Kraus.
Description: First edition. | New York : Henry Holt and Company, 2020. | Summary: Two
years after the disappearance of her father, seventeen-year-old Liv and her friend capture an
alien in the Iowa countryside, and instead of turning him over to the authorities, they choose
a different path.
Identifiers: LCCN 2019018801 | ISBN 9781250151674 (hardcover)
Subjects: | CYAC: Extraterrestrial beings—Fiction. | Torture—Fiction. | Conspiracies—
Fiction. | High schools—Fiction. | Schools—Fiction.
Classification: LCC PZ7.K8672 Be 2020 | DDC [Fic]223
LC record available at https://lccn.loc.gov/2019018801

Our books may be purchased in bulk for promotional, educational, or business use. Please
contact your local bookseller or the Macmillan Corporate and Premium Sales Department at
(800) 221-7945 ext. 5442 or by email at MacmillanSpecialMarkets@macmillan.com.

First edition, 2020 / Designed by Rich Deas and Mallory Grigg
Printed in the United States of America
10 9 8 7 6 5 4 3 2 1

Dedicated to

Joe Adam, Craig Brown, Matt Nelson, Jami Shipman

& Scott Slechta

And then it happened.

Amidst cosmic busting and booming

Gravity snapped,

That galactic rack and pinion.

Trees took off like rockets.

Cemeteries exploded.

The living and the dead

Flew straight up together.

Only up was gone. Up was away.

Earth still spun

As it stalled and drifted darkward,

Sublime,

An aspirin in a glass of water.

JAMES GALVIN, "RESURRECTION UPDATE"

FIRST STANZA:

ITALICS MINE

1.

LIV HEARD THE TOWN-HALL BELL GONG
seven times. Everyone knew it was ten minutes slow, which meant
twenty minutes until school started. Plenty of time. She stepped off
Hamilton Avenue, out of the shadow of the old J. C. Penney building and into the sun-splash of Washington Street. She was joined
by ten or fifteen other morning plodders, students bearing packs of
schoolwork and adults feeding meters before keying open Dittman's
Pharmacy, Bob's Shoe Barn, or First American Bank.

A flagpole stood at the northeast corner of the square. By habit,
Liv knocked on it as she passed. She heard the flag snap like wet
laundry, but for once did not look up at it, for she was a freshman
and had been walking this route for weeks now, and sensed right off
something awry at the southern edge of the town square. Everyone
else had stopped to look as well. That Liv could only see the backs of
heads—no faces—was itself unsettling.

A person had entered the square from the center of Jackson Street, a trajectory that only made sense if you'd emerged from the alley between Wilson Hardware and McAllister's Insurance, and why would you do that? Also strange: The person was pink. You didn't wear pink that early on a Tuesday—not in Bloughton, Iowa, population seven thousand, you didn't.

The person was pink because the person was naked.

He was a man, evident from how his genitals jounced with each lurching step. Walkers stopped walking. Schedules were forgotten. No one ran away, but neither did anyone run toward. The naked man's presence was so jarring amid the sweet birdsong and swishing trees that it was difficult to accept. Only Liv headed for him. Already she could feel in her veins the thrush of urgency.

By the time Liv had trampled through flowers and skidded to a stop in the dewy lawn ten feet from the man, one onlooker had screamed, as if hoping the noise might assure the lot of them they hadn't all gone mad. It worked: People moved. They were Iowans, luckless farmers, withstanders of bankruptcies, witnesses of machine accidents. They knew how to absorb shocks. A mustached guy approached the naked man. A woman stammered to a 911 dispatcher on her phone. An older gent limped up with a cane, coat outstretched, offering to cover the man's nudity.

The old gent succeeded on his third try, the first two times the coat sliding from the man's convulsing shoulders. It gave time for all present to memorize details that, over the next three years, would become local legend.

There was no indication why the man was naked. His chest was dirty. His calves were crisscrossed with underbrush scratches. His feet should have been bleeding, from rocks if not alleyway glass, except that he wore black dress socks—his only item of clothing. A fantastic detail for sure, though itself not enough to guarantee infamy; a few years back, a football play in neighboring Monroeville had been whistled dead when a young man, drunk and dared, had streaked the length of the field, and a week later it was old news.

What held everyone breathless was the man's behavior. His eyes were fish-wide, defenseless against both sun and cottonwood fluff. He jerked about as if being encircled by a threatening mob. Strands of spit swayed from his bottom lip. His upper lip curled back to reveal clenched teeth. Whines escaped, broken by tongue-tangled babbles. Finally, there was his knee-juddering stagger, as if the planet were fracturing beneath his socked feet. Liv felt it too, the loss of footing. There was no stabilizing flagpole within her reach.

"It's Mr. Fleming," someone said.

Had it come from a schoolgirl? The old guy with the coat? Bob of Bob's Shoe Barn? Or was it all of them, a choir of condemnation, shaming Liv for not making the identification herself? Whatever had led Lee Fleming to this state of degradation, she should have known about it, because Lee Fleming, in addition to being Bloughton High's senior English teacher for twenty-five years, and the director of every school play, speech competition, and community theater production for the past three decades, was also Liv's dad.

Her intestines knotted. She dropped to her knees and felt the dew soak through her leggings. The person closest to her in the world had been turned inside out. The flagpole was clanging again.

No, it was her heart, transformed into a hammer, driving her into the ground.

Liv was, in fact, mortified she hadn't recognized him first, though, in her defense, he was barely recognizable, stripped of his usual cardigan sweater, ironed slacks, and wire-frame glasses. Naked, he looked underdeveloped, even fetal. As the old man's coat closed around him and Liv heard sirens from the direction of the hospital, her dad's stabbing jabbers shifted to moist inhales and explosive, snotty sobs, noises louder and cruder than any she'd ever heard him make.

The actual event did not exceed five minutes. The hospital, like everything else in Bloughton, enjoyed a direct route to the town center, and an ambulance was the second thing to violate the square that day, rollicking over the curb and bouncing up the sidewalk, chewing up pretty green grass and ejecting two EMTs. They were all over Lee Fleming before Liv, still on her knees and struggling to breathe, could find the courage to reach him. They hoisted his forty-eight-year-old body of soft, but clenched, muscles onto a stretcher.

Certainly they would have beckoned Liv, the man's only child, into the ambulance if they'd known she was there. The medics began administering to her dad before he was even strapped down, and the last thing Liv saw was his limbs thrashing, spittle geysering, all ten fingers pointing at his wet, matted chest hair.

"Biologic evidence!"

They were the first words he'd managed.

The doors slammed, and the ambulance hopped the curb, surging the wrong way down Hamilton, its siren no match for the happy birds, its swirling red lights gulped up by the cheerful sun. Liv pivoted in the grass, knees muddying, and watched, thinking there was other biologic evidence here, the provable kind, that tied the raving, naked lunatic to the gasping, kneeling girl.

At least her dad was home, after four days missing.

Eight months and six days later, he would vanish forever.

2.

BONE CRACKED AGAINST GLASS. LIV
sucked air, wobbly, sick. She'd chased the ambulance and fought her
way through the back doors, only for it to overturn when it took a
corner too fast, and the sound was her bones, or her dad's bones,
shattering hypodermics. No—she was lying down, and it was wet.
The dewy grass? No, the wet was sweat. Was she in bed? Yes. In bed.
The dream again. That terrible memory, ending this time with a fic-
titious crash. The memory was never going to leave her alone.

The knock again, steady as a woodpecker's. Right: It was Sunday.
And not just any Sunday—the last Sunday before senior year began.
She'd been waiting for this week for so long. Liv opened her eyes to
the fiberglass ceiling panels her dad had installed eight years ago,
once upon a time cloud white but now tawny with water damage.
Orange was the closest color, given the quality of sun at that hour,
which was, of course, seven in the morning. Her father's hour—
seven would always be her father's hour.

For the third time, a hard knuckle against her window. The visitor's shadow was cast across the same ceiling at which she stared, not that she needed the shadow to recognize Doug. All week, her excitement to begin her last year at Bloughton High had allowed her, deliciously, to forget the pains of the past. But Sunday always came; so did Doug; so did the memories.

"Doug." She hated the whine in her voice. "Can't you be late for once?"

"Love you, too," Doug said from outside. "I'm going to steal some food, cool?"

Liv sat up and rubbed at the pillow grooves in her cheeks. Her tank top was soaked to her back. She grimaced, distraught like a child who'd wet the bed, and angry, too, for being unable to quit doing it. She peeled herself of damp clothes and kicked through the multicolored mess on her floor for sweatpants.

John, a mud-colored sheepdog mutt of advanced age, struggled to his feet and followed Liv through the house, his claws clicking across scratched hardwood, dull linoleum, and broken tile, and then through the front door. Across the skinny dirt road awaited a mundane panorama of nothing of note: undeveloped farmland stretched into the horizon, thin groves of overgrown trees, and just visible off to the east, a single hill topped with Major Dawkins's former place.

The major had once uttered the only inspirational phrase Liv valued: *Be the tallest you can.*

She spoke this charm to herself, attempting to draw her spine tall and straight, forcing the muscles of her torso to tighten and her eyes to open fully. Only after she'd built the best Liv she was going to get at this odious hour, she shifted her eyes left to the sight she knew would try its best to depress her.

Doug stood in the yard shoving an untoasted Pop-Tart into his face. The disheartening vision fit into the yard's ambience: a cemetery of dead saplings her dad had planted that, since his disappearance, no one had bothered to nurse. The sunrise, by contrast, was a great one, an electric tangerine that coaxed feathered textures from silver clouds. Doug, however, stared at the dirt, as he always did, as if there was something with his neck that hindered looking upward at what the world had to offer.

"You could at least close the cabinets," Liv said. "Every Sunday it looks like we were robbed."

Doug shrugged. Crumbs clung to the greasy tendrils of his shoulder-length hair. John snuffled at the ground for bits.

"Aggie doesn't mind," he said. "If she was up, she'd say, *Go hog wild, Doug.*"

Doug called her mom Aggie and had called her father Lee, a familiarity no other friend of hers had achieved. Liv felt her annoyance soften. She looked where Doug looked, at the dirt, and kicked at an anthill.

"She's never up, though, is she?" she asked.

Liv sighed, bothered by her early-morning urge to criticize Doug. She knew the kitchen cabinets at his house were empty. He didn't eat meals, mostly surviving off trail mix he made from ingredients he bought in military bulk—almonds, peanuts, pine nuts, sunflower seeds, raisins, and dried cranberries. It was a trait he'd picked up from Liv's dad in his final months. All day long, to the ridicule of class-

8

mates, Doug pulled feed from baggies he kept in the side pockets of the same army-green shorts he wore every day regardless of season. It didn't help that he insisted on using the hikers' term for trail mix, *gorp*, which was too close to *dork* for anyone to resist.

Doug didn't react well to sympathy; he eyed it like a snake he hoped would slither away. In fact, he behaved in ways that invited scorn, as if more comfortable with that emotion. He got to school late, slept through obligations, forgot to shower for days on end. Yet he was never, ever late for their Sunday morning ritual. His fealty to it was a fist that squeezed her heart. She was afraid of what he'd do if she ended the ritual—which is what she wanted to do more than anything.

"You sure you want to do this?" It was as far as she dared. "We could go back inside. I can do better than Pop-Tarts."

"Don't be lazy," he admonished. "You got the screwdriver?"

She held it up with the speed of an eye roll. He saluted the tool and indicated the clear plastic grocery bag tied to one of his belt loops. It was filled, as ever, with John's poop, a week's worth collected from the yard. Here it was, the day before her last year at Bloughton High, and this, ladies and gents, was her life: not blitzing through last-second school shopping with Monica and the gang, but perpetuating a fanaticism that, if anyone ever learned of it, would brand her as loony tunes as her dad. It meant everything to Doug, so she did it for him, in gratitude for the years when he'd been all she'd had.

She stowed the screwdriver in her pocket and set off for the backyard. She was tired and grumpy, but forced herself to smile; Monica said she'd read online that smiling actually forces your brain to be happier. Right then, something about the light reminded her of a walk she and Doug had taken when they were short enough to breeze beneath these same branches.

"Remember when we walked to the firehouse?" she asked.

"Those guys were jerks," Doug said through his last bite of Pop-Tart.

The backyard was in shoddier shape than the front. The push mower had rotted where it had died, searing the grass with gasoline. The swing set's collapse had contorted it into a briar of sharp steel. All over, there were piles. How else to say it? Piles of brick, piles of plank wood, piles of buckets. No one remembered why Lee had piled them. The grass had become shin-high bracken and knee-high sedge, a jungle gym from which ticks swung until they found John's belly.

"They were perfectly nice firemen," Liv said.

"They came at us with axes!"

"They were *holding* axes. They were firemen. Firemen hold axes. They just weren't used to kids showing up with a list of demands."

Doug chuckled. Now Liv's forced smile became real. The firehouse visit was the kind of jaunt that had made knowing the younger Doug Monk such a thrill. Doug was the best kid to play with; he always arrived armed with multiple proposals of stuff to do, each so original they made their sleepy Iowa burg feel like a place where incredible things happened all the time.

All kids heard things—from their families, on the playground. Only Doug took rumors as dares. *Liv, did you hear there was a barn on Sycamore where a guy built a "monster" from dead-animal parts? They say he lets people see it for a few bucks! Liv, did you hear about the guy who used to live above Fielder's Auto? He robbed graves. You think we should sneak up there and see if we can find anything cool?*

"There was a dude buying firecrackers from my dad once." Doug spoke in the animated voice Liv alone in the world got to hear. "And he said he used to be a volunteer firefighter, and he *swore* the firehouse had a chunk of meteor."

"I'm just saying," Liv said, "who would even believe that? I didn't think it could be real."

"A meteor hitting Bluefeather Prison? Why wouldn't that be real?"

Liv laughed, and the happy sound helped, now that they had waded halfway into the backyard. John held back. It was dangerous out there; his old master had taught him that. He whined, lay down by the door, and watched Liv, the closest thing he had now to a master, walk straight toward what he sensed was still a bad place.

What the homes at Bloughton's outskirts lacked in stores, gas stations, and reliable cell coverage they made up for in real estate. The backyard was a third of a football field long, the back half of which was nearly vacant. In the far southeast corner of the backyard was Lee's shed, a storage facility for gardening tools until the day he stumbled naked onto the town square. After that, he began to fill it with tools of a different kind.

The cobwebs over the shed's door were as thick as boards.

Even Doug knew better than to talk about it. He leaned into good-mood joshing.

"And what did we learn that day?" he asked in the voice of a snooty professor.

"Firemen hate kids?"

"That they had the meteor! Right there in a glass case like the firecracker dude said!" He shook his head hard enough for his greasy whips of hair to sway. "Man, no one ever believes me about shit."

A flimsy fence marked the southern border of the yard, though Lee had used wire cutters to expedite passage. Liv went first into the thicket, hoping her mood could survive it. It couldn't. The coolness of the shade made her grinning lips go cold. Jokes and nostalgia might get them through this Sunday excursion, and the next, and the next, twelve more months before she escaped to college. Was letting this continue mercy or cowardice? Because each Sunday hurt her, which meant each Monday was spent building herself back into the Liv Fleming that Monica and the others expected.

"Speaking of firecrackers . . . Mr. Tooney, Angie Tooney's dad? He came out Tuesday. I guess there's some anniversary party? Anyway, Mr. Tooney definitely did his research because he was like, 'Give me five girandolas, five roman candles, two chrysanthemums, two flying fish, and one giant peony.' He had this envelope of cash he tried to give me before I even told him what I had in stock. He acted like he was buying coke. He wasn't even listening to the safety instructions."

There was one reason Bloughton didn't wipe Doug's family from its mind. Unless you wanted to truck your ass to the Missouri line, the Monks were it when it came to illegal fireworks. They were stored in a separate garage, the only building on the Monk property kept watertight, air-conditioned, locked, and free of critters, and because Doug's dad set the prices, Doug had no room to haggle. It also meant he had no leeway to deny kids who forked over insults along with payment. Liv hadn't been to Doug's place in years and was glad. She couldn't stomach the notion that the Fleming household had caught up to the Monks'.

"I think he was nervous because he had this little boy with him. I think he was worried the kid would say the wrong thing at the party and expose him as an illegal-fireworks-buying criminal and he'd end up serving life in prison, hard labor. People are so dumb."

Fireworks sales were what kept the lights on and the toilet flushing. Doug's dad, a trucker, touched down in Bloughton six or seven times a year to dole out truck-stop trinkets and drop off fireworks gathered from across the country. He'd stay for a couple of weeks before getting itchy for the road and his various girlfriends. Doug's mom had never been in the picture. The only role model Doug had ever had was Lee Fleming. Now all he had was Lee's memory. Liv carried the responsibility of that, which was why she was here, kicking through stickerbush at dawn.

"So the kid starts crying how he wants to see something explode, and Mr. Tooney definitely didn't want this kid crying all day about it, so he asked if I could just shoot something off for an extra twenty. And I was like, 'It's two in the afternoon, man, you won't be able to see anything,' but he was practically begging. I didn't want to burn good fireworks no one could see, but remember when I cleaned out my car?"

Two years of Sunday safaris had tramped a thin trail through the woods. Liv banked right at the dry gulley, circled a towering black ash, and ducked under a marquee of threaded branches, eyes squinted for the flash of metal that marked their first stop.

"I found a flare in the back seat. I didn't know I had a flare. So I said, 'Here, how about I shoot this?' and Mr. Tooney said fine, and I did it, and we could even see it for a second. Pretty boring, but the kid liked it, and then they left, and I went back to my game, and then like an hour later I smell smoke and I look outside and there it was. A fire. You know that field of dry grass across the road? There's this whole line of fire where I guess the flare went down. I almost shit."

Liv looked over her shoulder at Doug. He was talking past gorp, grinning to his tale. Doug was on the short side, but not bad-looking, with a fox face and shoulder-length black hair so thick you couldn't see scalp, not even when wind split it. In middle school he'd bought dumbbells at a garage sale and, in classic Doug fashion, committed to a workout routine of pointless rigor, developing tennis-ball biceps while ignoring every other muscle of his body. Today, and nearly every day, he wore a sleeveless T-shirt to show off his arms.

"I went out there to stomp it but it was too big and I only had flip-flops, so I had to call the fire department. I'm not even kidding. They asked what happened, and I couldn't remember if I'd sold fireworks to any of them before, so I said I didn't know. But I must've sold one of them something, because he covered up for me and said it was probably lightning. I spent the whole next day out there making sure there weren't pieces of flare I had to hide. I don't need the FBI on my ass. Now I'm out a flare and my flip-flops are melted. Fucking sucks, man."

Doug pointed, his preposterous biceps flexing, as if Liv didn't know exactly, precisely, down-to-the-square-foot where they were headed. She faced front again, though her eyes dragged behind. Looking upon this ugly metal contraption hidden in the woods was as close as she got to looking at the corpse of her father.

3.

IT WAS A TRAP. TRAP ONE, AS LEE FLEMING called it, or, when stirred by the fever of creation, Amputator. Based on the centuries-old model used by fur trappers, it was a stainless-steel spring-loaded set of jaws chained to a tree trunk that, when triggered by pressure upon the center plate, would snap shut, its triangular teeth driving into both sides of the trespasser's leg. Whether the prey was fox, coyote, bobcat, raccoon, or possum, the pain would make it pull, digging the trap's teeth in deeper, tearing tendon and muscle until the animal could only try to gnaw off its own leg.

How many hundreds of times had Liv looked at this thing that Lee had hammered, jointed, screwed, soldered, and sharpened in the shed? And still she flushed with shame. If the rust blotches and the weeds threaded through the spring eye were real, and they were, then everything else had to be real, too, from her father's original town-square calamity to his plunge into delusion, paranoia, psychosis, and sickness.

Amputator was only the first of six traps Lee had placed at cunning intervals across the thicket, each one guarding an avenue of approach to the house. Reproducing a single trap design six times would have taken less effort, but who was to say which sorts of traps would be effective against his alleged abductors? He was determined to cover his bases. He'd rather die, he'd often said, than be dragged back into their hellish realm.

Trap Two, Hangman's Noose, was the simplest and, when triggered, the most dramatic. Constructed from wood Lee had sawed from nearby trees (to ensure that it smelled native to the location), the trap did, in fact, resemble an archetypal hanging post. It was tripped by a wire noose hidden in the grass. A camouflage-painted cinderblock acted as counterweight, so that when the wire cinched tight, the weight would sink and the boom would spring upward, and the prey would find itself dangling upside down.

Trap Three, Crusher, was brutality incarnate and scary to manage. A six-hundred-pound log studded with nails, each one sharpened to a point by Lee's diamond-stone file, hung ten feet in the air from a galvanized reeling cable wound through a mountaineer's carabiner to serve as its own trip wire. It was the only trap never to have gone off and that was lucky. Liv doubted that she and Doug could hoist the log back into place.

Trap Four, Hard Passage, was the only trap featuring bait, a stiff wad of Lee's unwashed clothing that, when the wind was right, still gave Liv a whiff of her dad's smell. It was a cage trap, the sort park rangers used to capture live animals, and the enemies of Lee's imagination would have to crawl inside it. This would disrupt a magnetic field and a guillotine-style door would drop. The only option then would be to move forward through a series of sharp, slanted rods that turned even an inch of retreat into a flesh-rendering nightmare.

Trap Five, Neckbreaker, was the woods' most elegant killer. It was a standard conibear trap blown up man-sized, two rectangular steel frames that sliced shut like a scissors when an invader passed through them, which anyone choosing this route would do, Lee said, since Neckbreaker was positioned beneath a fallen tree that was easier to duck under than clamber over.

Trap Six, Abyss, was Lee's tour de force of despair. Constructed beneath a fake "path" he'd created for the sole purpose of duping intruders into taking it—the path led nowhere—it was a seven-foot pit covered with a polyethylene sheet propped up by delicate braces, atop which, in each Sunday's most laborious task, Doug and Liv styled dirt, pebbles, moss, and sticks to fabricate a natural-looking forest floor. If you stepped on it, you'd fall, and the pit's floor was covered with dozens of punji spikes, which was why Doug brought the bag of John's feces. He dumped it over the spikes so that any delivered wounds would become infected.

Lee Fleming was the gentlest man you'd ever meet. Everyone in town said as much. Liv tried to remember that.

The illegality of this line of defense was as flagrant as it was moot. No one had any reason to wend their way through this half-mile arc of trees, though were some lost soul to do so, he might be seriously injured, if not killed. Liv's whole face was cold now. She thought, as she did every Sunday, that she might never smile again. Each of Lee's traps screamed insanity. How could Doug not see that?

Doug stepped past Liv, holding out a hand for the screwdriver, which she placed into it like a surgeon's scalpel. He knelt alongside Amputator and set it off with the screwdriver, just to make sure everything worked. Then he levered the shank of the tool until the steel jaws yowled apart. Loosen the spring neck. Pry the jaws flat. Fix the trigger. Liv hissed. There was always a second when Doug got close to getting maimed. More than a second, really. A full minute, a full day, a year, a lifetime. One of these days he'd be torn apart.

"Check out this rust," he said. "We need to soak this in oak bark. It needs re-dyed. It needs re-waxed, too."

It needs removed, Liv thought. *Destroyed, junked, smelted.*

He was up, smearing dirty hands on his shorts, taking the lead down the trail. Liv was hit by a surge of courage. Quick, before they reached the next trap, say something, break through the facade that everything about this was okay.

"How come you . . . like this so much?"

There, she said it. To his back, yes, but still. Doug's gait didn't change.

"*Like?* I *like* kung fu movies and porn. This is just something we gotta do, Liv."

"But . . . you know. It's a project. You like projects."

"Tell that to my Ds and Fs."

"But, like, the corn mazes."

Doug laughed once, bitterly.

"That was a long, long, long time ago."

It didn't seem that long ago to Liv. It was no coincidence that it'd been Lee who'd taken Liv and Doug, both ten years old, to Lomax County, where an industrious farmer had carved into his corn a thirty-acre maze in the shape of Abraham Lincoln. Liv thought there had been something sinister about the endless corners, intersections, and roundabouts, all while corn leaves shivered as if the stalks were snickering at her. As the sun began to set, only her dad's held hand prevented Liv from sprinting a straight line through the corn until she came out somewhere, anywhere.

Doug, though, had fallen in love. His father supplemented trucking and fireworks income by renting out fifteen acres of family-owned land on the other side of town, which he called the Monk Block. Most of it was being farmed for corn and, to Doug, that was proof enough of destiny. Maybe his wouldn't be the world's biggest corn maze, but who cared about biggest? The Monk Block Corn Maze would be the best.

On paper as small as napkins and as big as the backs of posters, Doug sketched hundreds of mazes. Early designs came in obvious shapes: skull and crossbones, a snake, the X-Men logo. Year by year, they evolved and refined. Doug became a connoisseur of confusion. Never much of a reader before, he checked out library books about patterns that challenged human perception.

Go slowly, Liv told herself. *Build up to it.* She raised her voice. "There was some pattern you used? To confuse people?"

"The Ebbinghaus illusion," Doug said instantly. "Tricks the mind into confusing relative size." He chuckled. "And then I blended it with the Ponzo illusion and the Hermann grid. Man, I would have had people lost for *days*."

He sounded too gleeful about this, but Liv couldn't blame him. People were shitty to Doug—folks who bought fireworks, kids at school, staff at stores who just didn't like the look of him. Of course he imagined them all trapped inside some brilliant labyrinth of his own design.

"What did you call it? All the patterns together? The Prank?"

"The *Trick*." He sounded irritated that she'd forgotten, even though, seconds ago, he'd been the one to claim that he'd all but forgotten it. "That's the thing about most mazes. They were such massive suck-ups. 'Oh, here's a big Abe Lincoln head.' 'Here's a salute to our stupid military.' Mazes are ancient. There's mazes carved on prehistoric bones. You gotta respect that. I used ancient runes and mathematic fractals in mine. That stuff is pure."

"I remember one of yours shaped like a spider. Real pure, Doug."

"It was! Humans are hardwired to fear things with long legs. I read that."

The conversation was as difficult as Liv had feared. She knew Hangman's Noose was just around the bend, yet wondered if she'd gotten that wrong, for it felt like the trap had slipped behind her and dropped its noose around her throat, slowly stealing her air as she walked.

"I'm just saying," Liv said, "that you left all that behind. Maybe, you know, maybe now's the time . . ."

"I didn't leave it behind. No one was *with* me on it. You certainly never liked it."

Now he was mad. It could happen that quick with Doug, and though she knew she had to stay firm, she heard herself backpedaling.

"That's not true. I thought it was really—"

"It is true, Liv. I tried to come up with ways for you to be involved."

This was bullshit, but just what Liv needed. Irritability fired from her brain, and she could almost see it, a cigarette lighter spark.

"Yeah, you told me I could sell tickets to the haunted house off the side. Sell cider and corndogs at the snack bar. Perfect for the little woman. Gee, thanks."

He stopped with an underbrush crunch and looked back at her. As quick as Doug could be to anger, he was even quicker to be hurt. His startled, wet-eyed look of betrayal made Liv feel awful, all at once, because what she'd said was unfair. Back when he'd made that offer, it'd been because Liv, scared of corn mazes, had been nervous about Doug's enthusiasm.

And what had happened after that? Doug's cardboard tubes of mazes had disappeared, and it had been her fault. Maybe if she'd supported him more, he'd still be working on those harmless plans instead of having shifted his energy to the absurdity of maintaining Lee Fleming's traps.

"That's not true," Doug said softly. "And you know it."

His eyes swept downward, rather pitifully, and he continued on, his bare knees not lifting quite so high now, the bag of poop on his belt not flopping so vigorously.

By the time she caught up to him, he should have been resetting Hangman's Noose. Instead, he was staring, and her stomach clenched. At least once a month it happened, and naturally it had to happen today: an animal caught. The Iowa timber was rife with underbrush scurriers that, unlike Lee's intended targets, actually existed. Liv didn't like to picture all the dead or dying animals they'd extracted.

They was the wrong word. It was Doug who did the deed while Liv squinted through the protective slats of her lashes. Today it was only a squirrel—*only*, as if that minimized the suffering, and suffering was what it was doing, the wire pulled tight around its tiny neck, its four feet scrabbling midair. The noose was designed for a bigger creature and hadn't cinched tight enough for a clean kill.

How many hours had the squirrel been hanging here? How many days? Doug glanced at Liv, his jaw jutted against reproach, and took the squirrel by the midsection, loosening the wire with the screwdriver and sliding the animal free. Doug stepped over to the oak tree he'd used for this very purpose so many times Liv could see the scarred bark, and brought the squirrel back for the head blow that would kill it.

Doug hesitated, waiting for Liv to turn away. She always did. But today she couldn't. She'd had a chance this morning to change things and had blown it. As screwed up as Doug's trapping and killing was, he did it out of love—for Lee, yes, but also for her. So her apology was this: not turning away. Liv would try again next week. Or the week after that. Surely she would.

Doug smiled, just a twitch of the lips, before whipping the squirrel forward in a brown blur. The snap of its head was crisp, and without pausing, Doug tromped past the tree and off the trail into brambles, because you had to bury animals away from the devices that killed them. That was just smart hunting.

Liv watched him disappear, then turned back to Hangman's Noose. She could reset the trap. She knew how. It would be a nice gesture. She hunkered down, took hold of the snare, and pulled against the weight. Two years had passed since her dad had vanished, but his traps, all six of them, still worked. Just look at the creature they'd trapped today. Look at her try to gnaw her leg free, silly thing. The creature's name was Liv Fleming.

4.

IT TOOK TWENTY MINUTES TO GET TO
senior year's first calamity. After parking her dad's too-recognizable
station wagon far from the building, the first nineteen minutes were
everything Liv had dreamed about. This was the thirteenth first day
of school of Liv's life, and the exhilaration of knowing it to be the
final one for her and her friends could only be countered by blatant
coolness. When Monica fist-bumped Liv hello, Monica was imper-
sonating the jittery theatrics of the younger classes. Liv took the cue,
and, while hugging Krista, who'd been out of state all summer, she
did so with a bored yawn that made Krista laugh.

"We're so over this," Krista said.

"We're doing the teachers a favor," Liv agreed. "Don't want to
hurt their feelings."

Darla and Phil swung by, Phil's hand already in Darla's back
pocket, placing his usual bet that no teacher wanted conflict on the

first day of school, thereby setting the precedent that Phil could have his hand on Darla's ass all year. Darla kiss-kissed at Liv, who made a facetious yuck face and tossed the kiss back.

Then Laurie, Amber, and Hank descended upon them in a sheet of excited shouts and hugs so forceful Liv could not tell who she was hugging at any given second. Except maybe Hank, whose hug was quick; the one-night sexual encounter she'd had with Hank last year still hadn't fully shed its awkwardness. The whole gang's coolness, so perfectly drawn a few minutes ago, broke apart, and they yielded to it. It was thrilling, being at the edge of whatever came after.

When the group began to disassemble to find their lockers and unload their stuff, Liv found Krista still clinging to her with two adamant fists.

"Just once, and then I won't mention it again," Krista said. "Just doing my fall check."

Liv sighed to convey that this wasn't necessary, but in truth felt a deep gratitude. Liv was a relative newcomer to this crowd (sports girls, mostly, and the guys who liked them) and sometimes still felt like a fraud: Hank and Phil going on about some grade school prank they'd pulled on an old friend of Liv's, or Monica, when she was feeling bitchy, celebrating old times with the others without letting Liv in on the joke. Krista, though, had a heart and, when Monica wasn't around to chide her for it, knew how to use it.

"Make it quick," Liv teased.

"Your dad—nothing?"

Liv shook her head. Still smiling. Keep up the smile. None of this hurts, none of it.

"And your mom—she's . . . ?"

Keep smiling. "She's fine. Same. I mean, she's fine."

Krista tilted her head skeptically, an angle sharp enough to dig under Liv's ribs and hit something soft. Liv grabbed Krista by both shoulders and pretended to shake sense into her like men did to hysterical women in old movies. The pain of that little cut, however, did not go away.

"She's okay!" Liv play shouted. "I'm okay! Everything's okay!"

Krista pretended to zip her lips. "All right! I'll shut up about it, forever and anon."

"Too much British lit for you. Get a life."

Krista nodded guiltily and slunk off for her locker. Liv heard the squeak of a sneaker stopping suddenly and turned to see Krista, who had leaned back to speak more quietly.

"I meant to tell you. I came in the back way, by the band room. And Doug Monk was there with a bunch of idiots. I know you and Doug . . ."

Krista trailed off—of course she did—because no one in Monica's group knew how to finish that sentence. Liv and Doug *what*? Liv herself wasn't certain. To the others, Liv supposed, Doug was a bewildering holdover from an older version of Liv Fleming, a Liv none of them were particularly interested to know. And it was for reasons just like this: first day of school, everything going great, and suddenly there's some situation near the band room.

Liv nodded an embarrassed thanks and took off for the stairs. The bottom floor at this hour was nothing but lonely halls. Away from watchful eyes, she sped up, past the shuttered home-ec kitchen and vo-ag wing, until she'd homed in on the southeastern bottom-floor stairwell, at the weird intersection of the chorus room and wrestling room. It was the hour of neither singing nor wrestling, and yet there huddled a group of four boys, just like Krista had said, their schoolbags slung across mom-ironed shirts so as to better record video on their phones. Each screen gave Liv a mini but unobstructed view of a scene that was as preposterous as it was predictable.

Doug was lying on his back on the floor, his hair spread out beneath his head like black tentacles. The parachute pockets of his shorts sagged to the floor with payloads of gorp. From all indications, Doug had been persuaded to bench-press Jackson Stegmaier, a kid who had what teachers called a "developmental delay." He was skinny with narrow shoulders, both of which, Liv hated to admit, did give him a barbell shape. The stunt was absurd, hence the laughter, hence the twist in Liv's gut.

The videos would be uploaded by day's end. By tomorrow, they'd be flickering from every gadget in sight. Jackson Stegmaier wasn't Liv's problem; he'd deal with it. Doug, though—Doug never made anything easy. Sweat rolled down his scarlet face as he pumped the kid up and down while a jerk named Billy shouted out reps. What Doug didn't get, what he never got until too late, was that the boys cheered only to mock him.

Liv sighed. It wasn't an indulging-Krista sigh. It was an extended, weary exhale, the sound of envisioning two more semesters of situations like this, every one of which forced her to keep a foot in a world she'd rather step beyond. Doug cutting power to the biology-class refrigerator to hide how bad he'd messed up his fetal pig, never thinking of the floor-wide stench that would result. Doug taking a dare to ride the bumper of a school bus, leading to stricter bus rules that pissed off everyone. And on and on.

Billy had taken a seat atop Jackson Stegmaier, pretending to ride a mechanical bull. Three cameras pressed inward. Some of these degenerates were whizzes at editing, and if they pooled their footage, the video could be split screen or multiple point of view, alternating between Doug's face and Jackson's face before cutting to the crowd-pleasing wide shot. It would be a smash hit, setting the bar for the whole semester, unless Liv did something.

She grabbed the closest boy's shoulder.

"Hi, Liv!"

That's what the boy said. It made her feel lousy about her risen social status over the past couple of years that anyone would think she had come here to enjoy the fun. She shoved the boy. He was too big to forcibly move, but the contact surprised him enough to withdraw. She swiped at the second boy's phone, intending to knock it free, but although she struck it perfectly, the boy managed to keep hold of it. The third boy, witness to Liv's onslaught, wisely evaded, tucking his phone into his pocket.

Three seconds had passed, and Liv now turned to deal with Billy, still astride Jackson. Infuriatingly, Billy laughed, seeming to enjoy making Liv use her full body weight to pull him off. Jackson, as seemed his lot in life, took the brunt of it, hitting the floor with one of his fragile shoulders and shrieking, then staggering away while clutching the shoulder. Billy fell straight onto Doug's stomach, still laughing. When Liv snatched for his phone, he easily dodged.

"C'mon, Liv." He fake pouted. "Don't be a bitch about it."

She kicked him in the shin. He chuckled through his pain, which drove her crazy. The other boys were retreating with their videos safely archived, less ashamed than they were aware that classes were about to begin. This event meant nothing to them; they'd already half forgotten it, as evidenced by their amiable farewells.

"Nice kick," said the first of them.

"You're on your period—we get it," said the second.

"See you at lunch, Liv!" said the third.

Billy got up and danced away from Liv's closing kicks, still laughing, and then it was just her and Doug, alone again at the scene of a crime. Billy's fall had knocked the wind out of Doug, and he was gasping for air, but calmly. He'd been squashed plenty of times before. This wasn't Liv's first time, either; she crossed her arms and glared at him.

"What," he panted, "is your"—gasp—"problem?"

"*My* problem?"

"We were just having fun."

"No, *they* were having fun."

"Whatever."

"Did it look like Jackson was having fun?"

"Until you showed up."

Doug winced and sat up. Sunflower seeds and pine nuts were everywhere.

"Oh no," he said. "My gorp."

He began sweeping food into his hand and funneling it back into the violated bag. He flushed a bit, perhaps realizing that if eating off the floor wasn't humiliating, what was?

"Floor's clean" was his excuse. "First day of school, everything's clean."

"It *is* the first day of school. That's right. And already look at you."

"I don't need your advice. Go find your stupid friends."

"You do need my advice. And my advice is to stop letting people do this to you! You do it willingly!"

"Oh, now you want to help. Yesterday, though, you barely wanted to check the traps. Probably thought it might mess up your nails."

That one burned. Because the thought had, in fact, crossed her mind. In the past, the branches above Hangman's Noose had scratched up her face, the gears of Neckbreaker had ripped out a lock of her hair, and, yes, the door of Hard Passage had broken one of her fingernails. Was it so horrible that she wanted to go to school not looking like a savage? She looked down. The knuckles of her right hand were scuffed, bleeding a little. The excited newness she'd felt upon entering the school had burned down to exhausted anguish.

"I know you think I ignore you here," she said.

"You do."

"It's just . . ." She shrugged miserably. "I'm trying to make everyone happy, all right? Including myself. *Including myself.*"

He said nothing, keeping his eyes on his gorp, pouring from hand to bag.

She turned on a heel. "I've gotta go."

"Hey," Doug said.

She stopped. Sighed. Didn't turn back. But she did lower the defensive set of her shoulders.

"I'll track down Jackson at lunch," Doug said. "Tell him sorry."

Liv listened and waited.

"Little weirdo only did it because we asked," he added.

Liv nodded at the stairs in front of her. "Let's just try to get through this year with minimum catastrophes. It's our last year, you know?"

"I wish it weren't," Doug said softly.

"Come on," she said. "You hate school."

"I know you want everything to change, Liv, but what comes after this? For me? I just wish . . . things could stay the same."

Liv closed her eyes for a second, absorbing another small slash of pain. She'd been able to prod Doug on Sunday morning precisely because she'd been looking at his back, not his face, and the same thing held true here. With her back turned, a speck of truth could be set free.

"Things can't."

Silence from Doug. The rustle of gorp had stopped. She couldn't even hear him breathe.

"Better get to class," he said, and his lack of acknowledgment that no one would care if Doug Monk made it to class on time was the last jab of pain Liv could bear. She nodded, grateful for being granted release, and rushed up the stairs while wondering what would happen if she turned around. What would it look like to stare truth in the face after two years of avoiding it? Maybe it would feel like freedom, like destroying old traps instead of setting them, over and over, despite knowing there was nothing new to catch.

5.

LIV SKIDDED INTO HOMEROOM AT THE
clang of the bell, earning applause from the teacher and hoots from
her friends, quite the opposite reaction Doug would receive. She
took the open seat, right in front, and was glad that the hour was
taken up with first-day preliminaries: going over schedules, the year
calendar, the sorts of things devoid of emotion.

She didn't realize how much she'd been dreading second period
until she sat down at a desk, this time way in back, to the confusion
of Phil and Darla, and felt her muscles tighten against the chair. It
was English, the class that should have been taught by her father,
in the same room she'd visited so many times as a kid. The teacher
who'd replaced Mr. Fleming, both as English teacher and drama
coach, Ms. Baldwin, had made the room her own, but Liv couldn't
stop seeing the shelf behind Baldwin's desk that had once held thirty-
five copies of James Galvin's *Resurrection Update*—the book that had
meant so much to Lee Fleming, right up until the end.

The shelf didn't even hold books anymore. It held idiotic troll dolls with multicolored hair. It shouldn't have aggravated Liv, but it did. She had avoided exchanging a single word with Ms. Baldwin in the two years they'd shared the same building, even though the woman had done nothing worse than show an affinity for ugly dolls. Liv knew it wasn't fair to Baldwin. It was only English.

Then Baldwin said the five words that earned any teacher ire: *Get to know your neighbor.* Next to the imbecilic Name Game, it was the most tedious of first-day time wasters, in which students were forced to pair off, interview a classmate, and then introduce that classmate aloud. Ridiculous, considering the size of the school and how long most of them had known one another. The shtick was likely for Baldwin's benefit, another reason for Liv to resent it.

Mired in disgruntlement, Liv moved too slowly. Darla chose Phil, of course, and every teammate Liv could see quickly paired off. She was recalculating when a fist knock-knocked her desk. She looked to her right and found the wide, dazzling grin of a boy she'd never seen before. He was tall and long-limbed. What stuck out most was his obvious sense of style, a rare quality in high school boys. His clothing was probably secondhand but actually fit, and was tucked and rolled where most guys would have ends flapping and flopping.

"I'm Bruno!" he cried, as if they were long-lost companions.

The grin kept going. He had great teeth, their bright white set off against skin further darkened by actual stubble. Hair, indeed, looked to be his biggest struggle: It puffed from beneath his shirt cuffs, and a gallon of gel must have been used to sculpt that swoop on top of his head. Liv looked all right today—she'd gotten up early to tie her hair in a neat bun at the nape of her neck. Bruno's unguarded gaze, though, made her doubt.

"I'm Liv," she said.

"Yeah, I know. Let's buddy up."

Buddy up? Liv threw out a desperate look for someone who might be less challenging than this guy, and, finding none, shrugged. Bruno scooted his desk; it bumper-carred against hers. Everyone else was doing the same, and the noise helped Liv relax. She took out a fresh notebook and inked on the first page *BRUNO*.

"Let's see: I'm Bruno Mayorga, I'm seventeen, I was born in Nuevo León—that's a Mexican state—but was still a baby when I came to Iowa. I only moved to Bloughton this summer, but I plan to work on the school paper, and do lots of drama, and also chorus, and hopefully a couple small groups. I'll probably join the tennis team, even though I'm not very good, but I hear the team is terrible, so maybe I'll actually get to play. I have three sisters named Mia, Elena, and Bianca, and three dogs. I'm into music, but that's super boring. Why did I even mention that? Who's not into music? Oh, my dad is still in Mexico. I basically don't know him. I know you don't really have a dad, too. I don't mean to be awkward about that. Sorry if that's awkward."

Liv finished writing before exhaling.

"You're an easy interview," she said.

"Yeah, but that's because I want to talk about something else."

Liv felt her shoulders close up as they did any time her past was questioned. *Don't do that*, she instructed herself. *Be the tallest you can.*

"And what's that?" she asked.

He clicked his own pen, gestured at his blank page.

"Let's get this done first. You're Olivia Fleming. I'm guessing you're also seventeen? You don't have any siblings, if I remember what I heard, and you're in like twenty-eight sports."

"Where'd you learn all that?"

"Oh, just from people this summer. I always do some ground-work before starting at a new school."

"Why do you keep starting at new schools?"

Another big grin, though this one looked strained. "Hey, we're done with me. Did I get all your details right? No pets?"

"Yeah, a dog."

"Oh! Tell me about the dog. Dogs go over great in these things. If you've got a picture on your phone we might not have to talk at all."

"Well, his name is John, and he's a blue-heeler mix—"

"His name is John?"

"My dad named him. After a poet."

"Which poet?"

"I can't remember. John somebody."

Bruno laughed. It fit with his grin—comforting, welcoming. He took a note.

"'Dog named after John the poet.' That's good stuff. Anything else?"

Liv sighed. "What's the point? All these people know me. We've been going to school together forever."

"You don't know me."

"Yeah, but you get the basic idea about someone, just by being awake. You can tell who's nice or whatever."

"Am I nice? Or am I whatever?"

"You're nice."

"Then why do you look so scared of me?"

"I'm not scared. I just—you're talkative. And I'm tired."

"Haven't had your coffee yet. You're definitely a coffee drinker."

"I guess you can add that to your notes. 'Drinks coffee.' God, that's why these things suck. You either sound boring or like you're desperate for attention."

"And it's probably hardest for you."

"What do you mean?"

"You know. Your dad. Like, that's interesting. I've only heard a little bit of it, and even I can tell it's *super* interesting. But because it's unhappy, we all have to pretend like it doesn't exist. 'I drink coffee, and my dog is named John' sort of pales in comparison."

Liv gave Bruno a careful look. Was the offhand way in which he mentioned her dad disturbing or disarming? Nothing duplicitous could hide behind such a smile.

"You said you wanted to talk about something," she said.

Bruno leaned closer and raised a conspiratorial eyebrow.

"I saw you bust up those guys this morning, and it was *amazing*."

Liv slapped down her pen and covered her eyes.

"Oh Jesus. Is the video out already?"

"No! I mean, I don't know. I saw it in person."

"There were people watching?"

"It isn't like there was a whole crowd. It was just me. You didn't see me because you were busy kicking all sorts of ass. Like I said, I want to join the chorus. I went down there to introduce myself to Mrs. Meachum."

"I'm going to end up in the video, I just know it, and then it's just going to be more . . ."

"More what?"

"More I have to deal with. Like why I'm still sticking up for Doug Monk."

"What's wrong with sticking up for Doug Monk?"

"In all your summer spying, you never heard anything about Doug Monk?"

"Not spying. Research. And no, he never came up."

"What am I supposed to say? I guess he's an old friend."

"And your new friends don't like him. That's how it goes."

"They just don't understand . . . I mean, unless you know Doug, he can seem . . . he's tough to talk to. His family life is weird. He's basically on his own. It's hard."

"Well, I think what you did was heroic. It was about the most heroic thing I've ever seen. You're a hero."

"Shut up."

"I'm serious here. It was really, truly amazing. You see that stuff in movies, but in real life? You tore those assholes new assholes."

"If I'd been a guy, it would've gone totally different. There'd be pride issues, and they would've beaten me up. See how heroic I am?"

"I think you're selling yourself short. If that's true, then how come more girls don't go on Liv Fleming–style anti-bully rampages? Because they're scared. I'd be scared, too. That's why you're my hero, and that's my final word on the subject."

Bruno crossed his arms and lifted his chin in defiance. Liv rolled her eyes, but there was a squirming in her stomach she mistook for dread before identifying it as dread's opposite. Her relationship with Doug had been soaked in stigma for so long that she couldn't trust any positive feelings anywhere near it. She stared down at the list of Bruno's sisters in a desperate hunt for a topic change.

"You were saying hi to Mrs. Meachum, huh? Really getting a head start on the brownnosing."

"Hardy-har. I actually happen to like teachers. Plus, I'm not above a little brownnosing. They're casting for *Oliver!* next week, and if I don't get a lead, these hallways are going to be ringing with my sobs. With my beautifully musical, pitch-perfect sobs."

A funny thing to say, but Liv didn't hear it. At the word *Oliver!*, it was like coal dust had been poured over her head. Her vision went dark, her brain darker. The word sat on the desk before her like a scorched, unidentifiable, yet disgusting object, something vaguely threatening and not definitively dead. She wanted to push her desk away in hopes that the object would drop to the floor and she could ignore it like a dead roach.

Bruno had quit talking. He ducked his head into her field of vision.

"Liv?"

She blinked, barely seeing him, then crawled her eyes through the room of oblivious natterers to the teacher standing before her stupid shelf of dolls. Mrs. Meachum might be handling the musical side of the play, but it was Baldwin who selected the productions, cast them, and directed them. Liv grit her teeth and let the feelings seep in.

"That *bitch*."

"Baldwin?" Bruno shrugged. "This assignment isn't *that* bad."

Only this boy's recent arrival made him any less ignorant than anyone else. *Oliver!* was intimately linked to Mr. Fleming's downfall. It had been his final production, the one that had proven to everyone that he had no place in civilized society. A mere five plays had passed in the interim, and Baldwin thought that was long enough to bring *Oliver!* back?

Ten minutes later, Liv's entire body quaked with a level of anger she could barely rein in. There was no need for Baldwin to fish around for volunteers to go first. Liv raised her hand and stood, to the surprise of Bruno, who, by his big grin, had clearly expected to launch their joint interview. Liv ignored him; she ignored the other students; she recalled lessons of speech classes past and focused on her audience, which numbered one: Ms. Baldwin.

"My name is Liv Fleming," she said in a trembling voice, "and the fact that you're doing *Oliver!* this year makes me sick. You don't have any sensitivity at all. You're a terrible, terrible person. I hope you go to hell."

6.

CROSS-COUNTRY PRACTICE WAS JUST
what she needed, though, sadly, the phrase *cross-country* was a mis-
nomer. When the two hours of jogging around the park were up, Liv
found herself still stuck in Bloughton, Iowa, with little rage burned
off. It was at least more time with her friends. Monica, Krista, Darla,
Laurie, Amber—the team was where she had managed, after her
dad's downfall, to find friends, and although there wasn't much to be
done in practice beyond gasp and sweat and shoot pretend bazookas
at Coach Carney, it was the best part of Liv's day, with endorphins
eclipsing all emotion.

She fell into the station wagon, her soggy shirt and shorts gluing
to the seat plastic, and did the twenty-minute drive home with only
slight attention given to stop signs and red lights. Only when the
white gravel cloud of Custer Road swallowed the world did she feel
invisible and safe.

John didn't lift his chin from the steps when she reached them. He rolled his brown eyes upward as if to warn her that there was nothing inside the house any better than what was outside.

Liv assumed that floors of beer cans and tabletops of bottles were more typical signs of insobriety, but Aggie Fleming's intoxication was signaled by tidiness. Her poison was wine, and her defense was to dress it up as something classy. You saw it on TV all the time. Girlfriends at a brunch, laughing over sauvignon blanc. Women in movies, luxuriating in bubble baths while candlelight made their Bordeaux twinkle. Aggie dressed to drink, in skirts, blouses, and pantsuits as if she were about to leave for a function, and to perpetuate the illusion, she neatened up before getting down to business.

The living room, then, was the antithesis of the jungled yard, as surface-clean as a cheap motel. Sofa cushions were equilaterally placed, magazines squared away in racks, tables cleared of detritus, and a single wineglass was centered upon a glass coaster. Aggie had missed only one spot, in the corner, an anthill of plaster dust from the crumbling ceiling. She was facing away as Liv approached, high-heeled shoe bobbing amiably over a knee.

"First day of school," Aggie sang.

She uncrossed her legs to look over her shoulder.

"How's my girl."

Her lips were too numb to make it a question.

Liv tried to will her sadness into anger. It would be easier. Aggie Fleming's life had been ruined by her husband's public fall from grace. The secretarial job at Sookie's she'd been on pace to parlay into marketing director had turned into an abrupt layoff; now she shopped there in disgrace, because where else was there to shop? She had two jobs these days, answering phones at the vet clinic by day and waiting tables at a steakhouse by night. Right now she was between the two. She used a pinkie to dab wine from her lip, and Liv suffered a contraction of sympathy. Why remove a single drop? She was afloat in it.

"They're doing *Oliver!*," Liv said. "The school."

"Hmm? Dickens?"

"No. Yes. The play."

"Baby, would you mind fetching me a paper towel? I think this glass has a crack."

Of course it had a crack—the constant picking up, setting down. Liv dropped her bag onto the dining room table hard enough to split it, ripped off a towel, and handed it over. Her mom took it, folded it daintily, and blotted at the black hose under her skirt. Liv didn't see wine stains, unless you counted the permanent ones on her mom's fingers. Liv noted the current bottle (a third full) as well as the previous bottle (empty) snugged neatly alongside the sofa, though not quite neatly enough to disappear.

"When's your shift?"

"Ugh, you're such an adult. People like a waitress a little loose."

"Mom. I hope you don't say that in public."

"I don't mean it in a vulgar way. Just . . . relaxed. Prepared for witty repartee."

"I also don't like you driving like this."

Aggie lofted her wineglass imperially in her left hand and with her right tugged Liv's wrist. Liv resisted.

"Sit with your old momma."

"I'm sweaty."

Her mom pouted and tugged. Liv inhaled, said nothing, and let herself be pulled down. The glass of wine sloshed, but Aggie was a virtuoso of liquid counterbalance. She sipped, then leaned into her daughter, nuzzling Liv's neck. Liv closed her eyes, anything to be able to melt into her mom's embrace.

Aggie wrapped her arm around Liv's waist.

"You're so strong," Aggie sighed. "Feel those muscles. You've got such a nice body."

"I feel like that's gross, Mom."

"Shush. I've been holding you since you were itty-bitty."

Liv, though, was holding her mother. How could Aggie not notice that? Aggie's free fingers ran through her daughter's hair, her long nails slicing through damp strands and sliding along the sweaty scalp. It did seem motherly, Liv had to admit, this acceptance of her child's dirtiness. Curled up against Liv, nearly in her lap, her mother looked tiny. The years revealed by the corners of her eyes and the backs of her arms only made her smallness more heartbreaking.

"I'd hold you," Aggie cooed, "while your daddy read you poetry. He wanted to turn you into a little . . . what's her name. Sophia someone. Sophie. Sylvia. Plath."

"Sylvia Plath killed herself," Liv said.

"Well, I'm sure he didn't want *that*. He wanted the whole town strolling around being all poetic all the time. He had this whole fantasy."

"Mom, I know. *Resurrection Update*, remember?"

"Oh mercy. If I never see another book-shaped package, it'll be too soon."

Lee Fleming's poetry push had solidified around the hardscrabble collection of poems by James Galvin, who scowled from the back cover in an old denim shirt, as if furious about being photographed. Lee had won some victories in broadening the curriculum—wedging Toni Morrison's *Beloved* into the mix of dead white guys, carving out a whole week for Philip K. Dick—but no one understood why you'd dump Frost and Thoreau for a living poet, despite Lee's insistence that Galvin being alive was half the point, not to mention his Iowa connection. When the school had balked at the purchase order, Lee bought thirty-five copies out of his own pocket, scouring the Internet for used paperbacks and, when they ran out, paying full retail price.

"He always wanted me to pick my favorite poem from the book," Liv said.

"Me too. I'd make it up. 'The seventh one.' Something like that."

"I always chose 'Sapphic Suicide Note,'" Liv said.

"Blarg. Suicide again. That's poets for you."

Liv shrugged against her mother's warmth. "I only liked it because it was short."

Aggie snapped her fingers in a pretty funny pantomime of a slam-poetry fan. She *was* loose. Liv could imagine her being plenty charming before steakhouse patrons, and wasn't loose and charming better than what she'd been during her husband's final year—tense, helpless, sick with worry?

"Recite!" Aggie cried. "Recite!"

Liv could have. Seeking a leg up on future classmates, she'd cracked *Resurrection Update* as a freshman. At seven words, "Sapphic Suicide Note" was the first—and only—poem in the book she'd read, one so short she'd unwittingly memorized it while trying to figure out how someone got paid for putting a mere seven words on a page.

> *day out*
>
> *no worldly joy*
>
> *italics mine*

The whole thing puzzled her, though it was the last two words that most baffled. When she'd asked her dad what they meant, he'd explained that "italics mine" was a phrase writers used when adding their own italicized emphasis to a quoted source. Fine, but there weren't any italics in "Sapphic Suicide Note."

"Dad always said poetry was full of secrets," Liv sighed into her mom's hair.

"I'm sorry, baby," Aggie said.

Liv didn't think Aggie was apologizing for the thirty-five copies of *Resurrection Update* missing from Baldwin's shelf.

"It's okay," Liv replied.

"One day it'll be better. You'll see. The house and the yard. The bills. Somehow they all got lost, but we're going to find them. They're around here. I'll neaten up the place. We'll find them. My phone has a flashlight. Does yours, baby?"

Liv's eyes swam in tears.

"Mm-hm," she said.

"Good." Her mother yawned. "Now what's all this about Charles

Dickens? *A Christmas Carol.* Tiny Tim. I remember George C. Scott as Scrooge. He flew through the night with a ghost. Doesn't that sound lovely?"

Liv looked from the pile of ceiling plaster to the ruptured ceiling above it, wondering if the fracture was big enough to permit her passage when, at night, a certain ghost in a certain memory tried to pull her through it.

"*Oliver Twist,*" she said.

"Your school is doing the play, hm?"

"The musical. The one Dad did."

"That's odd."

Liv sniffled hard, hoping the sharp inhale would spark her dampened rage. "How can they do that?" she pleaded. "It's only been two years."

"Has it been that long? Seems like"—Aggie clicked her tongue—"nothing."

"Everyone will start talking about it again. The whole thing."

"Nobody saw that show, baby. It was a . . . what do you call it?"

"Dress rehearsal. I know. But everyone heard about it. They still talk about it. Maybe you don't hear about it, but I sure do." Liv listened for any change in her mother's breathing. "Doesn't this make you mad?"

"I'm trying to be, baby. It's just . . . I'm so. I'm so. The wine, I guess."

"I mean, Ms. Baldwin—how could she? She's a bitch. Isn't she?"

Her mother yawned into Liv's neck. "That's right, baby."

"With me still in school? She couldn't wait one more year?"

"Shh, baby."

"They won't let it die. They won't let *him* die."

"We don't own the play, baby. We don't own people. We don't own anything. It's all just—poof. Dandelions in the breeze."

Hot sadness filled Liv's chest and burned to be cried out. Why was it only when her mother was drunk that she uttered words of such perfect, inadvertent beauty? Liv raised her hand, placed it on the back of her mother's head, and pet it. The hair was brittle and poorly dyed, but still pretty. Liv's hand, meanwhile, was not. Her nail polish was chipped to hell and her knuckles scabbed. She watched the scabs dive into her mother's hair, then resurface, then dive, and it felt like her life.

7.

TWO YEARS OF HEADING TO THE SAME
seat at the same cafeteria table had her legs operating with the muscle
memory that guided her to Amputator, Hangman's Noose, and the
other traps each Sunday. Though it wasn't unusual for other students
to greet her on her way to Monica's table, it was jarring to have one
cry out with such unbridled enthusiasm.

"Liv! Sit here!"

It was Bruno Mayorga. Her feet froze to her square of tile.
No one, especially not a new kid, dared broadcast such a naked
appeal—it could so easily be dashed. Liv glanced at her regular table.
Only Darla and Phil had noticed the situation, and they both chuckled at her predicament. When she looked back at Bruno, he was
already scooting over, making room. Others near him, a hodgepodge
of kids who fit nowhere else, inchwormed down the bench. Feeling
like every eye in school was on her, she walked over and cautiously

lowered herself beside Bruno. She kept her spine rigid, a signal that she wasn't getting comfortable.

"It's me! Bruno!"

"I remember," she said. "Three sisters, three dogs."

He gestured at her tray. "What you got there?"

Liv stared down. Most of the cross-country team brought lunches from home, healthy menus advocated by Coach Carney. The majority, though, had parents preparing those lunches, or at least reliably buying the raw materials. On that front, Liv never knew what to expect; it was easier to roll the roulette wheel of cafeteria offerings.

"I believe they call this chef's salad," she said.

"Is that a side of fried cheese?"

"Probably." She glanced at the brown paper bag spread before him, the scatterings of shredded cheese and salsa. "Taco?"

"Torta. Pork, avocado, peppers. Smells good, huh?"

Liv nodded. The morsels had a clean, sharp aroma that sliced through the cafeteria's meaty stink. She checked her usual table. Darla and Phil had moved on to feeding each other French fries, but Krista made eye contact, giving Liv an inquisitive, amused look. Liv replied with the mildest of head shakes—*I'll explain later*—before Bruno reclaimed her attention.

"Where's Doug?"

Liv frowned at him. "Doug?"

"He doesn't eat with you? Oh, I guess that makes sense."

"He's never here at lunch. I guess he goes outside."

"Tell him he can sit with me. I'm not picky."

"I don't really talk to him that much. But okay." She tried to imagine actually extending this offer to Doug next Sunday. He'd be embarrassed at his unpopularity being called out and ridicule the idea. Still, it was rare to hear so friendly an entreaty. Liv softened her voice. "I told you in Baldwin's class you were nice."

"Baldwin's class." Bruno whistled. "I've been to a lot of schools, Liv Fleming, and I have never, ever seen a student take it to a teacher like that. One hour you're rescuing Doug Monk, the next you pull *that*? *Eres una chica loca.*"

"Don't get too excited. It was probably my last stand. I have to meet with Principal Gamble after school."

"What's your beef with *Oliver!*?"

Liv stabbed her salad like she might a sworn enemy, stuffed a forkful into her mouth, and chewed it while giving Bruno a flat look. She knew what was happening here. Bruno raised both hands guiltily. His hands were large, with long, articulate fingers. He noticed salsa on one of them and nibbled it off.

"All right," he said. "I'll admit I've heard some things. Okay, *lots* of things. But there are parts of it that just can't be true."

"So you want the news straight from the source." She grabbed her tray and started to stand. "At least you're upfront about it."

Bruno rested one of his large hands on the edge of her tray.

"That's not why I asked you to sit here. We don't have to talk about it. Look, let's draw up a formal agreement never to talk about it. It can just be this big, mysterious thing sitting between us for all of eternity."

Liv laughed at the preposterous but flattering notion that this guy she barely knew was already planning for eternity, and that she was part of the plan. She glanced at her usual table, and this time it was

Monica who had fixed her eyes on her—not a good sign. Monica had on her most unbothered expression, which meant that she was plenty bothered.

But it had been a hell of a first couple of days of school. Liv was aware that if there was a pecking order in her group, she was at the bottom of it, but she didn't feel like thinking about it. She yielded to the gentle pressure of Bruno's hand on her tray and sat. She stared down at her unappetizing food and pushed a sigh from her chest. If the sigh was deep enough, perhaps it would expel the toxins that made this topic so poisonous.

"What, exactly," she asked, "did you hear?"

For the first time, Bruno looked less than confident. He winced, probably only now realizing the sorts of things he would need to say aloud, and exhaled in a blast, like this was hard on him, not her. That should have rankled Liv, but instead she hid a small smile.

"I heard your dad had some . . . strange experiences he worked into the play."

"You could say that."

Bruno put one of his sharp elbows on the table so he could face her more directly. "What I don't get is that, from what I heard, everyone knew something was wrong with him. Not just the drama kids. People told me he was just talking about his *Oliver!* plans right in the middle of class. I don't see how—"

"How no one did anything to stop it?"

Bruno gestured his confusion on this point. Liv had lost her appetite, but she picked up her knife just to have something to wield; it made her feel safer entering into this dialogue.

"I guess everyone had a clue. Just no one pulled it all together. I can't blame anyone. My mom and I didn't do any better. I heard things, for sure. How he was talking weird in class. How he'd stand up and just walk out of school. I know how it sounds. Like, how could we not have done something?"

"No, I get it," Bruno said. "You only know how hard things are when they actually happen to you. Everything's complicated. No matter what you do, it's always going to hurt someone."

It was the most sensitive statement Liv believed she'd heard spoken by a teenage boy. *Everything's complicated*—was there a truer, more graceful summation of life? Liv nodded, noting she was being too enthusiastic but unable to restrain herself. Speaking honestly about her dad was the rarest of things.

"So then he disappeared for four days," she said. "There were search parties and APBs. It was scary. But then he came back."

"Naked in the park. Everyone mentions that."

Liv screwed the point of her knife into the tabletop. "He acted normal at the hospital. Ashamed and embarrassed, all that. But the second he got home, that's when it got bad. He told us the truth. What *he* thought was the truth."

"Which was . . . ?"

Liv narrowed her eyes at Bruno. She didn't trust the gleam in his eyes. Her story wasn't a torta. So she kept the full answer for herself, as the awful scene screened in her mind. She remembered coming home with her dad and how she'd expected him to retreat to his bedroom as the implications of the town-square event hit him. Instead, he'd marched about the house, unplugging or removing batteries from

communications devices—the TV, the computers, the shower radio—
while John padded after him in jubilant fascination. Aggie perched on
the edge of the sofa, winded by the flutter of activity. Liv took a chair,
worried her knees would buckle from the press of descending doom.

Had her father actually said everything Liv recalled that he'd said?
She felt like she could recite his rant verbatim.

*I was in the woods. I couldn't even tell you where. There was a place,
like a clearing. And tubes—two giant tubes. I think these tubes suctioned
me up. That part is confusing. It felt like I was going downward, into
the earth, because it was cold. But I know I was going up. It was so dark
up there. Their eyes aren't like ours. They only need a little illumination
to see. And it was cramped. I didn't expect that. Something comes from
that far away, you'd think their ship would be gigantic, but it was small.
It makes sense if you think about it. Think about our space capsules and
space shuttles. All those little astronaut tunnels. No wasted space. That's
what it was like. Like they couldn't fit past each other fast enough to get
to me. But they did.*

Who? Aggie had asked, and Lee's answer was all that Liv gave to
Bruno:

"Aliens."

Bruno nodded in sage confirmation. "The skinnies."

Liv looked away from the sawdust the knife had dug from the
table to give Bruno a reappraisal. He sounded genuine enough. But
Lee Fleming had sounded genuine, too.

"Skinners," Liv corrected. "That's what he called them. He said
they had blue, wrinkled skin they'd shed every day. There were a few
specific skinners he was obsessed with."

She set down the knife.

"Don't you want to know who they were?"

Bruno registered her darkened tone.

"Yeah." He sounded hesitant. "I guess?"

Liv sniffed and realized her nose was runny, which meant she was close to crying for the second time in two days. What was wrong with her? She crashed onward, trying to outpace the sob. "Because to me, it's the worst part. I mean, anyone can get sick and see little green men. They're in all the UFO movies. But the skinners he dreamed up? He was really sick, you know? Really, really, really sick."

"Hey, let's stop," Bruno said.

But her voice was growing louder. "There was the Whistler. When the skinners were doing experiments on him, Dad said the Whistler stood out of view, whistling. That was weird because, guess what? Skinners don't have mouths."

"C'mon." He was looking around in concern. "Stop."

Louder now, losing control. "Then there was the Floating Pumpkin. This big, orange orb that floated over his body during experiments. He thought it emitted anesthetic rays. Oh, and the Green Man. The Green Man was the scariest one of all. Dad thought maybe the Green Man was what a skinner looked like after it shed its final skin. The Green Man was ten feet tall and just stood there, reaching for him with big green fingers."

"Enough, all right? I'm sorry I made you talk about it."

"But we haven't even gotten to your question. We haven't even gotten to the play."

"That's okay. I get it. He jammed all this stuff into *Oliver!* and it was weird. Right? Look, that fried cheese isn't going to eat itself."

"But you think that's the point of the story. How *weird* it all was. You probably heard all sorts of stuff about the play. The orphans wearing big, blue smocks—skinners, check. An orange disco ball—Floating Pumpkin, check. A huge green stripe down the stage—the Green Man, check. What else? Oh, how by the end of act one, all the actors were holding each other and crying. Does that about cover it?"

Bruno's regret had given way to a less charitable look. She was on the offense now, for no good reason, and they both knew it. Liv swiped the napkin from her tray.

"Is any of that true?" Bruno asked.

Liv blew her nose. "Some of it."

"Well, I'm sorry."

"The point," Liv snapped, staring through swollen eyes, "is that it wasn't a *play*. It was a crack in my dad's head, and we were all staring inside it instead of helping him. Everyone knew Dad wasn't okay, but we all let the play happen anyway. Because they already sold tickets? Because me and Mom hoped it would set everything straight? We were so stupid."

"You didn't know what to do. It was a new situation."

"Gamble did. He stopped the play."

"Principal Gamble?"

If there was a bearable part of the story, this was it. Liv embraced it, because it signaled the end.

"He went up onstage and made the orchestra stop, and when my dad came out all mad, Gamble just . . . he put a hand on Dad's shoulder, and he said, 'Lee.' And I know it sounds stupid, but it was like he was saying goodbye. Goodbye from everyone. And Dad knew it. He walked off the stage real slow. Someone lowered the curtain. It took a hundred years. I remember thinking that curtain would never make it, and I'd have to stare forever right into my dad's broken brain."

Liv threw her wadded napkin into her salad and pressed her palms into her eyes. She had a sense that Bruno's hands were near, one at her elbow, one at her back, but he probably hesitated, uncertain if he knew her well enough to touch her. He did not, Liv told herself, and she stood up, her thighs walloping the table hard enough to rattle cutlery. Talking had been a mistake. Maybe secrets didn't go away with words after all; maybe words were the invocation to bring them back from the dead. Baldwin's *Oliver!* would perform this rite on a scale Liv didn't want to imagine.

She glared down at him. "So now what? You're still going to try out for the play, aren't you?"

Bruno blinked up at her, his brown eyes wide and injured, because he was, of course he was. To make a stand against a frivolous school musical would not affect a thing. Right then, when Liv should have been her most upset, her brain betrayed her: She did wish, quite suddenly, that those lovely hands of Bruno's had settled on her elbow and back while she was still within reach, no matter what Monica might mutter to the gang when she saw it.

8.

SHE WAS PUSHING HERSELF TOO HARD.
The slopes of Custer Road were deceptive in grade. Out here, along their lonely ribbon of gravel road, the concept of neighbors was relative, but she was heading up the rise toward the former house of Major Dawkins, coiner of *Be the tallest you can*. The Dawkinses had been important friends of the family; Major Dawkins was an ex-military bigwig of gold-leaf distinction who'd thought the world of Lee Fleming. But after Lee vanished, the Major and Mrs. Dawkins moved away, as if there was nothing left in the sticks worth seeing.

Liv's heart was throbbing, and each exhale felt wet, like the kicked-up gravel shards had perforated her lungs. She kept going, though, up the winding driveway, past the rust-gobbled NO TRES-PASSING: YOU ARE NOW IN RANGE sign, and through a lawn grown out to a primeval state Major Dawkins would have abhorred. She slapped the garage door—her midway point—and started back down the hill. It was Friday; she'd made this run every day after school since Tuesday and had become wary of loose rock.

What a week. Liv gave begrudging credit to Baldwin for behaving like Liv hadn't told her off in front of the whole class, but Principal Gamble hadn't been so forgiving. Her mood, of course, hadn't helped. When Liv got to his office after the last class on Tuesday, her cafeteria conversation with Bruno had her nerves crackling again.

Gamble was at his desk when she got there. He was sitting with his hands clasped, devoting his entire attention to her arrival. Under another circumstance, it might be flattering. The second Liv arrived, he pointed a thick finger at a chair.

"What in the world was going on in your head?" he demanded.

"You only heard Baldwin's side of this," she mumbled.

"I didn't realize there could be another side to 'go to hell.'"

Her mumble got more mumbly. "Maybe there is."

"This isn't like you, Liv."

He raised his eyebrows and waited. Liv picked at her fingernail polish, praying for this to end soon. She figured she had a decent shot. Ever since the night Gamble had halted the abomination of her father's play, she had felt indebted to him, though she never knew how to convey it. But it must have showed; Gamble had been subtly protective of her over the last two years, smoothing over her misbehaviors, reminding teachers of the trauma she'd been through. Her hopes for that kind of charity sank as Gamble grabbed a detention pad and began writing.

"You know I've always tried to help you. But you're a big girl now. You're suspended from cross-country the rest of the week."

"What?"

"What did you expect? You're not impressing anyone."

"You think I was trying to impress someone? Baldwin is doing *Oliver!* How could you let her do that?"

"I have enough on my plate without worrying about which play Ms. Baldwin's doing."

"There are a million plays, and she chooses that one?"

"We still have the sets in storage. You haven't seen this year's budget."

"Which parts of my dad's sets are reusable? The orange disco ball? Baldwin's trying to make some point."

"Maybe that's a good thing—you ever think of that? It could be healthy. The school needs to get over that incident. The whole town does. Maybe Ms. Baldwin wants to take it on straight. Like an exorcism. Get all the demons worked out."

"At my expense. You know what kind of shit I'm going to have to deal with?"

"Whoa, whoa. You don't get to curse in here. Who do you think you are?"

"I'm Lee Fleming's daughter. And I'm going to get shit. Major shit."

Gamble put his pen back to the detention pad.

"When's your first cross-country meet?"

"Saturday. Why?"

"You're suspended from that, too."

"What?"

"And you're going to apologize to Ms. Baldwin."

"That's not fair! She's a bitch for doing this and you know it!"

"There goes another meet. You want to try for a third?"

Liv's face felt like it was in flames. Gamble ripped off the detention slip, and through the blurry heat waves of her vision she noted his sorry look but wouldn't accept it. She took the slip—she wanted to snatch it—and marched from the room without a word. Baldwin's room was just five doors down, and Liv planted herself at the threshold. Steeled as if to rip off a patch of duct tape, she performed what was, in a technical sense, an apology.

"I'm sorry about what I said."

Baldwin looked up from sending a text. The woman wore owlish glasses and a waist-long braid, the kind of thing Liv attributed to Renaissance fairs. Her wardrobe was composed of frowsy bohemian dresses in faux-patchwork crepe, which swept along the floor, hiding gross old sandals. These were Monica-like judgments, but right now Liv gave in to them.

"Liv," Baldwin sighed. "Let's talk."

"That's okay. I wanted to apologize, that's all."

"Come in. We have a couple minutes. I think you may have the wrong idea about this."

"No, I'm good. I'll see you tomorrow. Bye."

"Liv—"

But Liv was off, the distasteful task taken like a vaccination shot; she'd have to rub the pain away for a few hours, that's all. The silver lining of the outburst with Baldwin was that it competed with the Doug video as the week's top story. When the video hit her phone lunchtime on Wednesday, she watched it and judged that it could have been worse. The camerawork was woozy, and the acoustics made dialogue unintelligible. Her cameo at the climax was obscured, a small miracle she was happy to accept. No one would know she'd been involved.

Except, that is, Bruno. She scanned the cafeteria and found him with another random assemblage of kids, snarfing another torta, leading a gregarious conversation. Her secrets, it seemed, were safe with Bruno, and it surprised her that she was all right sharing them.

"I just heard about Baldwin," Hank said, sitting down with his tray. "Holy shit, Liv."

Liv closed her phone, killing the video. "All in a day's work."

"I was there," Phil boasted. "The baddest-ass thing I've ever seen."

Liv felt the prickling of a blush on her neck. She looked at the girls at the table. They seemed cautious, even suspicious. Darla wouldn't meet Liv's eyes. Amber and Laurie exchanged a look. Krista offered her a weak smile. Naturally, it was Monica who gave voice to the roiling undercurrent.

"That's two meets, Liv," Monica chastised. "We were sort of counting on you? We didn't train all summer for you to flake out, you know. I hope you at least got some jollies out of your little tantrum."

Monica smiled sweetly at the end of it, twisting it into a joke, but if you knew Monica at all, you knew no joking was involved. The flush of pleasure around her neck tightened into a burn. Liv swore right there, while picking at another tray of unpalatable food, that she'd make it up to the whole team. Just because she couldn't run with them this week didn't mean she couldn't keep herself in top shape for when she returned, at which point she'd rededicate herself to the new Liv, finally bringing the old Liv to an end.

So here she was, doing her part, running even harder than she would at practice. John, who'd jogged with her on Custer Road for a mile, was waiting on the shoulder where he'd given up, and he rejoined her as she headed back home from the Dawkins place. It had to be past seven. The forest line under which the sun had dipped glowed as if on fire from another of Doug's flares. In the time she'd been running, her mother would have gotten home, changed, drunk some wine, and departed for the steakhouse. Their home would be empty.

When Liv got to the mailbox, she kept running.

John followed her to the backyard, where he, as usual, halted. Liv ran past the perennial grave markers: the lawnmower corpse, the swing set cemetery, the cairns of loose brick, the garden-shed mausoleum. She vaulted the trampled back fence and hurtled through the woods, faster than she'd ever done it. Trees, upset at her unscheduled invasion, slapped her with leaves, which she ignored, and branch ends, which she fended off with elbows. There was a good strong branch, practically a baseball bat—she swiped it off the ground without breaking stride.

She wouldn't miss another cross-country meet. She wouldn't miss anything ever again. With the play unpreventable, as well as the affronts that would come with it, she would need to focus hard, do whatever needed doing, and to start with, that meant taking the step she'd failed to take on Sunday. The branch felt natural in her hand. It would do the job of destroying most of the traps, if not all of them.

All she had to do was keep running, because if she didn't stop, didn't catch her breath, didn't think, she couldn't change her mind.

There came a sound.

Louk.

Don't stop running.

Cleek.

Don't start thinking.

Hwolk.

Damn it, damn it. She slowed to a jog, then a fast walk. She winced from a stitch in her side. See? This was what happened in life anytime you stopped moving and started thinking—pain came crashing. She cocked her head, swiped sweaty hair from her ear. Was it a duck? Doubtful. A chicken? Not way out here. A squirrel? She'd learned the hard way that squirrels made all sorts of unexpected noises. The truth clobbered her. Trap One had caught something. That was bad news. Amputator was no Hangman's Noose. When its trigger was tripped and its jaws sprang shut, there could be blood, even bone.

She slowed her walk and tried to quiet her panting. Whatever it was had heard her and gone quiet, but the rustle of leaves carried. Under tree cover, it was practically night out here, as threatening as a corn maze. The idea that she would stride up to the trap in the dark and use the branch to finish off the animal was farcical. Only Doug would be so brave. She might even be forced to call him to come deal with this.

Liv circled around the final tree, her teeth clenched in expectation of blood. It could be a possum. Or a bobcat. She choked up on the branch. The animal might yet wriggle free. It might be chewing through its last tendon now. She held her breath, leaned to see better, and stepped into a clearer view.

It wasn't a squirrel, or possum, or bobcat. It was larger. Much larger. It had four limbs, but not four legs. Two of the limbs were arms. It had a round, snoutless head. Liv's innards flooded with nausea. Was it a man? Had the worst-case scenario of a wandering hiker stumbling into a trap finally come to pass?

She dared take a step closer. The thing spasmed. Liv gasped. A shiver shook out through the thing's body. Then, to Liv's revulsion, it sat up, its face swinging into the dim light, its inhuman features twisting to produce chittering sounds unlike any Liv had ever heard. *Cwelk. Slouk. Flech. Mwolk.*

No, it wasn't a man, and the worst-case scenario she'd feared wasn't the worst scenario after all, not by a long shot.

Trap One, Amputator, years after its construction, had lived up to its design. It had caught an alien being. It was the most abominable thing Liv had ever laid eyes upon, and she screamed, and screamed again, and screamed again and again, and as she sprinted back through the slashing woods faster than she'd run all afternoon, headed for home, for her phone, for help, one single thought raced even faster, stabbing her far more brutally than any stitch in her side.

Dad was telling the truth the whole time, and none of us, except Doug, believed him.

SECOND STANZA:

IN STUDY OF THE OBSCURE

9.

LEE FLEMING WAS AN INDOORSMAN, IF
such a designation existed, which made his rapid conversion into survivalist all the more bewildering. In the cold winter weeks following
his expulsion from Bloughton High, he did none of the things he'd
been told to do. He did not return to the doctor. He did not find a
therapist. He did not search for another job. What he did, beginning
on Christmas Day and continuing every day thereafter, was spend
most of his time in the garden shed.

Aggie watched from parted curtains. She said to Liv, "Your father
just needs some time," but Liv knew that she said it for her own
benefit. Each day her mother didn't investigate what was going on
back there, the glue holding their family together further dissolved.
It wasn't that Liv didn't understand her mom's mind-set. As long as
they didn't know what Lee was working on, they could perpetuate
any harmless fantasy they wanted. Pretty soon they'd have a cute little

fence for a new flower bed, maybe a fun novelty mailbox. Liv agreed with her mother's assessment that "time" was the operative word. The ethic with which her father worked suggested he believed he had little of it to spare.

When he did come inside, late at night, Aggie didn't ask the right questions, and Lee didn't volunteer answers. He didn't volunteer anything. Without washing the oil from his hands—the oil was a clue, but of what?—he'd hunker in a chair that had a forest view and study a library text about welding or soldering or riveting—more clues. He was distracted to the point of forgetting to eat or sleep, and often he'd be in the same chair, still reading, when Liv woke up. In some ways, Liv realized, her father *had* been abducted. In other ways, *he'd* become the alien.

Plus, he was sick. There was no pretending it wasn't true. Many nights, Liv was awakened by the sounds of vomiting. He went on coughing jags and didn't notice the specks of blood sprayed over his shirt. His clothes began to look like they'd gotten larger, an absurd idea, but easier to accept than the weight he was losing. His skin looked like putty. Sometimes he'd sweat profusely for no reason. He didn't have to say anything for Liv to know what he thought: The skinners, in their experiments, had infected him with something. He did not have forever to live. Whatever he was going to do, he had to do it now.

Aggie's attempts to get him to the hospital were ignored. She sank into quiet despair, only to speak up again after the packages began arriving. It was reminiscent of the thirty-five copies of *Resurrection Update* deluging the house years ago, except these boxes were much larger and heavier. Some Lee unpacked right there in the kitchen, tools mostly, pliers and calipers and straightedges and hacksaws, while the larger crates he muscled into a wheelbarrow and transported to the shed. It was Aggie who received the bills for these purchases.

While they fought about it, Liv did her homework, tracing the same words, the same numerals, over and over, until she sliced through the notebook paper.

"This isn't hundreds of dollars, Lee. This is *thousands*. If you won't think of yourself, your own health, think of us, Liv and me."

"It's necessary."

"None of what you're doing is necessary! You need to stop!"

"When I'm done."

"When will that be? We can't pay the bills, Lee."

"This is more important."

"Than eating? Than keeping our home? Our savings are disappearing."

"Saving—that's what I'm trying to do."

Aggie had forbidden any guests until Lee got better, but Doug called Liv all the time, positive that he could help this man who'd been more of a dad to him than his own father, and when Liv broke and said okay, Doug was tossing his bike onto their lawn an hour later, a five-foot-five fifteen-year-old hero in parachute shorts who apologized to Aggie for his unannounced visit and stated his intent to go check out the shed. His kid courage broke the final fiber of Aggie's self-delusion. One tear fell from the corner of each eye.

"At least take him a coat. And shoes. He went out today in pajamas and bare feet. It's February. This is *Iowa*."

The previous night's snow allowed Doug and Liv to follow Lee's footprints step for step. Scrap wood, chicken wire, fence rods, and sundry other debris had been tossed from the shed to free up room inside. They twisted through it, and Doug knocked on the door.

"Lee?"

He responded with viper quickness. "Doug?"

"Uh-huh. Can we come in?"

A pause. "Okay."

The door creaked open, and Liv almost sobbed with relief. The shed wasn't some wildly colored, strobe-lit phantasmagoria in the style of *Oliver!* The ten-foot-square storage space had been transformed, with surprising competence, into a functional work shed, lined with pegboards from which hung assorted tools and wedged with tables upon which sat the machines driving the Flemings to financial ruin. Atop other tables, far more ominously, sat other objects covered by dusty sheets.

Lee grimaced an apology while he finished taking a note. Not in a journal, but rather a copy of *Resurrection Update*, the autographed one his students had gifted him, covered with sawdust. Its presence seemed both perverse and natural. Her father found poetry everywhere; it made sense he'd find it inside his own madness.

He shut the book and looked up. It seemed that Lee Fleming, emcee of a hundred events, practiced hand shaker, had forgotten the basics of interaction. His hands tried his skinny hips, the tabletop, and other places to settle, before he crossed his arms, then uncrossed them. His grin, too toothy now inside his gaunt face, was just as faltering. Liv, though, found faith in it. Her father was looking at her and Doug, really looking, like he hadn't at anyone since going missing. Hope filled Liv's chest, so much of it she couldn't speak. Doug, though—today, no one could stop Doug.

"How you doing, Lee?" Doug asked.

"I . . ."

"Building stuff?"

"Well . . ."

"Looks like you're really into it."

"I am. I suppose I am."

Keep him talking, Liv prayed.

"We got a coat and shoes for you."

"Oh?"

"Although it's pretty warm in here."

"Yes."

"School's not the same," Doug said. "Kids miss you."

"Oh. That's nice. That's nice to hear."

"Other than that, you're not missing much. Same old junk."

"Well, yes, I suppose that's true."

"Anyway, I haven't seen you in a while."

"No."

"Guess I kind of missed you, too."

"Thank you."

"You're supposed to say, 'Doug, life has been meaningless without you.'"

Lee's upper lip twitched—the start of a real smile. Liv leaned forward, desperate to see it completed.

"You've been . . ." Lee searched. "Getting along?"

Doug shrugged. "I guess. Restocking from the New Year's blitz."

Lee gazed at the ceiling, as if he could see the sky, as well as things up there that might need scaring off with explosions. Doug took the opportunity to glance at Liv, and the sharp cunning of his look almost made her sob in gratitude. He gave her a quick nod; he was going for it.

"So, what are you making?"

Lee looked back down, blinked, and then, in a moment Liv knew she'd never forget, a warmth lit up his eyes, and he grinned like he used to whenever he saw Liv and Doug, then lifted a hand nicked with cuts and beckoned them closer, as in years past he'd done to show off costume designs or set blueprints. They crowded close, the sharp resin of sawn wood shooting up their nostrils, the blunt tang of fresh metal giving them headaches. Liv was so close to her father that their arms were touching. She had to force herself not to latch on like a little girl.

It was as if he hadn't realized how eager he was to share his activities. He introduced the machines like a crowd of new friends—lathe, grinder, drill, welder, table saw—and then ripped the sheets from the concealed objects and jabbered about his creations like they were model trains instead of deadly monsters of metal. He'd always been happiest, Liv recalled, when he was working.

They were traps, Lee said, to catch the skinners when they came back, which they would, though don't be scared—even though skinners were foxy, no way they'd get past six different kinds of traps. Liv was struck speechless by the long, lubricated teeth of Amputator and the sanded fulcrum and lever of Hangman's Noose. Back then, the other four traps were in fledgling stages, but already she could sense their menace.

She didn't have to feign interest; she only had to tamp down her dread. Her dad had made no positive progress since *Oliver!* He'd spiraled further into obsession. Doug, she thought, was laying it on too thick with his wows and questions, until an uneasy realization settled over her. Doug wasn't faking. He really thought this stuff was amazing. Later, she'd almost believe she'd seen him crumple his Monk Block Corn Maze plans right there in favor of this wilder infatuation.

Doug lowered his voice and asked the question that took the most courage to ask.

"What did they *do* to you up there?"

Aggie had shielded Liv from Lee's detailed chronicle, and until that instant Liv had found it belittling. Not now. She couldn't handle knowing, she abruptly knew it, and she mumbled some excuse before bolting from the dim, crowded space into the atomic-blast light of a winter's day. Her father's confessional tones chased her until she made it to the front yard, where she watched her exhalations turn into unidentified flying objects.

Doug ambled up twenty minutes later, his silence saying everything Liv needed to know about her dad's suffering. Doug was a blurter by trade; his sudden sensitivity to her feelings riled her.

"You don't actually believe him, do you?" she demanded.

Doug picked up his bike, leaving a shadow version of it imprinted in the snow. Liv felt like a shadow version of herself, paper-thin next to a friend newly heavied by her father's report. Doug slung his leg over the crossbar and gave her a maddeningly gentle look.

"How come you're so sure it's *not* true?" he asked.

How naive could you be? Still, she felt reproached, and by the

April thaw, all six traps were built, installed, and benefitting from Lee's regular improvements, which he made with a paranoid exactitude that he took pains to ingrain in them—now that he'd begun to talk to Liv and Doug, he wouldn't stop. *Put the prevailing wind at the trap's back, Liv. Use existing terrain as cover, Doug. Let's catch some critters and taxidermy their feet, then run them over the area so it looks natural.* Doug repeated each tip softly; Lee took notes in *Resurrection Update*; Liv wondered how any of this could possibly end well.

It couldn't: Lee next shifted to weaponry. He explained that it was impossible to know how many skinners would be sent to reclaim him. The craft he'd been taken aboard had carried maybe a dozen, but there could be other ships, even a mothership. Doug, eager to capitalize on his knowledge of explodables, suggested grenades, maybe dynamite, but Lee nixed them. Skinners would smell the gunpowder. Like the traps, the weapons had to be built from raw elements.

Weapons, Lee lectured, historically instilled fear in enemies on sight, as seen in the illustrated *Encyclopedia of Arms* he'd checked out from the library. Gold leaf, inlaid silver, and intricate reliefs were far outside his artisan ability; even getting components to be symmetrical was difficult. Yet it was this crudeness that instilled his armaments with a berserker's gap-toothed, punch-drunk intimidation. Within five weeks of bruising workdays, Lee fashioned over twenty weapons, all benighted with names to further gird them with power.

Everyone had a favorite. The weapon Lee slid into his belt before checking the traps was called Lizardpoint, a twenty-inch, fishhook-shaped fighting pick with origins in turn-of-the-century Ghana. The wooden shaft was wrapped in hyena hide (it had cost Lee a small fortune), save for the crocodile-skin grip. Doug's choice was Maquahuitl, an Aztec club that looked like an oar studded along both edges with thirteen stone blades. Doug's dumbbell exercises had made him strong enough to wield it, though his shortness made swinging it a tottering, top-heavy effort. Liv, against better judgment, was enchanted by a thrusting weapon favored by late-eighteenth-century Indian rogues, made from two antelope horns bolted together, both tips tapering to steel blades. Lee had dubbed it Mist for how the horns' ripples looked like mist settling over an imagined Indian horizon.

The shed became known as the Armory. Ever at the ready was a host of other amateur reproductions, each of which hung on a wall within a chalk outline. When space ran out, Lee dangled them from the ceiling on chains.

It was under a red-and-white sky of sunset and snow that Lee paused over his sharpening of the handle of a Russian poleax and gazed at Liv and Doug, snowflakes making his unshaven scruff cottony. Both Liv and Doug audibly caught their breaths, somehow aware of the magnitude and power of the moment.

"If anything ever happens to me," he said, "and you two have to deal with this on your own, you have everything you need. The traps, the weapons. You know what to do."

They nodded, so eagerly that snow scattered from their winter hats. They would do whatever he asked, and as soon as possible, so that this *anything* he suggested might happen to him would never, ever happen. Liv may not have believed in her dad's story as Doug did, but she believed in her dad, his goodness.

Liv squirreled updates on her father for her mother, concocting positive spins. Both Liv and Aggie agreed Doug's influence had been a godsend; when he wasn't coughing or vomiting, Lee was talking, smiling, interacting. But the sight of her husband, daughter, and daughter's friend in the backyard cavorting with lethal weapons appeared to be too much for Aggie. She began to turn away from Liv's reports, jabbering about the night job she was about to start at the steakhouse, won't that be fun?

She started the job on Lee's forty-ninth birthday. Before she left, the three of them sat around the table staring at a cake no one except John wanted. What do you give a forty-nine-year-old alien abductee who appeared to be dying? Aggie had chosen a seventy-dollar, water-proof, scratch-resistant, oil-filled compass with adjustable wristband. Her husband had disappeared for four days once; if it happened again, maybe the compass would help him get back.

Lee, however, seemed to take the compass as proof that Aggie believed him—at last, she believed him! He busted open like a dropped pumpkin, exploding with tears. With a bony arm, he reached blindly for Aggie, and she let herself be pulled in. Liv, watching this, felt ill—hers was the unhealthiest family alive. Then her dad reached for her, too, and instantly she revised her thoughts. How unhealthy could a family be that laughed, that sobbed, that embraced like this?

"This'll help me get those skinners," Lee wept. "I love you both so much."

10.

LIV'S FINGERS WERE ALL OVER THE place, drained of dexterity as if they'd been severed. Three apps, clownlike in their jolly, trivial purposes, popped open before her sweaty digits managed to hit the Contacts app. It leaped to her Recents, but Doug wasn't there—damn her for letting Doug slide off the edge of her world. Her finger hit Favorites, but Doug wasn't there, either. Had she deleted him from the list? Doug, who'd answered his phone every time in life it had mattered? She scrolled and found his name, those comforting four letters.

Of course he answered right away.

Of course he knew something was wrong.

"Liv? You okay?"

"There's—we—in the, in the—"

"Slow down, slow down. Is somebody hurt?"

"No—yes—there's—the, in the trap—"

"Oh my god, I knew it." Doug's voice, right off, was hoarse with emotion. "Don't move. *Don't move.*"

She still expected a bicycle's gravel skid, even though Doug had been driving a decade-old junker for a couple of years. Its skid was louder and throatier, coming ten minutes after the call. Liv sprinted the width of the house and unlocked the front door, and he came barreling inside, taking her by the arms, the kind of physical contact he would never initiate except that she'd clutched at him first, at his sleeves, which, of course, didn't exist, her ragged, paint-chipped nails digging into his biceps.

"I don't know what—it's back there, Doug, in the—I saw it, in the trap, it's—"

"Okay, shh, Liv, c'mon, shut up."

She pointed toward the backyard, the dark impossibilities of a hidden world.

"Yeah?" Doug's eyes shone like new pennies. "You sure?"

She nodded. He broke away. Doug still knew where everything was. He gathered the lantern flashlight from the laundry room, the softball bat from her bedroom closet, her old jump rope from the basement toy chest, a chef's knife from the kitchen drawer. He took the flashlight and bat and gave her the rest.

"No," she said. "We can't, we can't go—"

"Listen to me. We need to check this out. Make sure you're right."

"I don't want to see it again, I don't—"

"You'll be fine. Stay right behind me. Okay? Stay directly behind me."

The two cracks of the door's lock and knob were like double-barrel shots. Liv cowered, and when she recovered, she saw Doug leaping down the steps, his pale arms reflective in the night, the black lawn mowed by the flashlight's beam. His bold charge gave Liv a surge of confidence. She ran after him into a night the temperature and texture of sweaty skin, the dream objects of knife and rope transforming into actual physical objects in her hands.

Doug ripped a blue tarp from a rotten pile of wood, wadded it, jammed it under an armpit.

In the woods the flashlight was a chisel chipping through old black paint. Doug would scramble down a slope, and Liv would feel a hundred miles away, only to scramble down the same slope and crash into Doug, her brandished knife zinging against his metal bat. The night kept tensing, flexing, feinting. She felt pummeled, though nothing more lethal than a twig touched her.

The instant the flashlight beam struck metal, they both pulled back, but it was too late. All the expected colors and textures—brown, gray, green, rough, stony, leafed—were disrupted by a thing that was shockingly white and of slippery smoothness, a thing that, worst of all, *squirmed*. Liv took the knife with both hands. Doug fumbled the other tools, the bat clattering against the flashlight so that the light spun, and the whole forest appeared to tumble down eternity's hill.

"Stay behind," Doug gasped, and she did, placing her knifed fist against his spine and taking to the balls of her feet, knees bent, just like all her coaches taught her. She couldn't see anything beyond the outline of Doug's long, messy hair. She felt him shuffle a few steps closer, and she closed the gap so that her fist remained at his back. It was all that kept her from falling through a chasm into hell.

The light steadied. Doug hissed.

"Jesus. Jesus."

"Is it?" Liv begged. "Is it?"

"Rope."

She had to think about what the word meant, which hand held it, how that hand worked. He pulled the jump rope through her fist, burning her palm.

"Stay," he whispered.

Was he talking to her? Or it? Doug inched away, and Liv forced herself to remain still, the last human left in the black of outer space. The flashlight had been placed upon the ground, turning blades of grass into seven-foot shadow-spikes. There was rustling, first Doug's knees into leaves, second the snake rattle of the tarp being flapped out to full size. An absence of sound lasted forever, until forever broke and Amputator's jaws creaked. Doug was doing the dirty work, the same as he ever did, prying open the trap by hand—hazardous in daylight, treacherous at night—which meant he was right next to the thing, maybe touching it, and when she heard the clack of the opened jaws, her one thought was that he'd set it free, and like any wounded thing, now it would fight.

But the next noise was the soft crunch of the thrown tarp. Liv saw it, lit from below for a second, a radiant blue parachute. Doug leaped on top of it to bring it down hard, and for the next fifty or sixty seconds Liv was paralyzed by razor-thin sights and truncated sounds. The flashlight only caught Doug's feet, which dug into the dirt as he torqued his body, wrestling either the thing or the tarp itself. He exhaled in hard, isolated puffs and grunted with strain.

Liv couldn't hear anything else—definitely not the muffled *sweck, wourk, clirp*.

Liv flinched at a whip of rope. Doug was tying the tarp around the thing. The plastic ends of the jump rope clacked as they were knotted.

"I got it," he wheezed. "Get the light, the light."

The dragging was an awful, bumpy effort scored by fleshy squishes and birdlike chirps, with Doug on point, his back sickled, using the jump rope's knot to yank their cargo over roots, rocks, and weeds, obstacles ignorable on foot but oppressive when towing. A dozen times Liv could have helped, but she was holding the flashlight, wasn't she? And the knife, too? Doug, in the greatest mercy he'd ever shown, did not once ask her to grab the feet. Were they even feet? Would they kick if she touched them? She kept the light on Doug's back so she didn't have to know.

Liv wasn't sure where they were headed until Doug's shoulder rammed against the shed door. It wasn't locked; this was Custer Road. Doug freed one of his dragging hands to grope for the knob and wrench it. Time and moisture had done damage. The swollen door stuck, but Doug slugged his shoulder against it until it burst inward. Doug tripped inside, still gripping the tarp-thing, and Liv followed, a veil of cobweb settling over her face. She heard Doug pull a light string and nothing happened; he pulled another and nothing. Only in contrast to these delicate clicks did Liv notice John barking, an old dog but still possessing dog instincts, and she was so glad he was kept indoors at night, so glad he feared the backyard.

The last light bulb worked. The first item Liv saw was the light string itself, captured in balletic rebound. That same second, Doug rolled the thing across the floor, upsetting years of dust. The tarp half unwrapped, and the thing thumped into the far wall. Items hanging on the wall shook and swayed enough to remind Liv that this wasn't a shed, this was the Armory, and her father's weapons remained snug inside their chalk-outlined slots—Maquahuitl, Mist, every one but Lizardpoint, which had disappeared along with Lee.

Doug sprang up, backpedaling into Liv and gasping as if he'd done the whole operation—release the trap, lay the tarp, knot the rope, drag it home—on a single lungful of breath.

The bulb's rocking slowed, focusing its yellow parabola on the thing below it, collapsed amid the blue tarp and tangled in jump rope. The thing wore no clothing. What Liv could see of its skin looked like thin, pliable plastic, absent of pores or hair. Where the flesh was lax, it was an opaque white, like milk halved with tap water. Where the flesh was stretched tight, it was translucent. When the being writhed, she could see interior organs of shocking color—pink, green, yellow—strain against the abdomen.

"What do we do?" she hissed.

Doug seemed caught in a trance.

"Doug! Come on! It's moving!"

But he ducked to get a better look, and Liv, heart ramming, followed suit.

The alien was roughly five feet tall and humanoid. You could wrap a hand around its tiny tube of a neck, which somehow supported a spherical head almost reptilian in its lack of a forehead. Two eyes as large as baseballs protruded from shallow sockets and jerked in independent directions. The irises were of such crystalline blue that Liv had to force herself to look at the tiny nostril notches and mouse-hole ears. The being continued to chirp, though its mouth was no beak. It was a lathered, gnashing turmoil of wet palate and too much bone—the teeth were jumbled, askew, jutting at odd angles. What this mess of teeth might be able to chew was impossible to say.

"Let's *go*," Liv pleaded.

"It's not getting up," Doug whispered. "It's hurt."

How else, Liv had to admit, could you interpret the thing's writhing? Its chest, no wider than that of a child's, beat up and down under a set of exoskeletal ribs. What looked like a heart—a throbbing brown bag—was tucked beneath the sternum, as vulnerable as an unpunctured egg yolk. Farther down, Liv saw purple lungs inflate and deflate in fright. The ribs weren't the only exposed bones; yellow knobs crested from the flesh at the elbows, knees, knuckles, and shoulders. From the scapulas dangled two scrawny arms, the armpits webbed with veined membranes. The arms ended in thick, three-fingered hands, the left of which was squeezed shut, tight as a rock.

"There's zip ties," Doug said. "On the bench. Right beside it."

"Doug, no."

"What else are we going to do? It could crawl right after us."

Doug licked his lips, emboldened himself with urgent mutters, then crept forward. The alien's huge eyes twitched. Its heart flexed harder. Doug darted and snatched a handful of black plastic ties. The thing chirped and drew back against the wall, but its cycling legs couldn't find purchase in the tangle of tarp. Its kicking freed the lower half of its body; soft-looking cysts, maybe tumors, covered it from waist to knee.

When had Doug Monk become the bravest person in the world? With a strangled cry, he reached down and grabbed the alien's right arm. Liv gasped, wondering if Doug's skin would begin to boil, expecting long claws to switchblade from the thing's three fingers. Before anything so frightful could happen, Doug snugged a zip tie to its wrist, shoved it against the wall's crossbar, and locked it tight. The alien's rubbery neck twisted to see and its body torqued that way, too, and Liv got a glimpse of the bony, six-inch tail that extended from its spine.

The alien's pitch sharpened—*Louk! Louk! Louk!* Doug hopped on its body, took hold of the opposite arm, and zip-tied it to the same crossbar before scrambling out of range. The thing's yowls cut off, and its round head rolled left and right as its eyes skipped from point to point. It gave both arms an experimental shake. Its armpit membranes pulled taut.

"That's a skinner," Doug panted.

Liv fought to place the word. This all meant something, didn't it? Beyond the immediate horror and danger? This was a vindication. Proof of knowledge. Refutation of insanity. Doug and Liv had heard more than anyone else alive about Lee Fleming's skinners, the Green Man, the Floating Pumpkin. All things, she supposed, were uglier when removed from a high-school-musical set and exposed in their natural state.

"It's not blue," she managed. "Dad said they were blue."

"It's kind of blue."

"It's clear."

"Maybe the lights on the ship were blue."

"And they're supposed to be wrinkly. It's smooth."

"Because it shed its skin. He said that's what they do."

"He said they don't have mouths."

"That doesn't look like any mouth I've ever seen."

"Dad *said* they don't have *mouths*."

Doug glared, the first time he'd taken his eyes off the alien. "There was the Green Man, right? The Green Man didn't look anything like the skinners. Maybe there's different kinds? How am I supposed to know?"

"There was one called the Whistler."

"Yeah. Right. And it made a sound."

"This one makes sounds."

Even amid terror, she recognized the childish idiocy of her comment. She needed to wake the hell up. She shook her head. Still she felt muddy. She slapped her cheek. She bit her tongue. An extraterrestrial being was in her garden shed. No, it was simpler, broader than that. An extraterrestrial being *existed*. She was looking at something few people had ever seen, and if she didn't grow up and act like an adult, it might get away, and then she'd be just like her father—a madman raving about something no one else would believe.

She rooted her phone from her pocket. She brought up the keypad. She looked at Doug for support, but he was staring at the alien again. Fine, it didn't matter. She tapped in 9, then 1, then, because of her trembling figures, a 4, and had to kill the call, then tapped 9, but accidentally twice, and killed the call again, and then with ridiculous slowness tapped 9, then 1, and was poised to press the final 1, picturing the cavalry quickness of the ambulance that had bounded onto the town square the day her dad had lost his mind—or so everyone had believed.

But she didn't press the final digit, and that millimeter distance between fingertip and touchscreen would haunt the rest of her life. Doug was saying something, a single word, louder and louder until it broke through her absorption, and it took her looking up from her phone to make sense of it.

"Scalp," he was saying. "Scalp."

What a peculiar word, Liv thought.

Doug stood at the alien's side. He looked sick.

"Like a scalp," he whimpered.

She felt nothing when she stepped alongside Doug. She felt nothing when her phone slipped from her hand. She thought it probable she would feel nothing ever again. As reluctantly as a funeral-parlor guest might turn her eyes to a loved one's casket, she followed Doug's pointed finger to the alien's left hand, which, until then, had been squeezed into a fist. The three thick fingers were splayed now, perhaps because it had no strength left to hide what it carried.

What it held in its palm was not a scalp in the literal sense, but Doug was right. It was a souvenir of conquest stripped off a past victim. The two of them stood shoulder to sweaty shoulder, in silence but for the alien's wheezing, their ears tuned to the woods, for now it seemed quite possible they might hear the bangs, snaps, and crashes of five other traps being triggered, as there was no mistaking the trophy the skinner held.

It was her father's wrist compass.

11.

SKINNERS BLEED. **THAT'S WHAT FIFTEEN-**
year-old Liv repeated to herself, despite her disbelief, as she sprinted
through the forest, the uneven ground seeming to rush at her instead
of vice versa. Mist's antelope-horn handle was so sweat-slick she had
to use both hands, which meant no fending off the springy July
branches that slapped and pine needles that poked, nor the morning sun that fired like buckshot through the leafy canopy, the whole
world turned alien and enemy. Her dad was out of sight, but his
shouts echoed—*Doug, straight ahead! Liv, swing right!*—instructions
she couldn't follow, not moving this quickly, not being this scared.

This was not some test run. They were chasing a skinner, a thing
that did not exist, though that did not mean the chase itself, the
speed, the very-real weapons, her father's fever, the contagious madness, the danger of it all wasn't real.

She held Mist in front of her like handlebars. In the breathless dread of the moment, she nearly believed that her father was, in fact, chasing a skinner, and if that was true, and the creature popped up in front of her, it was best to lead with something sharp, wasn't it? Lee hadn't only assured her and Doug that skinners bled, he'd even described that their blood, like ours, was red. At that, Doug had winked at Liv. If Lee knew the color of skinner blood, that meant he'd managed to make a few of the bastards bleed.

Liv heard a whistle and caught the blur of a projectile. Lizard-point, her dad's African fighting pick, had been tucked, as ever, under his belt, but he'd also come armed with a cowhide-gripped Inuit bow and matching quiver of rosewood arrows, and he'd just taken a shot at what he thought was the skinner. Liv had known the bow was futile. With all the weapon forging, trap setting, and hunt planning, there'd been little time for her dad to master the thing. He would be, at best, inaccurate, and, at worst, dangerous to Liv and Doug.

Danger, though, was a concept leeched of meaning. Playing defense at home with traps had begun to wear upon Lee. If he'd been ill before, now he was hanging by a thread. Days passed without sleep. His voice was raw from the acid of frequent vomiting. Sometimes he would faint, and when he fell, his bones clacked like wooden blocks. Despite all of this, he'd taken the offensive in May, heading up hunting expeditions of escalating ambition, one every week or so, first into the same woods inside which he'd seeded the traps, and then beyond, hopping from one grove of trees to another in a haphazard path across the countryside.

Liv stayed on the team for one reason. Someone had to keep an eye on Lee Fleming. Doug was too rabid an apprentice to make independent judgments. Aggie's two jobs, meanwhile, had turned her into a rag doll—and a chunk of that income needed to go to wine, didn't it? Letting a horribly ill, unstable husband take her daughter on unsafe, probably illegal treks might have suggested Aggie was an unfit parent, but Liv understood her mom's perspective. Lee always returned from these hunts greatly improved, color returned to his cheeks, able to keep down several meals in a row.

Hope, a creature of tiny claws, hung in there.

Today, July 15, was the final hunt, the last day Liv would ever see her father, and though she didn't know that, a sense of doom blanketed the day like a thick snowfall. Finally her dad's birthday wrist compass had a purpose: Black Glade, only a half-hour drive from home, was Iowa's largest forest, a thorned and brambled repository for every cautionary tale told by adults and campfire shocker told by teens, and Lee's confusing, illogical tracking of the skinners had led them to it. The woods were worse than Liv imagined—still morning and already she felt lost inside sickening growth and pregnant death.

Lee had instructed them, through gruesome coughs, to keep one eye on the forest floor for skinners' shed skin, and fruitless though it was, Liv did it, which is why she didn't get a good look at the creature that dashed from beneath a bush to her left. She cried out, swinging Mist in its general direction. Leaves shivered and branches bounced as the animal raced through the underbrush. It was a rabbit or squirrel, she knew that, but her dad didn't, and he hollered back.

"Guard the perimeter, Liv! Flush it to me!"

She started running—and something hit her. It felt like a whip across her midsection, and a second across her thighs, and she was stopped as surely as if she'd hit a wall, her momentum blasting the air from her lungs and ripping Mist from her hands. Next she felt jabs of pain, three or four. She'd been shot, she was sure of it, her father having mistaken her for a skinner. How, then, was she still standing? She forced herself to look down, expecting an arrow. There, in the overgrown brush, lay the remains of a barbed-wire fence. She'd charged right into it.

She leaned back and felt two barbs dislodge from her belly. The punctures weren't deep, but her shirt was spotted with blood, and she felt stirrings of panic. She tried to withdraw from the fence, but her right leg resisted. It had managed to punch between two wires, tearing them from rotted posts, and now her leg was snarled in rusted barbs so similar to one of Lee's traps that, for a minute, she was certain the skinner was her.

"Quit wiggling."

Doug emerged from the trees, tracing the line of the fence. Despite the terrain, he hadn't altered his parachute shorts or sleeveless shirt, though he'd added to the ensemble an orange camouflage hat and painted his cheeks with streaks of black mud. In one hand dangled the stone-bladed Maquahuitl. With his other hand, he unbuttoned a side pocket of his shorts.

"You okay?"

Liv nodded, still shaken, and displayed bloody fingers.

"Ah, a wounded soldier," Doug said. "I'm afraid we're going to have to put you down."

He grinned, and Liv knew he was trying to set her at ease. She forced a laugh, and it did help break the paralyzing shock. From his pocket Doug withdrew a giant-sized Swiss Army knife. He set down

Maquahuitl, extracted from the knife a set of mini pliers, and knelt beside her. He took gentle hold of the wire and, after a couple of twists, a barb popped free.

"Maybe three more. Stand still and try not to bleed to death."

"As opposed to what?"

Doug pincered the next barb and shrugged. "Going back."

He didn't look at her when he said it. Radiating from her gut, as if released by the punctures, Liv felt the broil of abashment. Doug was far from stupid. He knew she didn't believe. But if anything was clear from the careful way in which he held her hips so as not to pinch her skin, he wanted her there anyway. With the quickness of a Black Glade wind gust, her every anxious emotion was overcome by gratefulness for this friend, who had, in some ways, given her back her father, and who, despite their divergent beliefs, had never quit believing in her.

"Freed," Doug announced, "to crash into other fences."

"So chivalrous of you, sir."

Doug pocketed the tool, picked up Maquahuitl, and handed her Mist, first using it to gesture into the shadows.

"We better catch up. He'll worry."

"Right." Her dad would indeed worry, but for a make-believe reason: It was an encirclement of skinners that had waylaid Liv, not a remnant of some farmer's failed attempt to keep Black Glade in check.

They followed bad, crackling coughs until they came upon Lee standing dead center in a clearing, taking readings from his compass. He blinked heavy lids, looking at Doug and Liv through yellowed, red-veined eyes.

"It got away," he said.

Doug nodded, accepting his culpability, and choked up on Maquahuitl as a promise to do better.

"What did I say about pocket formation, Doug? If you're on left wing, you need to stay ten or twenty yards ahead, not behind." *Cough.* "And Liv. We need to be quiet out there." *Cough, cough.* "The closer we get to one—and we were very, very close—the more critical it becomes." *Cough, cough, cough, cough, cough.* "You can't be screaming like that."

"She ran into barbed wire," Doug explained.

Gone along with the flesh that illness had peeled from Lee's face was his ability to hide any emotion. Liv watched the drill-sergeant points of his eyes diffuse as the dad she remembered resurfaced. He beckoned with a thin, trembling hand, the compass rolling loosely around his skinny wrist.

"Let me see."

He had, of course, a first aid kit in a coverall pocket, and as he set to cleaning and bandaging her gouges, he walked back his critiques. Maquahuitl was the heaviest weapon; Doug's slowed speed was understandable. Liv's startled yell was not, after all, entirely inadvisable; war cries were meant to immobilize foes with fear. Liv nodded but suffered a hunch that this was the last of their quests. The wildness of this hunt had to be some sort of climax.

Lee consulted *Resurrection Update*, as well as a topographic map folded inside it, then tucked both back into his pack. He then picked up the useless bow and quiver, weighed them in opposite hands, and placed them upon the forest floor to be left for future adventurers.

Lizardpoint was his natural weapon; anything else would only continue to complicate the hunt.

"Arrowhead formation," he said. "Doug, you up to taking point?"

It was dusk when the three of them crowded together at one of Black Glade's edges. It was a literal borderland, a taut wire fence separating them from an abandoned farm. The house's white paint had been shredded by time. The outbuildings were hammocks of rusted spoil. The dual silos had become dead gods wearing bird-nest crowns. The place was deceased, though it was surrounded by life: hilly grazeland for cows and rich, rolling cornfields. Liv had an eerie sensation that they were trapped inside a maze, bigger than the one Doug dreamed of mowing into the Monk Block and with a gimmick better than the Trick: They hadn't even known they'd entered it.

Liv looked to her dad for guidance, the last time she'd ever do so.

Lee's face, pale already, had gone a chalky white. His eyes had gone wide and unbelieving. His lips moved like a fish's mouth, unable to find enough air to breathe.

"I remember," he whispered.

"Remember what?" Liv asked, terrified of the answer.

"This place." He covered his horrified mouth with a hand. "This *place*."

Lee's eyes, looking big enough to drop from his skull, skittered across the outline of the farm, as if each building they landed on gave off invisible, painful rays. It didn't matter how old Liv was or wasn't; seeing a parent so terrified triggered a primordial response of equivalent terror.

"Dad," Liv said.

"There's so many," he whispered. "I forgot. I forgot how many."

"Skinners?" Doug asked.

"*How* could I have *forgotten*?" Lee's voice splintered.

"Dad." Liv's voice, too, broke into pieces.

Lee whipped around and gripped Liv's shoulders.

"I forgot. I forgot this place. I shouldn't have brought you. I have to do this alone. You need to leave. Both of you. See that field? There's a road on the other side. Go through the field. Flag down a car."

"No way," Doug said. "We're coming with."

Lee's arm lashed out, snagged Doug's shirt, and pulled their heads close together. He hissed furiously, spittle popping along his pale lips.

"You are not! You do *exactly* what I say and *get away!*"

It was the most aggressive Lee Fleming had ever behaved, and it nailed Doug and Liv to the trees. Lee released Doug and frowned at his own hands, perhaps at the person he'd become. Dusk light shone against his battered fingernails, and that was prodding enough. Quickly he retied his boots and pulled on his gloves. He worked his fingers around Lizardpoint's crocodile-skin grip.

Lee's lips trembled over clenched teeth as he took a shuddering breath, stood the tallest he could, and fired off a military salute to Doug, the same kind with which Major Dawkins had honored Lee at birthday barbecues. Doug, still stung by Lee's shouting, blinked in surprise. But what had Lee been teaching him if not to be a proper soldier? Doug's cowered back straightened, and he returned the salute.

Lee turned to Liv. He grimaced as if his legs were locked inside one of his steel-toothed traps. He opened his mouth to speak, but that, too, looked painful. What he did, then, was nothing, except look sorry, and out of time.

He whirled away, charged the fence, and lowered his ear within inches of the top wire. Liv felt eviscerated, barely able to stand, yet still understood. Her dad believed the fence to be electric, and some scrap of rural insight told her that electric fences ran in pulses, and her dad was listening for them. Liv thought she could feel them, each sizzling beat the mirror of her bruised, burned heart. Lee's hands hovered over the wire, preparing to make his move.

Liv ran, leaving Doug behind and colliding with her father so hard he had to roll to the side to avoid the electric fence. Lizard-point's metal pick clacked against Mist's sharpened blade. Somehow both father and daughter had turned lethal, too sharp to be held safely, but they held each other all the same.

"Don't go," she cried. "Please don't go, please don't go."

He held her cheeks in his hands, but all she could feel were his gloves' silicone grips.

"You have to let me go," he whispered. "I have unfinished business."

She tried to press her face into his chest, but he held her firm.

"I know you don't believe in any of this, Liv."

She was exposed, shamed, but also desperate to tell him that he was wrong, she *did* believe that *he* believed, and wasn't that enough?

"Dad, I—"

He shook his head, out of time.

"It's all right. Doug . . . he wants to believe. He needs to believe. He doesn't have the choices we've always had. You're a doubter like your mother. That's good. That means you're smart. Just listen to me, sweetie. Listen to me and then let me go. I want to say I'm sorry. For everything. How I ruined everything our life used to be. What I've done to your poor mother. I just . . . *forgot* things. And now it's all coming back."

None of it made any sense to Liv. She had a gutful of protests, enough to last all night, all day, all her life, but the stiff surfaces of his gloves slid down her face and took hold of her shoulders. He managed a pained smile and flicked his eyes up to the shadowing skies. His last words were not his, but James Galvin's, his favorite verse, one he told seniors on the final day of class, inspiration for their future.

"'Perhaps you didn't realize,'" he quoted. "'Anything can happen under a sky like this.'"

Gently, like Mr. Fleming the husband, the father, the English teacher, he held her away from his body. He unzipped his pack and withdrew his copy of *Resurrection Update*, wrinkled from study, bloated by rain, stained by coffee, studded with sawdust. He held it out to her. She stared at it. He prodded her in the sternum with the book until she felt her hands wrap around it. She stroked the cover. It was lightweight, she thought, for a soul.

When she next looked up, Mr. Fleming, the pariah, the lunatic, the survivalist, had one hand on a fence post, and having found the gap in pulses he was after, he climbed over the wires. To Liv it was a leap of unimaginable distance, the crossing from one world to another. He landed in a sloppy stumble, but righted himself and walked, then jogged, then ran in the direction of the silos, Lizardpoint at the ready.

By the time Doug joined her at the fence, Lee Fleming was a pale firefly. Doug must have known as well as Liv that they'd never see him again. He hoisted Maquahuitl over his head and brought it down on the fence, staving the wires downward, snapping some, bending the nearest poles inward. It was a mourning rage, violent as a cloudburst, and it would be minutes before it was through, fence posts dented to hell, wires pounded into the dirt, and Doug crying out, perhaps from electrocution, perhaps not, finishing by hammering the ground with his club until his red, grimacing face was lost in plumes of dust.

Liv felt the dry wind from Maquahuitl toss her hair, but she did not flinch. She could feel, extending from the muck of her sorrow, a different emotion, one that, like skinners, she didn't want to believe existed. The thing was called *relief.* Life would be difficult without her father. But wasn't it also true that, in some ways, life would be easier?

The book felt undeserved in her hands. Either her dad was a traitor or she was. She thought of "Sapphic Suicide Note," and wondered if the book itself, placed into her hands, was the suicide note of her father.

She thrust the book into Doug's arms. He tried to hand it back, but she shrugged it off. Doug was adamant; in future days, and weeks, and months, he'd keep trying to return it, telling her it was meant for her, assuring her that its poetry, just as Lee had always said, was full of secrets. She refused to talk about it, and as their relationship narrowed over the following two years to little beyond Sunday morning trap checking, Doug quit trying. Lee's italics, whatever they were worth, belonged to Doug.

12.

LIV LIFTED THE COMPASS INTO THE
moonlight. The box her father had opened on his birthday had
boasted scratch-resistance, but that claim had been disproven. A slash
ran across its face, northeast to southwest. She couldn't blame the
manufacturers, who hadn't worked into their calculations the trials
of an alien race. The plastic wristband was notched and discolored,
but the latch still worked, and she cinched it around her left wrist.
It was slimy against her skin, and she heard her father's town-square
shout: *Biologic evidence!*

She'd given Doug her father's notated copy of *Resurrection Update*,
but this gift was different. He had worn this. It was a part of him.
The compass still worked, wobbling in oil as she sharked her arm
through the pale light. It was a good distraction until the moonlight hit the glass wrong and refracted a blob of light onto Doug,
who lay curled on her floor among dirty clothes. The slow rise of his

back suggested he was asleep, a state that seemed inconceivable when they'd retreated to her bedroom hours earlier.

They'd come inside because of John. He hadn't quit barking, and who knew if Aggie, when she got home, would react to the dog's agitation by going into the backyard. They'd fed John a second dinner and led him to Liv's bedroom, and once there, nobody wanted to go back to the Armory. Here was a room packed with comforting, understandable objects, and inside it they'd huddled until Aggie had come home, shuffled about the kitchen, clinked wine bottle and glass, and retired to bed. Liv and Doug took the cue to lie down and stare at the ceiling. It was the innocent sleepovers of their youth turned inside out.

Doug, though, was a master sleeper, and never had Liv envied the ability more. Her eyeballs throbbed. Her chest ached from the fist-bash of her heart. Her mind raced through competing image streams of her father hopping the electric fence and the skinner zip-tied inside the shed. She had no emotions. Or perhaps had all of them at once?

She sat up. That felt better. She put her feet on the floor. The floor held. Her phone was right there. She could still call 911. Instead she stood up. Doug didn't move. John's eyes didn't open. She stepped over them to the door. Her muscles cried out in relief. She entered the hall, closed the door behind her. Her legs begged to run. She could. She still wore shoes. To sprint through the night, to drown in endorphins, what a release it would be. She unlocked and opened the back door. A billion excited bugs rubbed their wings.

Before leaving the shed, they'd piled lumber against the door. Lee Fleming had designed six intricate traps, but a pile of loose wood was the best his protégés could do. She undid the blockade, the wood sharp and real inside what otherwise felt like a dream. They'd also left on the lone light bulb, and already it was fading. What if it burned out and she was left in the dark with the thing? If there even *was* a thing. Maybe that's what she'd walked out here to determine.

It did not take long to confirm. The thing was right where they'd left it. It slid into view with the same dull inevitability of the TV when she entered the living room. The skinner's protuberant eyes scanned her, one rolling left while the other rolled upward. Its spindly neck shone from liquid that had oozed from its mouth. It didn't bother to struggle; its wrists were inflamed from previous efforts. Liv just stared at it, inhaling its garbage odor, acclimating herself to the shed as she might a cold swimming lake.

Liv did what only Doug had so far dared: She came closer. Her father's tables, weighed down by drills, table saws, and other metal corpses, offered slim clearance. If she stumbled, she'd fall right on top of the thing, an indescribable fate, and if she reached for the walls to catch herself, she'd bring down weapons that had waited two years to impale something. She tried to think like an aerialist, one foot in front of the other, until she stood above it.

"What did you do to my dad?" she whispered.

It blinked. Liv gasped; she hadn't known it had eyelids. They were transparent films that passed as quick as a wash of water. Its irises were big as quarters and so blue Liv believed for a moment it was daytime, and they were reflecting cloudless skies. Liv hissed in self-reprimand. This merciless thing would hold no sway over her. She held up her wrist and showed the skinner something it recognized.

"You never should've brought this." Hearing her own voice strengthened her.

The skinner's left hand, the one that had gripped the compass, sprang open its three fingers. Its bone-knuckles rapped against the wall, and the middle finger grazed Liv's hand. The finger was lukewarm and tacky, and Liv, senses heightened, took it as an attempt to reclaim the compass trophy. She leaned away even as she swiped with her right fist in defense. Her knuckle of flesh struck one of its knuckles of bone, and it hurt, and that hurt startled her, and on instinct, she kicked.

Her shoe struck the skinner where its waist was narrowest. The impact was revoltingly soft and punctured one of the gray tumors. The skinner made one of its chirps: *Yolp!* The sound was pitiful enough that she felt a quick, gasping release from her suffocating fear, and she clung desperately to that feeling to safeguard her sanity, to establish that she was stronger than this thing, and that she would be all right if only she kept it that way.

Her father's voice floated back to her.

If anything ever happens to me, and you two have to deal with this on your own, you have everything you need. The traps, the weapons. You know what to do.

Did she know what to do? She didn't think; she kicked again. Her shoe struck the thing's knee. It mewled, and its legs, with beetle speed, scrabbled to maneuver its lower half out of range. Its feet pulled free of the tarp for the first time, and Liv saw that they were three-digited like its hands, the undersides hard and segmented like chickens' feet. Its left ankle was in bad, bloody shape from where

Amputator had bit it. The skin was ripped into triangular flaps, and an inch of leg bone was visible.

She grasped at this detail, too, greedily. Only at this moment did she realize the full weight of fear that had dominated the past three years: fear that her dad was crazy, that he was deathly ill, that one day a policeman would come knocking to tell her they'd identified a pile of human bones. At the instant of striking the skinner, all that fear exploded into red rage, a feeling so much better to feel.

You know what to do.

She stomped her heel at the wounded ankle. The skinner skittered back, curling itself to a half-fetal position, thereby presenting the bigger targets of thighs and shoulder blades, not to mention tail and head. Liv stepped closer, lungs hot and churning, head on fire. She circled the skinner, mustering every warm memory of her dad she could—and kicked. (Her dad bathing her as a child, making her bubble-bath beards.) And kicked. (Her dad driving her an hour back to Iowa City to find the stuffed animal she'd left.) And kicked. (Her dad, during tricky middle school years, knowing when to be quiet and watch *Buffy* with her.) She kicked for her dad, her mom, but mostly herself, so that, for once, she would be the one delivering all the fear. She reeled back for more, reeled back, reeled back.

A hand took her shoulder. Funny for a girl wearing a compass, she'd lost all sense of direction and spun to attack. But it was Doug, sleepy-haired but not sleepy-eyed, holding up the white flag of his other hand. She cannoned her held breath, billowing hair from her face that resettled in a sweaty net. She focused on Doug's face. He looked so calm, so solid. Her knees shook. She looked at the skinner's pinkening bruises and spasming muscles and felt shame, perhaps for what she'd done, perhaps because she'd slunk from Doug to do it in secret.

"I'm tired; I'm screwed up," she mumbled. "I don't know what I'm doing."

She tried to move past him, but he sidestepped into her path and their shoulders collided. They were of equal height, but his shoulder, due to dumbbell drills, was bigger, and never had it been more apparent. Liv couldn't go backward without stepping on the skinner, and thought she'd never stood so close to Doug for so long. She could smell the dried sweat of their earlier labor, the grease of his unwashed hair. The fading bulb turned his face into a tiger-stripe mystery of light and shadow. The swinging of his straggles of hair told her that he had begun to nod.

He pushed himself into her, chest against breasts, not aggressively, not sexually, just a request for passage. Liv swiveled her body like a gate so that he could stand next to her and stare straight down at the skinner. Doug was front-lit now, his bright eyes searching the alien's body while the alien's huge blue eyes did the same thing back.

Doug called for Liv with his fingers—which closed into a fist.

"You need to put your back into it," he said.

He held up his fist so she could see it in the dim light. She lifted her hand, curled her fingers into a similar weapon. The tightening of skin across her knuckles felt good. Perhaps everything would feel good in a minute, for there was no more guilt in this shed, not when both of them were so eager to take back what they'd lost, not when both of them were so hungry to hit.

13.

EMERGING FROM THE ARMORY THAT
first night was hard. The gray predawn slid across their skin like cold
silt, gumming their eyes so they couldn't see the blood on their hands
and clothes, clotting their ears so they couldn't hear the thing's heaving on the opposite side of the door. Liv was reminded of every time
she'd crept out back to listen for her father's noises on the other side
of the same door, just to make sure his illness hadn't overtaken him
and he was lying there dead.

In stark contrast to the punishment she and Doug had rained upon
the skinner for who knew how long, they stood in the grass and shuffled their feet like strangers, until finally, using little more than grunts
to converse, they found a way to jam boards against the shed door.

"I'll buy a lock," Doug murmured.

"It's late." It sounded like her mouth was filled with moss. "Or
it's early."

Their exhausted nods goodbye were seen only from peripheral vision.

Then it was Saturday. She hauled John into her bed, a rare treat for him, and buried her face in his neck fur. Her head pounded and stomach lurched. Her mom, curious by midday, accepted Liv's excuse that she was sick. Liv didn't eat until her mom had left for the Saturday dinner shift, and then just crackers and water. So many possible actions and reactions whirled through her head she could not isolate any one of them. She didn't look out the back windows until it was almost dark, and only because she had to confirm that the boards were still in place in front of the Armory door. They were.

Then it was Sunday. How many Sundays in a row had Doug knocked on her window to get started checking the traps? Not today. She woke up early anyway. Her morning run—maybe if she went through the motions, she could wipe her brain for a little while, use adrenaline to alleviate the nausea. But as she got dressed, her back and arm muscles ached and she knew why, and she gagged over the sink and splashed water on her face and didn't dare look in the mirror. She felt as ill as her dad had been during his final year. She curled back into her bed, John's nose ice cold against her feverish skin.

Only in the afternoon did she force herself into the backyard, each step like a dare, until she got close enough to see that Doug had been there at some point to screw thick metal collars to door and frame and secure a giant padlock through both. Liv wondered if she should feel affronted that he had taken the liberty without her, but instead felt thankful. One of them had to hold it together, and apparently it wasn't going to be her.

She held her phone in her hand. It felt heavy with significance. She could text Doug, ask him how in the world he was dealing with this. She could call 911, get them out here to make the whole mess disappear, if only her mind wasn't so conflicted. Would she, who'd mercilessly beat up the thing, be damning herself to a life where any Internet search would bring up her face and details on what she'd done? She didn't know; she couldn't think that far. She needed another day. Or two, or three.

School was an assembly-line factory staffed by workers who produced pieces of paper of no consequence. To avoid morning interactions with her friends—was she even capable of speech?—Liv hid on the bottom floor, where no one would see her shaking shoulders, where the shadowy, indistinct hallways perfectly mirrored her mind's crowded confusion.

When the lunch bell rang, she headed for a far-flung bathroom inside which she could hide some more, but Krista intercepted her, waving excitedly like it was the first day of school all over again, like last week hadn't happened—if only that were true. Liv forced a smile; the lines of her face felt carved into her cheeks with a putty knife.

"You okay?" Krista asked.

"Mm-hm." It was the only sound she trusted herself to make without her voice cracking in half, after which who knew what might happen? Sobs breaking out in hot, wet splashes? Jags of ugly confessions splattering like acid?

"Something's wrong," Krista surmised.

"Nn-nn," Liv lied.

Krista put her hand on Liv's elbow. Flesh against bone—Liv had to bite down to keep from jerking away and kicking out, transported back into the nightmare of the shed. Instead of Krista's kind smile and patient gaze, it was the skinner's whorled jaws and bugged eyes. Liv told herself to be calm, be calm, be calm.

"I think I know what it is," Krista said.

Of course she knew, Liv thought wildly. The evidence must be pressed into every detail of Liv's face. Guilty, shifting eyes. Veins ballooning her temples with a panicked pulse. Literal blood and fluid crusted in her hair. Liv felt her spinal column slump, the beginning of a full collapse, and could feel the truth frothing at the base of her throat, ready to fizz upward and spill. Unconsciously she gripped Krista back and opened her mouth with a gasp, ready to confess.

"Don't let Monica get to you," Krista said.

Liv blinked at Krista as if she, too, were an alien being. Krista smiled gently.

"So you miss a couple meets. You think anyone's going to care in a few weeks?"

Liv processed Krista's words individually, like unwrapping mysterious packages. Had she said *meats*? Liv pictured the skinner's damp, piled organs. No, *meets*—cross-country meets. Liv distantly recalled a personal history as brittle as ancient papers. She thought she might like to forge a path back to those delicate, insignificant concerns, but couldn't see the way. She was lost, as if inside one of Doug's proposed mazes, and she was so scared.

"People get so wrapped up in their little dramas," Krista continued. "I mean, it's *high school*."

Liv nodded, wobbly. "Uh-huh."

"You'll come back, we'll win a meet, and you know Monica. She'll be kissing you on both cheeks."

Nodding was a way to keep Liv's heart beating. "Yeah."

Krista squeezed her arm. "Good. So let's eat? Or are you sitting with Mr. Latino Dreamboat again?"

Bruno Mayorga hadn't crossed Liv's mind in three days. Nothing good in the slightest had. Memories of his face, voice, and body language touched her like John's nose had in bed, unpleasantly pleasant, a good thing that she, having done bad things, no longer felt she had permission to accept.

"I just—" Liv pointed. "Bathroom."

Inside a toilet stall, she pressed her hot forehead against cool paint, listening to other girls come in, do their thing, and leave, everything so wildly typical, while a force inside her told her to start running through the halls, screaming to everyone that they were all sheep blind to the existence of wolves, and that they'd deserve what they got if they didn't listen to Lee Fleming's warning, albeit three years late.

She saw Doug once, slouching down the hall and clutching a textbook like a shield. Even from afar, Liv could see Doug's knuckles were torn the same as hers. He moved along, avoiding everyone's eyes as usual, but when his gaze swept across hers, he held it. Liv felt faint, but thought she could read his thoughts.

They had to feed it. Unless they wanted it to starve.

And that's not what they wanted, was it?

Krista had reminded Liv of the two cross-country meets from which she was banned, but according to Principal Gamble's edict, she was back on the practice squad today. Liv didn't waste time deliberating over whether or not to go. She bolted from school at the final bell, got in the station wagon, and on the way home held her phone in a sweaty hand, desperate to call Doug but distressed by the vague, criminal ramifications of establishing phone records.

Instead, she got home, sat trembling on the front stoop, and waited. She knew him. He'd come. A half hour later, he did. His junker pulled into the driveway, and he got out, and she stood up, instantly feeling a bit stronger, and they nodded as if this were the five hundredth day of this new life together rather than the second. They convened in the kitchen, where Doug fished out a Pop-Tart and gnashed it.

"How was your day?" He sounded tentative, hypersensitive to her reaction—all new tones for him.

"I don't know." It was the truth: Her head, her heart, her gut were in tangles, but she had no hard recollections of the day's events. "I just keep thinking . . . No one else at school . . ."

Doug nodded excitedly. "I know. No one has any idea. Of what's here. Of what's in the *universe*. It's incredible. Only we know. Liv, we're the *only ones*."

Liv smiled weakly. Doug's eyes were as brilliant as they'd looked back in the days of designing the Trick into corn-maze schemata. His life, Liv knew, had been one of lack: no real parents, no close relatives, no other friends, no money, no worthy possessions. Here, at last, he had something no one else in the world had. He would have a plan to go with it. Of course he would.

Doug grinned and unpacked a bag of food from home. A dented

can of green beans. A half loaf of bread. Freezer-burned chicken tenders. A bag of frozen mixed vegetables. Liv, glad for a task, explored her own kitchen crannies. A box of frozen mozzarella bites. Nilla wafers. A banana. A bag of Skittles. On impulse she added a foil pack of Pop-Tarts.

The walk out back was easier with Doug. Together they hauled away the pile of wood from the shed door, and Doug selected the padlock key from his key chain. They shared the same sort of glance, Liv thought, of detectives about to bust, guns blazing, into a drug den, and then entered into a familiar dark swirl of dust, a familiar fetid stink, a familiar terrible sight. She could do this. She could do this.

The skinner's eyes came alive at their intrusion, the same as before, but everything else was different. Its body, hanging slack from its wrists, barely moved in its congealed filth and blood. The hard clench of its heart had become a butterfly flutter, and the lungs inflated slowly. The pink wounds and red abrasions they'd caused had swollen and discolored to purples, browns, and blacks. Liv was breathless, frightened all over again. But these changing colors—they did, in a way, feel like progress.

They were as quiet as if in a church. Doug edged closer to the alien, kneeling alongside it while being careful to avoid its puddle of muck. He emptied his bag, unboxed and unbagged each item, and placed them on the floor in a straight line, as if this was a science experiment, which, in a way, it was. Bread, mozzarella bites, chicken tenders, wafers, mixed veggies, green beans, Pop-Tarts, banana, Skittles: Which, if any, would it lean over and eat? Lastly he took out an old dog bowl of John's and filled it from a water bottle.

At that, Liv and Doug retreated, latched the padlock, and split up, as prepared as possible for another night of queasy anticipation.

The next day, Liv skipped cross-country again and Doug did not delay, and they returned to the Armory for assessment. It was the first time Liv didn't feel like the mere sight of the skinner might crumple her. There it was, same as before, horrible and helpless. She didn't wait for Doug to go first; they both crowded close.

Its choices were unexpected. Liv and Doug scurried outside to whisper about it, easier to do in the dusk light and under a wide-open sky.

"The dog bowl was dry," Liv hissed.

"Makes sense. Everything needs water."

"It ate the banana. The *whole* banana. With just its teeth, no hands. I didn't see the peel anywhere."

Doug hadn't blinked yet. "Same with the chicken tenders. There weren't even crumbs. And I couldn't believe the Skittles! I thought—"

"I thought it would choke on them!"

"That's what I thought! And all the safe stuff, the soft stuff, the bread and beans and Nilla wafers, it didn't touch them. You think it's the colors? It likes bright colors?"

"Did you see the Pop-Tarts bag?"

"Chewed right through it."

They panted together beneath marmalade clouds, faces darkening until they looked like the shadow versions of Liv and Doug that they had, in fact, become. The surrounding insects took the opportunity to establish dominance, chanting louder in rhythmic mockery.

"It doesn't look good," Liv said at last.

"The skinner? No shit."

"I mean . . . when we found it, it was sort of . . . clear."

"And now it's kind of cloudy," Doug said. "I know."

"And the . . . I guess its membranes? On its elbows and knees? They're yellow. A bad yellow."

Doug's sigh came from a still-obscured face. "It probably has, you know, excrement in its wounds. It's inevitable."

Liv retched. This was too much when she could still hear and smell the skinner. She aimed her throat at the lawn, then managed to choke back the sick surge. Doug was probably right, which meant one more confirmation of Lee Fleming's theories: The feces-covered punji spikes of Abyss made sense after all. Liv coughed to clear her throat. She knew Doug's concern by how close he edged.

"I'll take care of it," he said gently.

"How? Doug, no."

"I won't get too close. Lee used to water the saplings, right? I know I saw a rolled-up hose somewhere."

She coughed some more, wiped her mouth, and nodded. Doug—thank god for Doug. How had she taken him for granted for so long? He was patient and quiet until she felt stronger, and then they walked together into the shed, where they refilled the water bowl and decided in low voices that Liv would acquire more chicken and bananas, and Doug more Pop-Tarts and candy. It was a good distraction from the skinner's writhing. This must have been what had kept her dad going despite a whole town's disbelief and disdain: having a course of action was energizing, even rejuvenating.

Wednesday came, growling around every corner. Would she tell someone about the skinner today? An adult who might take action? Did every hour she didn't put her into some legal jeopardy of which she couldn't even conceive? Yet she didn't. Still sizzling like acid at all edges of her conscience was fury over what the thing had done to her dad, fury at the sacrifices it had forced upon her and her mother.

Until she could create a clearer picture, it seemed wise to behave normally, so that day after school, she joined the cross-country team in the locker room. Monica, via artificial warmness, was predictably cold, but Liv was otherwise affectionately received, and she had to cover the tears that sprang to her eyes. In this room, with these girls, in these clothes, she could almost imagine that everything was the same as it had been last year.

Running was hard. Just five days without exercise and it felt like her heart, like the skinner's, hung vulnerable outside her body.

She was over two hours late to the Armory. She followed the trail of a long, green hose and found Doug squatting at the end of it. The concrete floor was dark gray, wet from having been sprayed down. The skinner was wet as well, having received the same crass cleaning.

"Hi," Liv said.

Doug nodded but didn't look at her. He kept spraying. Foam sloshed along the room's perimeter. Liv pet down her hair, stiff from dried sweat. There was an alien presence in this room, and yet the atmosphere felt like the previous week's check of the traps: Doug upset and her saddled with the duty to make it better.

"Sorry," she said. "I went to practice. I thought I—"

"You want to jog around in circles with your friends, be my guest."

It was a dart into her chest. He made running sound so meaningless. And it was; there was no arguing the point. Doug, however, knew nothing about the burdens of keeping up appearances. Doug Monk could go straight home after school if he liked. No one expected anything of Doug Monk. Liv evened out her breathing, hoping to diffuse the pain in her chest.

"It looks good," she offered.

"The floor?"

"*It.*"

Not only was the skinner clean, it had consumed its fill of food and water for a second day. The organs visible under its translucent skin seemed to have brightened and quickened. Its bruises had smoothed into duller, less alarming colors, and Doug had wrapped its ravaged left ankle in gauze and medical tape. Smaller white spots of bandage dotted the alien where the worst of its wounds had refused to heal—wounds that Liv and Doug had dealt.

The skinner chirped.

Liv thought it had to be a sign of returned health. She shut the door and came closer. One factor contributing to the skinner's seeming return of vitality was that Doug had replaced the dead bulbs overhead with bright new fluorescents. Pockets of the shed long obscured were as bright as if painted white. Doug had pushed Lee's power tools into a corner and lugged most of the tables behind the Armory to be disassembled. Overnight, the place had become twice the size, ready to accommodate two people's full ranges of movement. Why they might need so much space worried Liv.

Doug seemed to sense it. He sat against the wall and studied her.

He looked different. Not mad, exactly, but no longer patient, either. It looked as if he were trying, and failing, to understand how cross-country practice had served her any purpose.

"Don't be scared," he said.

"I'm not," she lied.

"In a way, I'm glad you're late. Gave me time to think. I'm sure you want to tell your friends about this, or your teachers, or your mom. Or the cops. I get it. But we cannot—we *cannot*—tell anyone. There's stuff we've got to figure out first. Important stuff." He grimaced at the skinner. "Look at this thing. We're never going to be able to communicate with it in a normal way. It can't tell us anything."

"What would it tell us?" She felt young and stupid.

"Jesus, Liv. It might know stuff."

She locked her jaw shut, abashed. "About Dad."

Doug raised his eyebrows as if to say *finally*. He clasped his hands.

"What it could tell us," he explained, "is if your dad's still alive."

Dad, alive. Did she repeat these words aloud, or were Doug's words echoing off the walls? Regardless, she frowned at the sound. The idea was obscene, little better than dragging Lee Fleming's corpse from a grave and proclaiming that he'd come home.

"It's not like his body ever turned up," Doug said. "Maybe the skinners have had him all this time. Maybe that's why they've come back here. Maybe the skinner had Lee's compass so it could follow his scent."

Liv tried to think through this idea, but the gears of her brain, as in all matters regarding her father, grinded against burrs of rust. "Is that what you really think?"

Doug jabbed a thumb at the skinner.

"You think this thing came here to make friends? It's here on a mission. What we have to do is turn that mission upside down."

Liv's eyes whirled across the shed's daggers, swords, maces, axes, tomahawks, and clubs. What wasn't there, but she saw nonetheless, was barbed wire tacked onto her stomach; Black Glade's colossal, spidery trees; a purring electric fence.

"You want to go back out there?" she asked.

"No, Liv. What I'm saying is we need to communicate with this skinner in a language that every single living thing understands. What did Lee say, way back when? 'If anything ever happens to me, you two know what to do.'"

So Doug remembered it, too. Liv's knuckles panged, and she looked at them. All week they'd ached, and decent scabs had only begun to build. While she'd been, as he said, jogging in circles with her friends, he'd overhauled the entire Armory, and for an action-able purpose. Here in the bright hospital lights she made a fist and watched the scabs bend, segment, and begin to seep.

"Blood," she said.

"We make it bleed," he said. "And shit, why not take that blood and—"

"We spread it around," she guessed.

Doug snapped his fingers. "All over the woods. If more are out there, they'll smell it. They'll know what happens when you send a skinner to the Fleming house, and they'll stay the fuck away."

"Hang on." Her vision was rocking. "Shouldn't we . . . the police, someone—if we called them, and we explained . . ."

"Explain what? You think they'd give a shit about Lee? Think

116

about it, Liv. There's nothing important about Lee Fleming. About us. About anyone out here in Buttfuck, Iowa."

"Please." It was a beg, and she hated its sound. "We're not . . . qualified, or equipped, or—"

"When it comes to Lee? We're more qualified than anyone in the fucking world! They'd take this skinner away from us, study it or whatever, and Lee'd just be forgotten. Roadkill on the highway."

So many things already hurt, but this was a blow right to her heart. Bloughton had forsaken Lee Fleming at every turn. Wouldn't the wider world do the same?

"You think . . . the other skinners . . . they'd bring him back?" Nine words, but she was out of breath, as if completing her Custer Road circuit. "Like . . . a prisoner exchange?"

Doug looked away from the skinner but not at Liv; instead, he craned his neck to gaze into the thicket of weapons, the closest things they had to Lee's remains. Doug's lips curled downward and trembled.

"If they don't, then—well, I don't really give a shit, you know? Because this thing, or this thing's friends, or this thing's whole planet . . ." His voice faltered with a heartbreak he never once betrayed at school. "They hurt Lee. Hurt him bad. Humiliated him. Made him sick. Stole him from us. And I am *not* going to sit here and take it. I'm going to *give it back*."

Doug had sat there and taken it from Billy and other bullies for years. Could that be part of why he was so starving now to react? His teeth were bared like an animal's. He blinked up at Liv, a single tear glistening down on each of his cheeks, two stripes as vivid as war paint.

"So are you with me? Liv? Are you?"

From both her father and Doug now: *You know what to do.*

There were bigger, more important teams than cross-country. There was the human team, and here was a chance to step forward like few other people had had the chance. Liv felt a flood of affection for this most loyal of boys, who'd do anything to honor or avenge her father. He stood, shifting from foot to foot like a boxer, and the energy that crackled off his skin landed on her. Doug was flexing his fingers now, another boxer's trait, and this time she believed it was her influencing him—she was already clenching hers.

Weren't boxers in movies always fighting for what they believed in? Doug moved toward the skinner. Liv couldn't see it clearly, but she could hear the moist slither of its limbs as it retracted against the wall, as well as its blank, belligerent chirps. She felt fury, she felt disgust, she felt exhilaration. She followed her friend, fists tight, prepared and willing to break some scabs.

14.

THE CONCEPT OF A CROSS-COUNTRY
meet, all those situations she knew so well—girls pressed into the
starter box like slaughterhouse cattle, the kindergarten chaos of the
first two hundred meters—not a single thought of it occurred to Liv
over a weekend of skinner food prep and feverish dreams. Nothing
of the event touched her until Monday morning while walking from
her parked car to the school, the keys in her hand making her fist
look even more like the weapon it had become.

"There she is. Our jailbird."

Liv looked up, half-blinded by the rising sun, and saw Monica,
wrapped in a sleek jacket, standing like the bow of a ship with Krista,
Darla, Laurie, and Amber fanned out to either side. It was windy, and
Monica's long, highlighted hair whipped like a flag, beautiful and
savage. Liv woke up nauseated every day now, but at this instant was
glad she'd skipped breakfast; her stomach flopped, like it did anytime
Monica turned on her.

"Ha," Liv said, hoping to play it off.

"Forty-nine," Monica said.

Liv had a sense where this was headed, and she felt a falling sensation, like the balance she'd kept in the face of the captured skinner had been but a few toes on a narrow ledge.

"Monroeville: forty-four," Monica said, and the inference was clear: Had Liv, one of Bloughton's top runners, been racing, they would have won handily. For Monica, coming in second was worse than coming in tenth. Such nearness infuriated her.

"Oh," Liv said, the most pitiful syllable.

Monica shrugged like she didn't care, the biggest tell that anger had been eating at her all weekend. "At least we won't have the stress of maintaining a perfect record all year."

"I'll be back in two meets." Outside the reverberating box of the Armory, Liv's voice was a dead leaf, whisked away with the breeze. "I'm sorry."

Monica tapped her chin as if in thought, before gesturing at the girls behind her. "That's good to know, since none of us got a *way-to-go* text about the meet, or anything, really."

Krista winced at Liv, a look of apology, but how much was that worth? Krista said nothing and made no motion on Liv's behalf. Liv considered that old saw, *I've been busy*, but Monica would ask what, exactly, was keeping her so busy, and Liv didn't have the strength to generate the necessary lies.

None were required, at least this morning. Monica whipped her head, a show-horse gesture, and the wind threw her hair into a whirl of daggers. She said one more thing, which Liv missed—no doubt one of her practiced dollops of sweetness laced with arsenic—and then headed for the school's back door. The girls, tapping gadgets to pretend to have missed the conversation, trailed after Monica, wiggling goodbye fingers at Liv. Only Krista lingered, raising her eyebrows as an invite to join them, but Liv felt like her ankle had been snared in a big metal trap in the woods. The difference being that she didn't struggle. She wondered why as Krista walked away.

"That was cold."

She looked back to see Bruno Mayorga striding along the line of rusty, dirt-crusted teachers' cars. At the edge of the student lot, she could see what must be Bruno's vehicle, a rectangle-shaped jalopy with a replacement trunk of a different color, currently swallowed in noxious blue exhaust. Bruno, though, looked as clean as ever, his collar so sharp it must have been ironed that morning, his silver belt buckle a minor sun. What shocked Liv was how quickly his brightness, of buckle but also of eye, punctured her dark matter and began to bleed it out.

He stood an inch closer than he ought to, something Liv noticed immediately but decided was all right.

Bruno nodded toward the rear exit. "Did you kill their cats?"

Liv sighed a sequence: "Baldwin, Gamble, suspension, cross-country."

Bruno tsked. "You sports people. So competitive."

"I bet the drama kids have knives hovering over each other's backs."

"I'll let you know. Auditions are today. Oh, sorry. Maybe that pisses you off."

Liv barely had energy enough to shrug beneath her backpack's weight. "Doesn't matter. I can't do anything about it."

"Look, I'm just some jerk auditioning for a play. But those girls? Not to be all parental, but shouldn't your friends be nicer to you?"

Liv couldn't hold her head up. She found herself staring at Bruno's shirt buttons, pearlescent discs popped through tidy, seamed holes, everything in its place.

"They like me how I am now. They didn't think of me before."

"Before your dad did the play," Bruno surmised.

"Before all of it." She wanted to take one of his shirt buttons between her fingers, relish its small, containable cleanliness. "After my dad disappeared, I only had Doug, you know? I was the crazy man's daughter. So I got into sports. Made friends. All that." She squinted at him, way up there, his poof of hair like a bird's plumage, something to cradle. "They're never going to understand what that was like."

"Not to restate the obvious," Bruno said, "but *I* know."

This boy's newness in her life, ignorance of social orders, and refreshing distance from her backyard shed must have been the qualities that put Liv at such ease. It was like being in a hot bath; anxieties dripped from her pores and became steam.

"Be the tallest you can," she said.

"Well, all right," Bruno said. "I mean, I'm five-eleven. I'm trying."

She smiled. "We used to have these neighbors, the Dawkinses. There's a pond between our places, and my dad dragged Major Dawkins's daughter out of it once."

Bruno's forehead pinched, and Liv read the look: the realization that Lee Fleming wasn't just some irrelevant wacko being disgraced by Baldwin's *Oliver!*

"Dad always said she would've been fine," she added. "She was just caught up in the cattails. But the major didn't believe it. He'd have a birthday barbecue every year with all his military friends, but the only one he saluted was my dad."

"I think right this second is the nicest I've ever felt about our military," Bruno said.

Liv laughed. "Yeah. Major Dawkins was good. The last barbecue was right between when Dad said he was abducted and when he disappeared for good."

"When he was sick."

"*So* sick," Liv replied, grateful that he remembered. "And the major pulled him aside and it was . . ." She exhaled loudly. "I guess because the major was so big and strong, Dad just looked . . . I mean, the major had to hold him up. I don't know if I ever saw two friends more . . ."

Bruno gestured at the school. "That's what I'm saying. Those girls. How hard is it to be supported? If you were *my* friend . . ."

Liv met his brown eyes, several shades lighter in direct sun. It was the second time she'd caught him off guard, and the fact that she could be amused by it made her feel human, no matter what was going on in the alternate world of her backyard. She gazed at the football practice field, the sun turning the goalposts into bars of gold, the tufts of sod into gold nuggets.

"I couldn't hear what the major was saying," she said, "but whatever it was, my dad was crying and nodding his head, and then I heard one thing: *Be the tallest you can.* The major told him that. I've always thought it was a lovely thing to say."

"It is," Bruno said.

"Thank you."

"You're welcome." Bruno paused. "I feel six feet tall just hearing it."

Something in her chest fluttered, gentle and grateful. She felt tingling relief in her fingers and toes. Not every second had to be lived at a blade's edge. The first-class warning bell rang, and, the spell broken, both she and Bruno looked down at their bag straps, which required sudden adjustment.

Bruno extended an arm for her to go first, some chivalrous instinct, and she went ahead, with him following, an inch too close this time as well, though again she didn't mind it.

"There's Doug," he said.

Liv stopped, her hand automatically gripping the railing hard enough for her palms to gauge the layers of chipped paint. Trained to identify Doug's slouch, the antithesis of Bruno's perpendicular posture, Liv spotted him at once, a sweatshirted, shorts-clad smudge trundling beetlelike across the lot.

Doug, in turn, knew her shape. She could tell he was watching her. It was in his diagonal trajectory, how he slid in her direction while leaning in the opposite, the same way he always edged closer to her on school grounds despite knowing that she was a different Liv Fleming here, one who hung out with different people.

Except right now she was not with those people, but rather a boy Doug wouldn't even recognize. Even at this distance, Doug would file away Bruno's height, body type, clothing, and hair. Doug was, above all things, observant, and just under that, canny about knowing when to use those observations. His leaning lope scolded her. Wasn't this a dangerous time, Liv, to be befriending new people?

"You want to wait for him?" Bruno asked.

Liv turned back to the school. She had to hold on to the version of herself that Bruno inspired, whatever scraps might survive this.

"No," she said.

15.

THEY SETTLED UPON A METHODOLOGY.
Or Doug settled on one, and Liv agreed, because she could not think clearly, not when she looked at the thing that had, one way or the other, been party to her father's eradication from earth. Their stated goal was to get the skinner, through pain, to express tangible information about what had happened to Lee. If he was still alive, if he was definitely dead. Unstated was the catharsis of simply doing something about Lee, no matter what shape it took, after years of just taking the hurt like punches.

At Doug's direction, they gathered what objects existed that might still smell of Lee Fleming. Aggie had gotten rid of a lot, but she'd done it as she did everything—in fickle, fitful impulses. Lee's gardening gear still hung from a garage hook. His winter hats, gloves, and scarves remained in the hall closet. A box in the bathroom was a veritable time capsule: his last-used bar of deodorant, his razor, his toothbrush. What could smell more like him than those?

They also gathered pictures. Most family photographs, Liv came to realize, focused on her. She had to dig out albums curated from before she was born, filled with photos shot on actual film. There was Lee Fleming at grad school graduation, pretending to weep in joy. Further back: Lee on the beach, looking up from a book at the photographer, his wife—or maybe, back then, only his girlfriend. Further back: Lee, impossibly sharp-boned, his hair full and whipped by wind, wearing a jean jacket, atop a picnic table, happy. *The blessing of ignorance*, Liv thought, remembering when she had it.

They entered the Armory with a shopping bag of these items. The skinner had had days to improve. Raised welts had lowered. Scratches had sealed over with crystalline crust. Wounds on exposed organs had faded from furious, red blemishes to dimmer blots. None of these improvements would last.

Doug spread Lee's personal items around the skinner in a half circle. While the skinner goggled in instinctive fright, Doug donned a pair of work gloves and Liv her mother's studded gardening gloves. Doug picked up a hollow metal leg he'd broken off one of the work-tables. It was as hard and lightweight as a police baton. He tested several grips, then looked at Liv.

"Ready?"

No, she'd never be ready, not for this. She nodded.

He nodded back, blasted out a breath, inhaled quick, and whacked the skinner's left hip with the baton. It made a loud clucking noise, metal on bone. The skinner's strangely jointed legs scrabbled away to move its hips as far from Doug as possible, which, because of the zip ties, wasn't far.

Liv knew what to do. They'd discussed it. She picked up the razor, a dull thing spotted with rust but still clinging to Lee's hair and particles of his skin. Hunched by the skinner's opposite hip, Liv held the safety razor in front of its face.

"Closer, Liv," Doug said.

She blew out a nervous breath and scooted forward until she could feel the skinner's warm flesh through her jeans. She positioned the razor inches from its face.

"Closer," Doug pressed. "Get that thing in its nose."

Liv didn't want to hear a third critique. She shoved the razor into the alien's face. Her reward was a queasy thrill, watching the skinner whip its rubbery neck to evade contact. A pointless struggle: Liv pressed the razor's handle over the thing's mouth, while the blade rested against its nostrils. The skinner flopped and, sure enough, the blade nicked the small, delicate flap of its nose.

Liv recoiled on instinct, but tried to push aside the nausea. A little blood was nothing at all. It might focus the skinner, help it get a big whiff of her father's smell.

"Talk to it," Doug said. "Like we said."

Liv nodded and cleared her throat. This was nothing like speech class, and yet she found herself strangled with nerves.

"Lee Fleming," she said. "Where is Lee Fleming?"

Skinners had mastered interplanetary travel. Doug's rationale was that they therefore must be highly intelligent and capable of recognizing sounds if not words, though he did leave room for an alternate theory that, to Liv, felt plucked from science fiction: that individual skinners were indeed dumb and that their collective intellect rested in overlord figures like the Whistler or the Green Man.

Doug's baton connected with the skinner's hip a second time, and the alien's body jiggled as if electrocuted. Liv jerked, too, and couldn't help but notice where blobby tumors on its hip had been squashed flat, where whitish skin there had gone hot pink. She tried to focus; she'd missed her cue. She swiped for one of the photos of Lee and held it so close to the skinner's eyes that, when it contorted, the stiff photo paper dug red scratches across the eyeballs' plump white surfaces.

Keep going, don't stop, don't think, she told herself. She pushed the safety razor harder against the thing's mouth. The plastic handle clattered off crooked teeth.

"His name was *Lee Fleming*," she said.

Doug let loose, harder this time. The skinner thrashed about. The flesh of its left hip was rising like bread.

"Lee Fleming," Liv repeated. "Lee Fleming, Lee Fleming."

The violence drove everything from Liv but the anxiety that these three syllables were losing meaning, degenerating from words that symbolized her beloved father into nonsense prattle that meant nothing but oncoming agony. Doug hit the skinner a few more times, and Liv watched the thing learn to bear down in anticipation, muscles thickening before each strike.

Chirp, she wanted to tell it, and the surprise notion screwed up her chant: *Flee Lemming, Leaf Femming.* If the skinner would only make one of its small, sympathetic sounds, it might give her and Doug the excuse they needed to pull back and reassess the possibly flawed plan under which they labored.

To her utter shock, the skinner did what she hoped.

"Car."

Liv's head snapped back so fast a neck muscle cramped. This wasn't just an alien chirp. It was recognizable, an English word that might have been said by her mother, home early, needing the station wagon. Liv looked to the door and listened, but heard nothing from the direction of the house. She looked up at Doug, but he didn't appear to have heard. He had the raw, busted end of the table leg pressed against the skinner's hip and was grinding it in a circular pattern, shaving off a curlicue of skin.

"Bow."

This time Liv hissed. She didn't mean to. Doug quit twisting the table-leg baton and frowned in uncertainty. Liv's mind spun into the rafters, among the dangling weapons. *Bow*—her dad had brought an Inuit bow to the climactic hunt through Black Glade. Could it be that the animal that had rushed through the underbrush that day hadn't been a rabbit or squirrel, but rather this ghastly thing?

"Hole."

Doug scrambled back, taking the baton with him. His motion startled Liv and she stood; their shoulders collided. *Hole*, Liv thought, could refer to so many things. Could the skinner be alluding to Abyss? Had the trap caught a second skinner? Or did this skinner wish to be tossed into Abyss so that it might impale itself upon the spikes and die?

"It's talking," Liv said.

Doug shook his head. "Just noises."

"Those are words."

"They just *sound* like words," Doug insisted.

They were words, Liv was certain of it. Simple, single-syllable, preschool words, and for an instant Liv entertained a fantasy of Doug sneaking into the shed every night to read picture books to the skinner. What might the alien parrot next? *Boy? Dog? Tree?*

"Car," the skinner repeated.

Liv pointed a finger and shook it.

"You can't tell me that's not a word!"

Doug broke away with a snort of disgust, wiped sweat from his forehead, and looked at the trail of Lee's belongings scattered across the concrete floor. He checked his watch and then bent over, gathering the toothbrush, deodorant, and winter hat. Liv could tell by the set of his lips that he wanted to say something, and after snatching up Lee's old scarf, he couldn't resist it.

"You're losing it," he said.

"What's that supposed to mean?"

Doug gave her an impatient look.

"You think it said *car*? You really think, Liv, that this thing knows the word *car*? *Car* is probably its word for 'fuck you.' *Car* is probably some god it's praying will get it out of this mess. Well, it can say *car* all damn day. Nothing's going to change what it's got coming."

Liv felt fireworks going off inside her. She turned and grabbed their first aid kit off a table. She nudged past Doug and squatted next to the skinner. Its writhing had gone slow-motion, a pained rotation of its injured hip. Carefully Liv held the area in place with her gloved hand and removed from the box antiseptic wipe, gauze, compress, and tape.

"Bow," the skinner said.

Liv ground her jaw and opened the antiseptic wipe.

"Hole," the skinner said.

Liv glared up at Doug's stubborn chin.

Doug threw up exasperated hands. "You think when a dog goes *ruff, ruff,* it's saying *rough,* like a rough texture? No! These are coincidences."

Suddenly the shed felt like an oven. Liv began unspooling gauze, but her face, then body, was sluicing sweat. Doug paced around her and the skinner, gauging Liv's ministrations. When he reached the skinner's opposite side, Doug halted.

"So, what? You're not mad at it anymore?"

"I'm not *not* mad," Liv said. "I just know when I've heard words."

"I guess mad can burn itself out," Doug said. "Even if something does the worst thing in the world. Like kills your dad."

"You're jumping to conclusions. I'm tired, okay?"

"*I'm* jumping to conclusions? I got news for you, Liv. We're both tired. This is tiring work."

"We don't have to do this all ourselves. We could still call someone. Maybe not the police, if you don't want to. But, I don't know—a teacher?"

"An adult, is what you're saying. Because adults have been so fair to me in the past. So kind and understanding." He held up the baton. "Oh, they'll definitely understand *this.* Liv, think about what you're saying."

"No, *you* think. We could clear Dad's name. We could finally do it. The proof is lying right here. We show this thing to the world, and no one would call Lee Fleming crazy again."

"One person sees this thing, five minutes later it's gone. The FBI, CIA, whatever. Then we're the ones who seem crazy." Doug looked exasperated. "You're looking for a way forward that doesn't hurt, Liv. That doesn't hurt you. But it's going to hurt. We have to live with that. This is about Lee, not us. 'If anything ever happens to me, you two know what to do.' He *said* that, Liv. Lee *said* that."

"Why not take a few weeks off? Get our heads straight?"

"A few *weeks*? You want to waste that kind of time? This isn't a pet."

"I know that. I know that better than anyone. It's at *my* house. It's in *my* backyard."

"Then your responsibility is double."

She yanked a length of medical tape. The gauze was already soaked with blood.

"Then why don't I even have a padlock key?" she asked.

Doug crossed his arms. "Maybe I'm waiting to see if you're serious."

"Are you kidding me?"

"Fine. Great. Be mad at me, if that's what it takes. Do what you have to do. As long as you're mad. Because if you're not mad, *that's* a problem. A big problem. A problem with you."

Liv stared at the skinner. The spindly limbs, bent like triggers in expectation of pain. The huge, round, bulging eyes. The spumous mess of its mouth, reverted back to silence. It was inscrutable, obstinate, unsympathetic. Doug was right. She had to hate this thing, for her dad. She pictured him and searched herself for anger. Nothing, so she tried again, pushing herself toward specific recall, precise details that might bring Lee Fleming screaming back to life.

Up leaped a memory she'd long forgotten. Watching her dad put on a tie for a community theater matinee of *Annie*, jabbering about poetry again. Liv, in middle school back then, had scoffed, and Lee tsked at her as if she was missing the time of her life. *Writing*, he'd said, *is the most dangerous thing there is. Because when you write, you're only creating half the ideas. The reader brings the other half. And when you have two people involved in a plot, what's that called?*

Her answer: *boring*.

His response: *a conspiracy*.

Then she'd asked what the conspiracy of *Annie* was, and he'd replied that it must have something to do with how lousy kids are at keeping orphanages clean. Liv had laughed and said that if Miss Hannigan really wanted to punish Annie, she should have made her read poetry, and that made her dad laugh. There was no clutching bellies and rolling on the carpet; it was a small moment, one of a million, and that's why, Liv figured, it hurt so hard. There would never be another moment like it. Because of this thing. This ugly, awful thing. And Doug was right—no adult, no matter who they were, would ever understand that.

In that way, she was trapped. She knew a lot about traps. The only way to get out of one was to fight and accept the wounds that came with it.

She had the first aid kit's scissors in her hand. It was there to cut the medical tape. But in that moment, she could see herself plunging its blades into the center of the gauze, maybe the pulsing brown sack of the skinner's heart, perhaps the softness of its neck. Hate returned. It had been waiting behind three small, unimportant sounds that bore a vague resemblance to English. Liv slapped the tape on the skinner's bandage, but did it unkindly, and when she next glanced at Doug, he looked proud of her.

He went outside to fetch the hose. This was a responsibility, he'd said, and he didn't shirk it. He came back and started to spray, creating a pink tide that sent clots of flesh like bitsy rafts into Liv's shoes. Doug's loathing of the skinner was all over him, and Liv was jealous. They ought to bear equal loads. There were, after all, two of them involved here. In Lee Fleming's words: a conspiracy.

16.

THEY HAD ONLY FINISHED THE HOSING
and floor scrubbing when they heard the gravel crackle of Aggie's car
pulling in. Liv and Doug had discussed this possibility before and
switched into damage-control mode, turning off the shed light and
huddling in shadow until the kitchen light turned on and another
ten minutes passed. Only then did Doug and Liv slink around to
the front of the house so that, when they did make their presence
known, it would not bring attention to the backyard.

Doug got into his car, fired its sputtering engine, and drove off.
There was no quiet way to do it. Her mother, of course, had eyes and
ears, but Liv dallied outside anyway, muscles throbbing, hoping she
might still evade conversation. She waited another fifteen minutes,
listening for the clatter of a toilet seat so she might dart into her bedroom, shut the door, and get to the hard work of pretending to sleep.

It didn't work. Aggie was a mother, and Liv's sneaking appeared

to remind her of it. What Liv had thought was the *thunk* of the
toilet seat was the settling of a plate. Her mother sang out from the
kitchen.

"I'm making you cookies."

"I don't want cookies," Liv said.

"You love cookies."

"It's ten o'clock."

"The perfect time for cookies!"

This felt to Liv like a penchant Aggie attributed to a long-gone
child, one who could be appeased with easy remedies of cookies,
dolls, park visits, and fairy tales. Instead of feeling irritated, Liv felt a
dragging sadness. She'd give anything for all of it to be true.

The microwave kicked in. The realization that these were store-
bought cookies took Liv's sad heart and dropped it. She'd wanted to
grow up so fast for so long, but it seemed that exhaustion was even
more endemic in adulthood. Well, she'd got what she wanted: She
was stuck in a deep, adult hole now, the crawling from which seemed
impossible.

How could a plate of cookies mean so much?

Her mom set the plate on the table along with a jug of milk. Liv
couldn't believe it. No wine. Just milk. Aggie poured two glasses and
brought hers to her lips. She was trying. Tonight, at least. Liv's throat
filled with the sticky raw materials of tears she no longer felt young
enough to produce.

"Okay, I *warmed up* cookies. Eat them anyway."

Liv picked up one. It melted to her fingers.

"School going all right?" her mother asked.

Liv knew the thin, worn pages of this script.

"Yeah."

"They're still doing *Oliver!*?"

"Yeah." A word as short as *car*, or *bow*, or *hole*, containing even less meaning.

"You want to talk about it?" The subtext: *While I'm sober.*

"It's fine. It doesn't matter."

Aggie chewed a cookie and nodded.

"That's a good attitude. Few more months, all this"—she waved the cookie at the disheveled kitchen, but also at Bloughton—"will be in the rearview mirror."

Liv knew it was college that Aggie spoke of, and she tried to visualize it, the independent future that, only a few weeks ago, had tantalized her. Now all she could picture were the shiny college brochures that kept coming in the mail, plastered with multicultural mixes of young people with smiles that were easygoing, inspirational, and determined. Such glossy dreams now felt out of reach. Her story was doomed to dead-end with her in handcuffs, juvie, prison.

"Is that your dad's compass you're wearing?" Aggie asked. "Where'd you find it?"

Liv shrugged. So many lies would suffice. "The garage."

"Huh. That's nice. He'd be glad to see that."

Would he? Everything Liv was doing out in that shed was for her dad, though increasingly, it had begun to feel like it was just as much for Doug, and for her. Liv glanced at her mother. The loss was all right there, in the lines of her face, the unchanging apologetic slant of her eyes. Liv could tell her. Right now. How the thing that took her husband was a few hundred feet away. Only Doug's warning about adults halted her: They did things in ways that might account for laws, but rarely justice.

"Yeah" was what Liv said instead. "Still works."

Aggie wiped chocolate from her chin.

"So," she said. "You and Doug are spending a lot of time together."

Liv set down the cookie and took hold of her glass of milk. Chocolate smeared across it like blood on pale flesh.

"Not really."

"Not really? I hear you guys tromping around; I see his car."

Now it made sense. The soothing setting. The comforting cookies. She thought Liv and Doug were fooling around, possibly out back in the shed. It was so unimaginatively romantic: childhood friends finding love right under their noses. Liv's stomach hurt as it had while Doug clobbered the skinner's hip. Her mom, after all, was right. She and Doug *were* experimenting, just not how she thought.

"It's just—you know. We're just friends."

"Well, either way. I want you to know that I'm not a shrew. I'm a modern woman and all that. If you need advice about anything or whatever, I'm here. I'm right here."

Her mother wanted so badly to give that advice—Liv could tell. It would be proof that Aggie's existence had meant something, that all her upheavals and losses weren't in vain. Liv thought of her mother's photo albums, now missing pictures of her husband Liv had used to taunt the skinner. Aggie had been in plenty of those old pictures, wild haired and red lipped and short skirted, ravenous in a way Liv thought she herself had never had the chance to be.

The problem with her mother's advice was that it came too late. If it were indeed sex, and not violence, that she and Doug were sharing, they'd be far beyond the sort of innocent bumbling Aggie was imagining. They'd be engaged in the filthiest of perversions, past rescue of any mother-talk chat.

"Got it," Liv said. "Thanks."

"You tell Doug he doesn't have to speed off like he's not welcome. He's welcome. He'll always be welcome here."

Liv wasn't hungry—she felt, in fact, like she might be sick—but she picked up another cookie and pushed it into her mouth in self-punishment. What if it was inevitable? What if the secrets Liv and Doug shared, deepening by the day, locked the two of them together forever? Maybe this was it. Maybe *he* was it. Maybe, once you crossed certain thresholds, there were no more options left. No cars, no bows, only a hole.

THIRD STANZA:

PHILOSOPHIES OF SUFFERING

17.

LIV COULD NOT GET THE WATER OF HER
daily showers hot enough to cleanse her, and once in class, she so
closely studied her fingernails for skinner flesh that she missed being
called upon. She continued to move alongside Monica, Krista, and
the gang in the halls, and sat with them at lunch, but interactions
felt blurry and muffled, as if performed through a fiberglass pane. If
only they spoke fewer words, like those three she couldn't get out of
her head, the three the skinner continued to croak every time she saw
it: *Car. Bow. Hole.*

Her interactions with teachers followed the same model, and
when Coach Carney called Liv into the crowded office she shared
with other coaches, Liv expected role-model boilerplate: *Is there
something troubling you? There are counselors trained to help you.* Liv
declined the seat Carney offered and adopted a pose she'd be able
to hold long enough to cycle through a short series of lies. Instead,
Carney ambushed her.

"You're off the team, Liv. I'm sorry."

Runners were dutiful by nature, and Carney wasn't practiced at tasks like this. She crept a hand over her mouth as if prepared to cry if Liv cried; the coach was a noted weeper, liable to shatter into sobs when a runner scored a personal best. Liv, though, felt no mirrored emotion. The fiberglass was still there, slotted between her and a world that seemed increasingly unintelligible. At least Carney's pointed words cracked the pane. Liv narrowed her eyes and tried to peer through it.

"It's just too many missed practices," Carney said. "It's not fair to the other girls."

"The other girls." Liv echoed it only to get her mouth moving, but once uttered, the words hung there like soot. "What did they say?"

"They didn't have to say anything," Carney said.

But that was an artful dodge. Girls *had* said something, and Liv believed she knew which girls. Monica, for sure. Or Darla, Laurie, and Amber if Monica convinced them to do the dirty work. That was it, then: Her legs were cut off from under her, severing the last link she had to her friends. How quickly it happened, Liv mused, thinking back to the first day of school, just a few weeks back, all those cheers and hugs. A different time, and she a different person. Liv examined herself for grief, and it was only the carefulness of this search that alerted her that her hands were balled into fists.

She looked down at them. They were the same fists that had twice assaulted the skinner; that's what fists were for. Liv snapped her head up and looked for something to hit. Letter-jacket emblems, paper inboxes, a coatrack—nothing with the sort of bulk that would be satisfying.

So instead she kicked. Her foot punted the metal folding chair Carney had offered, and it flew backward, clanging shut against the floor. Carney leaped to her feet.

"Liv!"

"I don't want to be on any team," Liv snarled. "None of you understand anyway. *No* one understands *anything*."

"I don't know what you're—"

But Liv was out of there, slamming the door to cut off whatever bullshit Carney, who was probably weeping already, hoped to shovel at her, and just so the crying coach would have something to stop her from giving chase, Liv ripped a bulletin board off the wall. It hit the floor with a giant *whap* while individual papers took flight, each promoting more bullshit. It was like Doug had said, all of it just running around in stupid circles.

Liv careened in the direction of the parking lot. Get out of here, get back to the shed, where actual events of consequence were going down. She fled downstairs and heard voices banging about the auditorium. Baldwin herself—all Liv needed right now. Actually, it was. It was exactly what she needed.

The auditorium was dark except for the middlemost seats, dusted pollen yellow by sun shaving through the lobby entrance. The stage itself was bright, as if carved from the dark by a knife, and hosted several kids moving like robots while reading from scripts. So here they were, the cast of *Oliver!* Liv figured that they, too, whispered about her every time they passed her in the hall.

Liv hurried along the front row, not seeing Baldwin until she sashayed in from the wing, her billowy skirt moving like a jellyfish, to take the girl by the elbow and restage her. Liv stopped, throttling the railing over the orchestra pit. It was Baldwin up there, but it could have easily been Carney, or Gamble, or anyone who'd done her wrong.

"I hope all of you are happy!" she cried.

They were illuminated; she was not. The actors squinted, trying to recognize her by shape and sound. Off to the left, or stage right, or whatever the hell thespians called it, stood an actor instantly recognizable by his exemplary posture. Bruno Mayorga—and it was the final indignity, this boy she'd come to like, even trust a little, incorporated into this sham of a show.

"You're all shitting on my dad's memory by doing this," she raged.

Baldwin was the only one who looked to have identified Liv right off. She heaved a sigh big enough to be appreciated in the balcony.

"I offered to discuss this with you," Baldwin said.

"Everyone thinks they know what happened to him!" Liv shouted. *If only these assholes could lay their eyes on the skinner*, Liv thought. *If only Doug would agree to show the skinner to all these ignorant nonbelievers.* "You have no idea, none of you. He was *not* crazy, not even a little. You just didn't listen to him. No one did. And they shut down his play, which could have been really important to everyone, just so we could have this, this . . . shit?"

Her splintered voice scared her.

"This is not the time, Liv," Baldwin snapped. "If you want to talk about it, we can talk about it. But tomorrow. Not now. You have to be an adult about this."

"Why would I talk to you? You're the one to blame for all this!"

"That's right. I am. So I'd appreciate it if you spoke to me privately and left everyone else alone."

Liv spread her arms to appeal to her fellow students.

"If any of you had any guts, you'd quit!"

"Oh lord," Baldwin muttered. "Enough with the mutiny routine."

"Well, don't be surprised if your sets end up busted."

"That would be destruction of school property." Baldwin was starting to sound bored. "At least then we'd be done with you."

"You'll never be done with me."

"Our own Phantom of the Opera, I'm honored. Now will you leave?"

Liv's lips moved, but she was emptied of comebacks. Had Baldwin won this round? The idea infuriated her, even more so for Bruno standing witness, but her muscles were tightening as they did in the Armory, a dangerous feeling, so she headed for the red exit sign. She ducked down some stairs, shoved open a door, and was blinded by a blast of sunlight from which she didn't recover until her hip collided with the station wagon. Then she was in the front seat, vision blurred with sweat, but the engine didn't turn, and then she was outside the car again, kicking the door as hard as she'd kicked Carney's chair, as hard as she'd wanted to kick Baldwin.

She stomped from the parking lot toward town. Summer had fought back, and it was gallingly hot, and she kept her eyes on the sidewalk until she sensed a car crawling beside her. *Car*: The word had a dark magic now, straining for *bow*, reaching for *hole*. She ducked and looked at the driver. It was Bruno. And for the first time since she'd met him, he didn't greet her with a smile.

"What?" Liv demanded.

"What is with you?" he asked.

Liv ground her teeth and resumed walking. The car crept alongside her.

"That's creepy, you know," she said. "That's stalking."

"Get in. I'll drive you."

"Even creepier."

"I'm the one who should be worried! You're acting like you're going to knife someone!"

"I am." She stopped, and the car stopped, too, chuckling exhaust. She breathed it in on purpose, craving the toxic taste. It was too much and she coughed, leaning over with the force of it, and when she rose, wiping her mouth, she was weaker. Her muscles still ached from the skinner interrogation, and she was tired of pretending they didn't.

"You don't even know where I'm going," she mumbled.

"To the knife grinder, obviously. Get in—you can tell me."

He pushed open the passenger door. She gave him a lengthy warning glare, but he was the least threatening boy she'd ever met, and besides, what did it matter? She almost wished he did try something, so she could bite off his finger.

"The vet clinic. By the Best Western. My mom works there. She'll drive me home."

"Yes, ma'am."

He got the car moving again. The interior smelled like its own foreign land, as strangers' cars always did, and though it rated only a notch below her own clunker, as well as Doug's, it was, like Bruno, exceedingly clean. Not so much as a gum wrapper obscured an inch of the sun-roasted upholstery. Liv futzed irritably with the air-conditioning until she sensed Bruno beginning to enjoy her futile effort. She turned her face to the wind. Inside a car was, at least, out of the sun.

"Fuck," she sighed.

"You're a barrel of monkeys today."

"I didn't ask for this ride."

"Will you take ten chill pills?"

Liv took a deep breath. She'd been so heated minutes ago she'd been lucky she hadn't punched a fist through the station wagon window. Here Bruno was doing her a favor, and she was being a bitch about it.

"What's a knife grinder, anyway?" she asked.

"It's an old-fashioned job where you sharpen knives. There's a song in *Oliver!* that mentions it."

"So you got your wish. You're in the play."

"You really have it out for Baldwin, don't you?"

"Aren't you skipping out on practice?"

"It's called *rehearsal*, Fleming. And no, they were done with my scenes."

"Then why were you still there?"

"I don't know. Just to hang out?"

"Seriously? You have nothing better to do?"

"What are you doing that's so important?"

The car slunk into a shadow the exact shape of the Armory.

"Don't take this the wrong way," Bruno said, "but were you always so mean?"

"No." There: honesty. It felt good. "I guess I made myself this way."

"And are you happy?"

She gazed out of the window. Even their speed of travel couldn't make Bloughton, a town that moved at a creep, go any faster. Bruno's question was so simple, yet was one she'd never been asked. There had to be a way to be strong without being horrible. *Be the tallest you can*, Major Dawkins had urged, and maybe sitting inside this car, where no one could gauge her true height, was the best place to try.

"I don't want to make things weird," Bruno said. "I'll just drive."

"It's not weird. It shouldn't be."

"I mean, I get why the play would make you sad. I just don't get why it makes you *mad*. That's not a productive emotion. If you were sad about it, then, you know, you could kind of work through it, and then it'd be over. You know how it is after you cry. You feel better."

"So be a girl, you're saying. Cry it out."

"Man, you're unbelievable."

"Sorry. Sorry."

She was. Every conversation she'd had with Bruno had been a revelation of disarming candor. Another conversation like it was suddenly all Liv wanted in the world.

"What's *Oliver!* about?" she asked. "I mean, I saw my dad's version, but it was a little confusing."

"The story itself? It's idiotic. I only like it for the songs. I've been reading the book to see if it's any better."

"The book? The Charles Dickens book?" She laughed, and the laugh, coming as it did so abruptly, made her smile. "That's like grade grubbing in a class where you don't even get grades."

"It's about this old guy Fagin, who lures all these orphans to his house to become his army of pickpockets. Now *that's* creepy. Makes a guy like me picking you up on the road pretty harmless, huh?"

"And Oliver's one of these kids."

"Right. He gets caught pickpocketing, but it ends up helping him find his parents."

"And who are you playing?"

"I'm the Artful Dodger. He's like the old man's assistant."

"So you're a tall, Mexican Artful Dodger. What would Dickens think?"

"Dickens calls Fagin 'the Jew' for like half the book. He would've lost his shit if he ever saw a Mexican Dodger."

"Maybe I should audition. Be an understudy in case someone keels over. Really blow Baldwin's mind."

"I wouldn't bother. It's a crap play for girls. There's not a single female main character except Nancy."

"Who's Nancy?"

"She's a hooker in love with an abusive maniac."

"What happens to her?"

"He murders her."

"It's so nice the school keeps supporting this inspirational drama."

Bruno laughed. "Well, they always cast a girl as Oliver. Guys can't hit those high notes."

Liv's stomach seesawed as Bruno turned into the vet clinic lot. She hadn't realized they were already there. She'd been distracted, honestly amused, and only realized the extent of her smile when she felt it retract into the afternoon's established scowl.

She didn't move for a moment too long.

"What's wrong?" Bruno asked.

"Nothing. Thanks for the ride."

She bucked from the seat back, but there was a hand on her upper arm. Her instinct was to recoil, rip it away, and swing at it with Doug's table-leg baton. Instead she looked at its owner. Bruno's bright white teeth were hidden. The honest brown eyes, though, did not change.

"I just want you to know that everyone knows how you feel," he said. "I mean, as much as we can. We've talked about it. Everyone's sympathetic. If there's anything we can do to make you feel better, just tell me. We're not bad people. We're theater geeks."

Anger had so overwhelmed Liv lately that a trickle of gratefulness was enough to drown her. She gripped the door handle in hopes of keeping her head above it.

"I'm sorry I yelled at you guys. Everything is confusing right now." Liv gestured at the clinic. "My mom's got two jobs and can't pay the bills, and I'm not helping at all. At all. I don't know what I'm doing. You don't understand."

"Yes, I do. My mom's got two jobs, too. Plus four kids, and my dad's doing shit work in Mexico, and we move like every couple years, and what am I doing to help? I'm in a stupid musical."

"Why do you move every couple years?"

"Why do you think? My parents worked for nine years at a factory in Monroeville squashing pumpkin into little cans for people to make their stupid Thanksgiving pumpkin pies until one day there was this sweep and my dad ends up in Mexico and mom ends up basically on the run through a series of shithole towns where it gets harder and harder to get hired because her résumé is full of jobs she quit without notice. So, yeah, I think I understand."

The only pumpkin Liv had ever given thought to was the Floating Pumpkin. Bruno's vehemence made her feel like the insensitive dunce she was, and she had to suppress the urge to tell him that she wasn't just another privileged white girl, that she knew what it was like to remake yourself into a different person. However garish her hardships, Bruno Mayorga had her beat. And yet what he'd offered her was something she suspected he'd never told anyone. The final thing Liv wanted to say, but didn't, after nodding and apologizing and getting out of the car, was that he shouldn't worry—she, more than anyone, knew how to keep a secret.

18.

THAT BIRTHDAYS STILL HAPPENED ON
the dark side of the earth surprised Liv. Doug was a Virgo, and she
remembered a birthday seven or eight years back, as he read out
of a kids' guide to the signs, announcing with pride that he was
loyal, analytical, kind, and hardworking. Virgos were "all work and
no play"—that fun fact she remembered. Sitting there on the cool,
patchy grass beside the Armory, gazing up at the stars, she wondered
if there were, in fact, rules and orders even in these bent heavens.

Liv could see Doug's car asleep and peaceful on the road, as well
as the front bumper of the station wagon, fortified by a new battery
Aggie purchased but couldn't afford. The heat, so high yesterday, had
bottomed out to an early-autumn chill, but Doug wore his usual
shorts, which meant there was enough pale flesh exposed to see him
coming from the house. He sat next to her, handed her a glass, kept
another for himself, and planted a wine bottle between them. Liv
stared at it.

"You think my mom won't notice that's gone?"

"One bottle? On a Saturday night? Aggie won't mind."

Doug had no idea what to do with a corkscrew, though, and handed it to Liv. She made a mess of it, but a little cork down their throats wouldn't kill them. She poured the red wine, and they clinked their glasses together.

"Happy birthday, I guess," she said.

"When you put it like that."

They drank. He winced, not seasoned to the taste, and she winced, worried that she, like her mother, would like it too much. And she did like it. She gulped until she had to come up for air, and discovered all around her a night of unnatural stillness. The treetops looked like photographs. The clouds in front of the moon stayed in place like a shroud. Even without wind, her flesh tingled. She wished the wine were any other kind of drink. Wine felt celebratory, and celebration felt wrong.

"You get anything from your dad?" She was careful not to slur.

"A call. Caught me before I came here. He's in Colorado. He said he's got something for me, but won't be by for a few weeks. He doesn't have shit for me. Not that I care. Which reminds me: We'll have to figure out how to handle it when he's here. If I'm gone every night, he'll think it's weird. You know how he gets. He tries to make up for being gone; he gets all dadlike." He paused. "It would actually help if . . ."

When he stopped talking, he seemed to vanish into dark waters. Liv held the wine in her cheeks so she could listen for any sign of a drowner's struggle. She could feel the effect of the alcohol. Her emotions were truncated, and she was so glad. Finally she swallowed.

"What would help?" she asked.

"Nothing."

"Just ask. It's your birthday. I'll probably do it."

He sighed. "If I told him I had a girlfriend, he'd be cooler about it."

Either the wine was acidic or her gut had other reasons to revolt.

"It'd just be pretend," Doug rushed to say. "You wouldn't have to do anything, like, at school. He's got so many girlfriends, what could he say about me going out every night? It was just an idea. It'd get him off my back is all."

Stars did not reflect in the wine; the liquid was as black as ink. She swirled it and felt as if the glass was stationary and it was she who spun, round and round through the ink, until she was heavy with it and she could see nothing at all, not even Bruno Mayorga. Maybe if she said yes to Doug, as a favor, he'd owe her a favor back and might reconsider allowing others to see the skinner as a way to save Lee's reputation—and, somehow, save both of them as well.

"All right," she said.

He nodded like it was no big deal but sipped his wine too fast, too hard.

"I might have to tell a couple other people, too. Just so it, you know, checks out."

Liv nodded. It made sense. If Mr. Monk, in a spate of parental concern, called Mrs. Fleming to get a read on the situation, Mrs. Fleming would confirm the relationship. *Why, yes, our kids are a couple, though they're shy about it. Isn't that the sweetest thing?* Liv could foresee each development. Aggie would begin mentioning her daughter's boyfriend to coworkers. Eventually it would reach school, regardless of Doug's guarantees. And Liv wouldn't be able to dispute it, not if she wanted to conceal what she and Doug were really doing.

Some traps, like those built by Lee Fleming, were inescapable. Her panic was wine-doused and quiet.

Doug ruffled through his bag, eager to move on. He extracted a few pieces of rumpled paper filled with indecipherable notes.

"I've been reading all these message boards. To see if anyone else has spotted one of these things. What if we're not the only ones?"

"Are we?" Liv's own voice sounded distant to her.

"Well, yeah. So far, anyway. There's tons of these sites. Thousands of people write their stories in the forums. They think they see UFOs or they upload pictures of things they see in the sky. Some of them do hypnosis and say their abduction memories are exactly like the memories of people they've never met. Some of the most popular ones go by aliases. The Washington Construct, TR00TH with two zeroes, some guy called Mr. Brown. I know most of it's crazy, but who knows? You have one Lee, you can call him crazy. But thousands of Lees? Anyway, I'm watching out for anything from the tristate area."

He crammed the paper back into his bag. It was overfull; Liv could tell, even by moonlight.

"What's that other stuff?"

Doug considered the bag. Chewed at his lip. Then, impulsively, hauled out a file folder, unable to stifle a grin. Perhaps, thought Liv, this was the face of a guy with a brand-new girlfriend. This might disturb her if she could feel anything, but tonight, halfway to drunk, she could not. The folder bulged with multicolored paper. She recognized the bottom pages—recent homework he'd repurposed—before he flipped over the stack, and she saw the telltale tray smudge of the school library printer.

"You said before that we should think about telling someone. And

I understand that. We haven't been getting the results we want. I know it, and it's my fault. But I'm not giving up. I'm never giving up. So I did some research. If we're going to get results, we need to do this how the pros do it."

"Pro what?"

Doug paged until he found a stapled sheaf. Entire paragraphs, Liv was surprised to see, had been highlighted. Doug had never highlighted anything in his life.

"This is called the Third Geneva Convention Relative to the Treatment of Prisoners of War. It sort of defines what a prisoner of war is. They're enemy assets, basically, and you're not allowed to mess with them. When the war's over, you send them back."

Liv repeated the bewildering words: "Prisoner of war."

"But it was written in 1949. Wars were totally different back then." Doug selected another packet of printouts. "This is from 2002. It's by President Bush, and it's called 'Humane Treatment of al Qaeda and Taliban Detainees.' It basically says the Geneva stuff is fine, but if I'm reading this right"—he tapped a line both highlighted and underlined—"it says not everybody is *entitled* to the Geneva stuff, not if we think they're bad enough. See what I mean? When we're in a war, our authority overrides everything else. I don't know about you, but I don't remember us ever *not* being in a war."

Liv's head felt fuzzy. Doug's eyes looked too bright.

"We're doing everything right so far. The first rule of detention is isolating the prisoner. Even the Geneva convention said you could hold prisoners as long as you wanted if you could prove military necessity." He brought out a second folder, twice as large as the first.

"Look. I printed out this whole thing. *Army Field Manual 2-22.3, Human Intelligence Collector Operations.* Four hundred pages. Took me like three days. I thought they were going to yank my library privileges. This thing lists nineteen ways to get information from prisoners. This is from our government. It's a hundred percent legal. Just so you don't think we're doing something criminal here."

Liv's glass was empty again. She grabbed the bottle and poured. A word formed in her mind. She wanted to ask about it. She hesitated. She swallowed half of the glass at once, gasped, wiped her lips with the back of her hand, and decided to try.

"Torture," she said. "You're talking about torture."

Doug looked injured.

"We're just following orders," he explained.

"Whose orders?" The question came out as a whisper.

Doug shrugged. "Lee's? The country's? Ways to deal with prisoners already exist. We shouldn't have tried to reinvent the wheel, you know?"

Liv licked her teeth, filmed with wine, and sucked on her tongue, soaked in it. Nothing being said tonight should be a surprise. Doug's dad missed another birthday. Liv's mom, and soon Doug's dad, would think Doug and Liv were having sex. They were torturing an alien. Tonight, it all made sense. Any other way she'd chosen to look at their backyard activities had been a joke.

Doug adjusted his voice to the quiet night. "*Nineteen methods.* Proven methods. Legal methods. They have names. Incentive Approach. Ego-Up. Ego-Down. Emotional-Futility. We Know All. And those are just the listed ones. The guards were authorized to augment them. *Augment* was the official word. Did they cross the line or whatever? Some people think so. I don't. Because what else do you do? If you have a prisoner unlike other prisoners, how do you know the nineteen approved methods are going to work at getting the info you need? You don't. But it's your job to keep trying if anyone is ever going to be safe. You can call it torture if you want, but torture's just what happens in war. You cannot, under any circumstances, pity the enemy."

Liv let herself be lulled. Doug's soft voice seemed to have rocked the trees awake. They swayed and shushed, and she was tossed along with the first leaves beginning to fall. Doug had never sounded so confident, so prepared. Like one of Lee's skinners, he'd shed a skin and stepped from it as something stronger, with a new voice that made hers even more useless. How many times now had she pressed him to get others involved? He'd deflected the idea at every turn, and now they were too far down the path to turn back, even while they knew, better than anyone, how some paths held vicious traps.

"Tomorrow's Sunday," Doug said. "Good day to get started. *Really* started."

The words made her feel like the wine might come back up. She had no rage left, except for herself. Instead of trying to climb out of her personal Abyss for the past weeks, she'd only dug herself deeper into it, as if searching for an appropriate depth of grave. She saw no way out that didn't ruin both her and Doug and betray everything, no matter how regrettable, she'd entered into with him with eyes wide open. Her mother cooked with wine sometimes; Liv imagined herself sizzling inside it, disappearing.

"Here," Doug said. "A present."

He dug a hand into his pocket and withdrew a tiny object held between thumb and forefinger.

"You're the one having a birthday," she protested.

But she took it anyway. It was a key to the Armory padlock. When she closed her fingers around it, it was like absorbing the metal directly into her bloodstream. It hit her like two more glasses of wine. She was abruptly moved, almost sobby. She knew it was the wrong feeling. She should have had a copy of the key all along. She leaned back on her arms and stared up at the stars in hopes of purging herself of every feeling, as none were to be trusted. A plane, or satellite, or something unidentified eased its way across the night sky.

"It feels like a dream," she said. "All of it."

"Sometimes I wonder what it knows about the universe that we don't."

"You think there's more things like it up there?"

"Doesn't there have to be? Think of all those Internet posts."

"You think Dad's up there, too?"

"In space? Or in heaven?"

She let her arms slide to the side until her back was flat on the ground. She wished, in a childlike way, that space and heaven were one and the same, and she closed her eyes and imagined it until there was a thump from the shed, the skinner rolling over. It stirred awake Liv's practical side, not quite soppy with wine, damp and sullen in the knowledge that outer space wasn't heaven. If anything, it was hell.

19.

THE NEXT DAY, HER NEW LIFE BEGAN. IT would be one with no Monica, no Krista, no coaches, no teachers. Those who'd always believed Liv had made a brisk comeback from the tragedy of her father would now believe she'd succumbed to the same mental deficiency that had brought him down. Bruno Mayorga was the exception—he didn't know enough about the past to see it saturate her. Every time she talked to him, she felt better, filled with unearned hope, and so she'd just have to stop talking to him. She'd just to have stop caring, about everything and everyone—or almost.

Her Bloughton narrowed to Population: 1, Doug Monk, and it was a realm in which he held absolute control. As with the corn mazes he'd plotted as a kid, he put every ounce of his energy and creativity into building something even he could get lost inside. Before leaving her beneath the stars on Saturday night, he'd claimed he had the whole week planned out. And he had.

On Sunday, Doug followed the *Army Field Manual*'s humiliation tactics and chased the skinner around the shed, spanking it with the table-leg baton until it collapsed.

On Monday, Doug dug up Liv's old Chicago Bears helmet to protect the skinner's skull and rigged up a pulley system that would dangle it like a rabbit for skinning. He'd hunted with his father; these things were second nature.

On Tuesday, Doug brought in John as a "force multiplier," only to be driven to fury when John tucked his tail and whined.

Liv helped, tried not to think, tried not to feel. *Why do we have to?* she wanted to beg, but she felt she'd burned up all rights to ask that question by participating in activities that also had no good reason *why*. The skinner jabbered from within its Bears helmet—*Car bow hole car bow hole car bow hole*—and Liv smiled and said, "Shh," to reassure it that the furry four-legged beast, unlike the two-legged ones, wouldn't harm it.

It was a smile she'd regret on Wednesday. The daytime was like that of the previous two days: hiding her face from anyone at school who might talk to her, hiding her whole self outside at lunch. Time decelerated to a glacial pace the second she entered the Armory and her foot booted the Bears helmet across the floor. Doug was already there, which meant he'd ditched school early. He stood before the hoisted, dangling skinner, holding a pair of pliers and a paring knife and wearing a barbecue apron streaked with blood.

Things crunched underfoot. Liv looked down, expecting a plastic piece from the helmet. Instead she saw most of the skinner's teeth, those irregular, misshapen gravestones. Closer to Doug, plopped red and meaty on the floor, was its tongue.

Doug shook his tools to clear them of blood.

"It's done talking," he said.

"Doug." Her head thundered. "What did you do?"

He glanced back at her with wobbly, bloodshot eyes.

"This isn't a *buddy* for you," he croaked. "You gotta remember what we're *doing*, Liv."

Liv braced a hand to the wall so she wouldn't pass out. This was her punishment for cooing at it, petting it. Doug had noticed, of course he had, and now there would be no more words from the skinner, not ever, and it was all her fault, because she had forgotten their respective roles: torturer and tortured. Liv fought down nausea and sent a silent plea to the skinner to try to not make any new noises, not ever. It might be its lips that went next.

Doug staggered away from the skinner. He peeled off his blood-soaked gloves and dropped them to the floor with two squishes. He shambled for the door while ripping the wet apron from his body, as if shedding a final skin. His expression tried for pride, but it was a mask nibbled away by an underlying acid of revulsion.

"See if you can stop—"

He gagged. He may have used his knowledge of hunting and trapping to perform his crude surgery, but it didn't look like he'd found pleasure in it. Maybe punishment for Liv was not how he'd viewed it. Maybe he'd been trying to rescue Liv from feeling too much for the subject. Maybe this was standard procedure, buried somewhere in *Army Field Manual 2-22.3*.

Stop what? *Stop the bleeding? Stop me? Stop yourself?* Liv didn't know: Doug was gone, their shortest session ever was also their most brutal. With the door still wide open and banging, Liv grabbed the first aid kit and rushed to the skinner's side. This was beyond contusion, bruise, or scratch. She knew how to lower the skinner from the pulley system and did so, arm muscles straining, until the skinner struck down. Instantly, blood bubbled from its mouth like hot tar. It was choking on it, hard and fast.

Liv reached for it with both hands before hesitating. She'd touched this thing dozens of times, but gloved and with bandages between their skins. This would be a touch of a different order, but there was no time to blanch. She took the skinner by both its arms, her fingertips sinking into its squashy skin, and tipped it onto its side. A cannonball of blood fired from its mouth, followed by other, smaller blasts. But it was breathing, air scraping hoarsely over the craggy remnants of its teeth.

How in the world, how in their *worlds*, could it be that Liv wanted to lean down, place her dry skin and clean clothes against the mucky, tumorous flesh of this inside-out monster, which had perpetrated who knew what violence against her father, and embrace it with all her might, never minding the slime of its earholes, the fishy wobble of its eyeballs, the blood-stench of its mouth? It was a shock of a thought; instead, she pulled the gauze from the kit and began unwinding a large strip into a ball it could bite on, the only thing she could think of to do.

"You'll make it," she whispered. "I believe in you."

Thursday, the day that would change everything, Liv strode directly from her final class to the station wagon and sped through spitting rain under the yoke of a blasting, all-day headache. It was the headache, though, that had given her the idea: The skinner needed drugs. There was no telling how it would react to them, but if it could eat their food, maybe it could process their pharmaceuticals. She could not let it exist at this level of pain any longer.

In the bathroom, she read the ibuprofen label. Headache. Muscular aches. Toothache. Menstrual cramps. Fever. Some of it had to be applicable. She tapped a couple of pills into her palm, stuck her face beneath the faucet to swallow them, and then tapped a dozen more for the skinner and put them in her pocket. Only then did she recall an old prescription of Vicodin she'd once spotted in Aggie's bedside drawer. She darted there, found the bottle, and took most of the pills—perhaps her mom would be as fuzzy about pill count as she was wine.

Back in the bathroom, Liv gripped the sink and wondered how she'd gotten this far so fast, able to visualize interacting with the skinner without disgust. She glanced at her reflection in the mirror. There was her answer: The face that disgusted her now was her own. She watched her eyes grow tears. Tears had plagued her since the first day of school, yet so far this week had vanished, and she knew why. Because Lee Fleming had vanished, too, from her mind, from Doug's mind. What they were doing in the shed no longer seemed to have anything to do with Lee; it had become its own self-perpetuating machine, powered by its own bad fuel.

She heard Doug's car rattle and gasp into the drive beneath the lulling patter of rain. She considered sprinting to the Armory and using her recently gifted padlock key to get some Vicodin down the skinner's throat before Doug appeared, but it was too risky. She stared out at the shed, small and innocent in the rain, and watched

Doug enter, the lights go on, and then, quite ominously, nothing else about it changed at all.

She entered the Armory to find the skinner still cuffed and curled into its usual crumple, and Doug seated on a table. The last she'd seen him, he'd been gagging over what he'd done to the skinner. He looked to be fully over it; he was now reading. Not military memos, either, but Lee's personal, autographed copy of *Resurrection Update*, the water-warped one he'd forced into Liv's hands before he vaulted the farm's electric fence.

Doug had his nose deep in the book's gutter; Liv could see the faint squiggles of the notes her dad had made over his final months. Liv shook off the rain and walked past Doug without a word, choosing to ignore the sight. It was impossible; it was like her dad was in the room. She checked behind her to make sure he wasn't. It was just Doug, not only reading but *writing*, as if he were the author chosen to complete a master's unpublished work.

Liv picked up the first aid kit and knelt so her body blocked Doug's view of the skinner. Instantly, its arm, that three-fingered, bone-knuckled deformity, strained toward her. She sensed nothing of menace in the move. In fact, if the thing's wrists weren't tied, she felt that its hand would be pawing her like John's when he'd been a scared puppy, as if to beg, *Please, please, please never leave me again.*

Liv's emotions splashed into one another: moved, repelled, dejected, alarmed. She swept them away and got down to the business of pretending to conduct a typical nurse's survey. She knew she should wait until Doug left before slipping the skinner painkillers. But its big, scared eyes bulged at her, pleading, and anxiety screwed into her gut. She tilted her head slightly to listen. The *scritch-scritch* of Doug's pencil was a knifepoint along her skin, but she couldn't let that stop her.

She slid the water bowl closer in case the skinner choked on the pills. She finned her hand and forced it into her pants pocket, a difficult maneuver while squatting. She shifted a bit, hoping it looked natural, until her fingertips touched the curved plastic of the Vicodin bottle.

Blackness enveloped them.

"What are you doing?"

It was Doug, blotting out the fluorescents, and Liv screamed, though somehow she kept it inside, her ribs shaking painfully from the gulped decibels. Her instinct was to fling herself over the skinner and cry for Doug to get the fuck out of the shed and off her property, but it wasn't an instinct she had time to evaluate or understand. She slipped her hand out of her pocket with what she hoped looked like nonchalance and resisted the urge to turn.

"What does it look like?" She tried to sound affronted. "If you're going to sit there reading, I'm going to see how its mouth is healing."

"I'm only reading because I was waiting for you."

"You didn't wait yesterday before cutting its tongue out."

Doug sighed. "I'm sorry. But caring about its stupid sounds wasn't going to help, you know? It was just going to trick us into feeling sorry for it." His voice became gentler. "I just thought we could work on A together. Like we did at the start."

Now Liv did turn, pivoting on a sneaker.

"Did you just call it 'A'?"

"Huh? Oh. I've been"—he gestured vaguely—"taking notes. It's just shorthand."

"Shorthand for what?"

Doug shrugged. "Subject A."

"What's the point of A," she asked slowly, "if there's no B?"

Doug grunted with exasperation, turned away, and swiped up *Resurrection Update*.

"I'm doing everything this book tells me to do."

"The poems? My dad's *notes* on poems?"

But for the first time since she forced Doug to take the book by the fateful electric fence, Liv wanted to know what her father had written in it, not to mention what Doug was adding. She looked hard. From here, she could see her dad's handwriting, but also Doug's, along with Doug's sketches—the kind of tidy designs he used to make for the Monk Block Corn Maze.

Liv flinched when Doug slapped the book against his opposite palm.

"You're supposed to be behind me in this. We're supposed to be together."

"We *are* together." She said it but couldn't make herself believe it.

"Then you shouldn't have to ask why I call it Subject A, Liv! Of *course* I call it Subject A. We have to be ready for that possibility. We have to know what works on Subject A to know what'll work on Subject B and Subject C and Subject D and Subject E."

"This isn't a prison, Doug."

"Yeah, Liv, it is. Some places have always been prisons and always will be. Like high school? Like Bloughton? But right here, this shed, is where we rearrange all of it. This is a prison *we* run. This is where *we're* in control. I read you those military memos! Weren't you listening?"

The Armory was silent but for a bug suiciding against a bulb. Liv did not speak, did not move. This boy looked like Doug. The long black hair, thick as carpet. The vulpine cheeks, the bulging arms. But was he still the Doug Monk she knew? And her, down here on the floor, was she still Liv Fleming? Or had the things that had gone on in this shed changed them as deeply as if on a molecular level?

"I just want to stay on track," Doug said. "There's a lot coming up to look forward to. I'm just barely into the army manuals. I'm going to try Fear Up Mild this week and then Fear Up Harsh next week. I can't do them alone. It takes two agents to play the roles. We'll get all the way to Shock and Awe, I promise, but I can't do it alone. Okay?"

"What," she asked, her voice trembling, "are you trying to accomplish?"

The appalled, betrayed look Doug gave her was like the forward-slanted blades of Hard Passage, digging into her flesh the second she tried to back her way out of the trap. She could feel her skin pull and tear. Her next words came out from a voice not only trembling, but falling apart, a crumble of octaves and inflections.

"Why don't you just . . ." She swallowed and it hurt. "Doug, why don't you just kill it?"

His eyes flooded red with anger, but also tears.

"That's not what Lee meant when he said, *You know what to do*," he said in quiet disbelief. "That's not justice. That's not revenge."

Liv turned away and dug into the first aid kit. She pulled on the gardening gloves with shaking hands and reached into the skinner's mouth to extract the blood-hardened gauze. She saw Doug's shadow slip away, heard the scuffle of his shoes, listened to the purr of paper as he readjusted his grip on *Resurrection Update*. His steps to the entrance were slow, as if the book's 280 pages weighed a pound each. The door creaked open. Liv pressed her eyes shut.

"You know what I think?" His voice was as soft as the misting rain. "I think you've been right all along. Maybe there's other skinners out there. Maybe there's not. But what A can do, what A can *definitely* do, is change everyone's minds about Lee. You're right— *that's* what we owe your dad. And I don't think it's too late to make that happen, you know? And in a way where someone can't just see A and suddenly haul it away like it never existed."

Liv opened her eyes. The skinner's blinkless orbs were fixed upon Doug, and so she looked that way, too; it seemed important to see what A saw. Doug was paused at the threshold, his face tilted into the drizzle. The shed's blazing bulbs slid like liquid fire from his back as he exited. A silver sheet of rain rippled, and a gust of wind began to close the shed door behind him. Liv was frightened by his silent exit, yet did not pause. She stuffed her hand into her pocket and yanked out the bottle of pills.

20.

BEING AT SCHOOL WITH KIDS WHOSE biggest problems were sorting through crushes and achieving arbitrary academic objectives was difficult to comprehend. When Liv got to school Friday morning, she got out of her car and stared at her warped reflection in the door for twenty minutes to avoid going inside. But when the day's final bell rang, she found herself equally reluctant to go home and confront Doug. She tried wandering the halls, but they were a minefield: Monica over here, Coach Carney over there.

Liv made her way to a lower floor. The auditorium, to her surprise, seemed the safest place—there she could sink into the black sea of seats. All she had to do was control her temper about the play being rehearsed. She settled in, halfway back, hoping no one saw her. A few did, of course, and word was passed actor to actor, creating a heightened electricity. Liv recalled from opening nights past her dad saying that a few nerves weren't a bad thing for acting.

It seemed true. As if trying to prove something to Liv, the cast appeared to shift to a higher energy level. The first couple of scenes were hard for Liv. The actors danced through choreography ignorant of the blood they tracked around the stage. They belted songs without recognition of the people haunted by those melodies. It had to be comforting, Liv thought, to know the precise parameters of your three-walled world, to know exactly what words to say, when to enter, when to exit, when to laugh, when to die.

It amazed her how quickly her trauma receded. Perhaps she needed a diversion, and, given one, she attached herself to it with claws and teeth. Bruno had insisted that the drama geeks were "not bad people," and no matter how hard she looked, she saw no indication that he was wrong. The girl who played Oliver was decent, despite the dull, angelic role. The kid playing Fagin, however, was amazing, bounding over props, flipping his cane like a twirler's baton, and behaving as if herding pickpockets was the funnest thing ever. Liv recognized this kid from classes—a quiet notebook scribbler— and never would have thought he had it in him.

Bruno Mayorga was the best of them all. His lanky frame was extended by a stupendous top hat, which he rolled up his arm with a magician's dexterity until the hat broke in half. He spoke dialogue as if it were a rope holding him back. Words were irrelevant; everything was conveyed through his agile tone and body language, the manipulation of his big eyes and expressive mouth. Liv could read them from a mile away.

Baldwin's gaze was warier, and Liv understood. These were her kids, and she had to protect them. When rehearsal was through, the cast and crew filtered into the auditorium, lingering to gab. Bruno, as usual, made no effort to conceal his interest in Liv. He took the stage steps by twos and ambled up to her. He was in casual clothes, as they all were, but still carried his collapsed top hat.

"I think Baldwin's braced for a bomb. Where'd you put it?"

"You were good." It came out before she could stop it. "I mean, everything was good."

Bruno looked touched. "Aw. I didn't expect you to say that."

Since becoming A's nurse, she'd developed some expertise at evaluating bodies, and what joyful respite there was in observing one that worked as perfectly as Bruno's. His body needed nothing from her—no antiseptic, no medical tape, no painkillers. She longed to place both hands on his chest, feel how his heart beat evenly, how his lungs breathed steadily, how his ribs rose and fell *beneath* the skin, where ribs ought to be. She pictured herself doing it and leaned forward.

With that small arch of her back, everything became as simple as if they'd rehearsed this scene a thousand times. The subsequent exchange didn't feel canned, but rather exciting, each word of dialogue in its proper place.

"What are you doing now?" she asked.

He held up his busted top hat.

"The costume room," he said. "Need a new chapeau."

"You want me to come?"

"Yes, I do."

The costumes were kept in a low-ceilinged, concrete-walled dungeon beneath the auditorium, a labyrinth of overstuffed clothing racks arranged at odd angles. It was lit by overhead bulbs, just like the Armory, and when Liv clopped down the steps into the stuffy, mothball air, she was struck by a worrisome displacement, as if all paths led to the backyard shed. She hurried, sending puffs of dust upward and rains of sequins downward.

She found Bruno standing before a large bookshelf arranged with fedoras, bowlers, newsboys, berets, beanies, sombreros, pillboxes, visors, cloches, and crowns. He was staring up at the top hats, but even faced away from her, Liv could tell he wasn't seeing them. He turned at her approach and looked at her with a sense of disbelief.

"Did we come down here to make out?" he asked.

The lean into him she'd started up above continued here down below, her hips and breasts pressing against his opposites. She placed her hands on either side of his torso. His T-shirt was pitifully thin. She could feel ribs, individual moles. She tilted her face up to his, making it simple—all he had to do was lean down a couple of inches—but his hands settled on the sides of her shoulders, and there was nothing sexy about that.

"You're gay," she guessed.

His lips were so close that his laugh fluttered her eyelashes.

"Mono's going around. I have to sing with this voice."

Mono was farcical to Liv. A's blood, tumors, teeth, tongue, spittle—all of it had landed on her, hot and frantic, festering with extraterrestrial microbes worse than any kissing bug. She exhaled in frustration, dug her fingers into his back, and mashed her lips against his. This time, there was interest. She felt it in the grope of his lips and a slight tilt of his hips. His hands slid from the safe zone of her shoulders and pushed into the sides of her breasts. She found the hem of his shirt and raced her hands up his bare back. This is what she wanted: to feel, against her own skin, a skin that wasn't sticky or gelatinous, and to hear hoarse pants of excitement, not foreign chirps of pain.

Bruno moved fast once he'd begun. He yanked down the nearest three costumes for cushioning and lay back on them, folding Liv down atop him. She closed her eyes and opened her mouth, and felt Bruno's tongue—still there, not severed—slide across her teeth— every tooth still rooted in place, not cast across the floor. Revolting, invading images; she pushed them away and buried herself in Bruno's scents and textures.

Their clothes shaved off in alternation, just like skinners were supposed to shed skin. His warm thumbs ran under the elastic of her underwear, unsealing it, inch by inch, from her sweaty skin, and that did it—her mind blacked out in spots like when she took a hard body-check in soccer. She manipulated his penis from his boxers and stroked it. She'd done this only twice before, but was eager. He had a hand down the front of her pants when he climaxed all over some peasant tunic that hadn't seen action in decades.

For a while they lay with legs interlocked, listening to the distant thuds of faculty leaving the building late. Liv pictured a janitor pushing his mop bucket toward the costume room, and she tried to care that she was half-naked. She couldn't. Maybe it was Fleming genetics: She thought of her father, naked in the town square, and an oily puddle of bad mood bubbled inside her. She'd have to leave soon, tunnel through the darkness of Custer Road, and brave the shed. She swiveled her face away from Bruno.

"We don't have to make this a thing," she said. "My life is weird right now."

"Are you kidding me? I wish this was a thing, like, three times a day."

He was looking at her, she could feel it; she could also feel herself draw away. He had no idea who she really was.

"You need a ride?" he asked.

"So gallant," she joked.

He shrugged, jostling her sweaty shoulder. "My car is cleaner than your car."

"Car," she sighed, and the rest came unbidden: "Bow. Hole."

Bruno humphed. "Who's that?"

Liv felt herself blush and wondered how far down her bare chest the pink went.

"It's nothing."

Bruno turned to face her, grinning. "Ooh, another Latin lover on the side. I'm jealous."

She stared at him. "What do you mean?"

"It's a name, right? Carbajal?"

He said it phonetically: *Car-bah-hall.* Liv felt her throat swelling shut. Could it be that, all this time, *Car-Bow-Hole* had been a person's name? Had A had been trying to give them somebody's name? It made no sense, was bizarre beyond anything she'd ever considered.

She pulled her phone out of jeans still warm from friction.

"Well, this isn't very flattering," Bruno said.

"Shh," Liv replied. Two years of high-school Spanish gave her the foundation to guess the spelling of the name, but to type it she had to take a slow breath and peck each letter with an index finger.

Results sprang up, the usual screed of heartless hits and cold-blooded URLs. A municipality in Spain, a California congressman, a street photographer. None of them felt right. Liv used her index finger again, added *Iowa*. A basketball coach, an obituary.

"Did you forget Señor Carbajal's full name?" Bruno teased.

Liv closed the browser. She stared into the dark ceiling, feeling disjointed and cold, while her heartbeat thumped hard, like a table-leg baton against helpless flesh. *Carbajal, Carbajal, Carbajal, Carbajal*—A had repeated it endlessly until Doug had performed the oral surgery to make it stop.

"It's a word I heard in a dream," she said. "Doesn't mean anything."

Bruno reached for her phone and gently took it, and for some reason, she allowed it. Carbajal was a Spanish name; maybe he knew a variant way of spelling it. Instead, she realized he was only inputting his number. It felt as personal as the physical acts they'd just shared, and Liv looked away. The low, cobwebby ceiling, the janitorial thumps above—these mundanities shielded her from the expansive awfulness beyond.

She shivered and wanted her shirt back. Bruno's long arm reached behind them and came up with what she'd wanted, plus bra. She sat up and began the upper-body gymnastics of getting into the garments, a routine she'd done thousands of times but that was made newly complicated by watching eyes.

"I know you've got problems," Bruno said.

Liv paused in the adjusting of her bra, but knew it was better not to. She picked up her shirt, grabbed it through the neck hole, and pulled it right side in. He might be correct, but that didn't mean he had any clue what the word *Carbajal* had just done to her world.

"You don't quit your team and start hanging with drama dorks because everything's going hunky-dory," he continued. "You're running from something. And that's fine. I'm not one of those people who say you shouldn't. My family sure has. Sometimes running's the only thing you can do."

Liv lost sight for a scramble of seconds as she pulled the shirt over her head. Bruno's role of the Artful Dodger, she thought, was fitting: He'd dodged from town to town with his mom and sisters. More miraculously, he'd dodged the gloom and pessimism he'd earned twice over. And like the Artful Dodger with Oliver Twist, Bruno, if given the chance, might lead Liv somewhere better, if only she could scrounge courage, or desperation, enough to follow. She already had the wrist compass.

She was fully dressed and looked down at herself in disappointment. There had been excitement and possibility to her body when naked. The way it had stretched and flexed, anything had been possible; she could have been any Liv Fleming she'd wanted. Dressed, she was the same hopeless girl she'd been at the start of the day, except for that one unpleasant new thought: *Carbajal.*

"What happens to Dodger at the end?" she whispered.

"Let's see. In the movie, he gets back with Fagin, and I guess they keep on stealing. In the book, he gets sent to prison in Australia. In the play, though, they don't say."

"What do you think?"

"He's pretty nice in the play. I think he stays friends with Oliver. Reforms himself. Becomes a proper gent."

"That seems good. Maybe Nancy doesn't die, either."

"And the workhouse hands out better gruel."

"And Oliver finds his dad. His dad's not dead after all."

"Yeah. That'd be nice. Maybe we can convince Baldwin to rewrite it."

He sighed, zipped his pants, and sat up, reaching for his own shirt. Liv felt a yawning chasm of longing as he leaned away. He was beginning to stand now, angling toward the hat shelves to resume his original task. She wanted to crook her arm across his chest, quick while she could, and pin him back down on a cold floor they could turn warm. She wanted to pull her face into his beautiful neck and inhale the smells of fusty top-hat hair and over-laundered shirt, and then, nursemaid now by trade, kiss around until she could find his pulse in every spot where it beat.

21.

BRUNO HAD TO SPLIT AND PICK UP HIS
sister. Despite the lateness of the hour, a clutch of *Oliver!* actors still
milled about the parking lot beneath the darkening dusk and a second day of rain. It was three girls from the orphan chorus, bumping
umbrellas and thumbing gadgets while talking out of lips almost too
blasé to move. Liv, focused back on *Carbajal*, suspected her presence
at the rehearsal was the topic and wished to sidestep all of them, but
that would be too obvious—they were directly on the way to the station wagon. Liv snugged her hood down, took out her own phone,
and pretended to text.

As she passed the girls, Doug's name snagged her ear like a fishing
lure.

A *thing*, one of them said. *Doug Monk* was having a *thing*.

Liv's body went stiff as a corpse, and she stumbled. One girl was
polling the others on whether they were going to go when Liv caught

herself directly in front of them, one of her shoes crashing down in the center of a puddle. The girls stared, too shocked for mockery. Liv forced a chuckle, though it felt now like her stiff corpse had been pitched into the crematorium.

"You're taking about . . ." Liv tried just repeating it. "Doug's thing?"

The girls regarded her skeptically. She couldn't blame them for being unforthcoming. They knew her views on Baldwin's play. They kept their responses cool.

"He's inviting people to something?" one of them ventured.

"We heard it secondhand," another clarified.

"I'm not even sure it's real," the third insisted.

"Oh, right," Liv said, a blather reply, before continuing toward her car. She opened her phone, dried the screen on her coat, and checked her call records, email, and texts for any notifications. There was nothing. Had she fallen out of favor of so many cliques at once, including the two-person faction of her and Doug, that she would be the last to hear about this? How was it getting out?

Liv climbed inside the station wagon and slammed the door. She turned the ignition, and as the vehicle cycled through its near-death rattles, she swiped through her apps, including the search results for *Carbajal*. Her social-media presence had fallen fallow in the past four weeks, but no one had yet unfriended or unfollowed her, and she began to skate through the traceries of interconnected profiles.

Searching for clues was like sifting through glass—too many pieces, all of them sharp. There: the word *Doug*. There: *Monk*. And there: *that psycho* and *freak* and *Popeye*, the last a reference to Doug's biceps. No firm details, but inference suggested it was happening soon. Then Liv saw a word she would never forget.

Show.

The context was a conversation between two former teammates. *Guess i'll go to dm's show*, wrote one. *We hav big crew coming!* wrote the other, to which the first responded, *Show and tell!!!* Liv knew she had to keep reading, but she thought she might throw up, or pass out, or both, so she tossed her phone into the passenger seat, shifted the gears, and lurched from the parking space.

Once she hit the main road, she called Doug, whose contact had migrated back to her Recents since the capture of A. She'd rather text, but she was driving, and so tapped his icon, while swerving to avoid a car exiting Burger City. Her cheeks hurt from wincing, defense against the voice she expected to hear.

Instead, she got a leave-a-message beep. Liv exhaled in frustration and relief.

"It's me. I don't know what you're planning, but don't do it, okay? I'm glad you think A could change people's minds about Dad, I am, but this, whatever it is, isn't the way to do it. I know we fought. I know we hurt each other's feelings. But listen, those sounds A was making? They're a name. I don't know whose name yet, but—"

Another call was coming in. Liv tried to ignore it. Emotion was pouring from her, clean and pure, and she needed to finish describing to Doug the aches she felt in her heart. But the second caller was Bruno, so recently entered into her phone, and his was a name that carried its own new weight. The speech she had going for Doug cracked at the stern. What she'd already said would have to do. She ended the call, and the signal changed.

"It's Bruno!" he said.

"Uh-huh," she replied.

"Hey, I just got this text about Doug."

The ferocity of her reaction blinded her. She pictured herself racing through the rain and finding Bruno and shrieking into his face how he was never to mention Doug again, and if he knew what was good for him, he'd run home, pile his mother and three sisters and three dogs into the car, and keep on driving, keep on dodging.

Bruno continued, "He's having some—I guess it's a show?"

That word again: She tore into it, dreading confirmation of her suspicion. "Where? Do you know where?"

"Your place. At eight." Bruno paused. "You don't know about this?"

Liv's heart crashed around. She couldn't breathe.

"Yeah," she said. "It's—I don't—"

"Anyway, I mean, I know you just saw me—saw a lot of me—but maybe we can sort of go to it together?"

Please, no, she thought, and that's what she blurted out: "No."

The signal tsked for five seconds, a second, hissing rain.

"Why not?"

She felt physical pain, of course she did, because in the costume room she'd managed to scale a hill of happiness she hadn't deserved and now, right on schedule, she'd been toppled from it. So many people were lost to her already: her dad, her mom, her friends. Did she have to lose Bruno, too?

She gasped, drowning in rain. Even here and now, steering through slippery streets, the answer was clear: Yes, she did have to lose him, and right away, like forced vomiting after the ingestion of a poisoned delight. If Bruno came to her house, that site of unfathomable secrets, he might learn what she'd been doing for the entire time he'd known her. She didn't think she could bear having him know the monstrous truth.

"I just . . . I don't want you there."

More signal loss, tsking, tsking.

"Is it . . . because of what we just did?"

Liv imagined saying *yes*—it would be the most shameful word she ever said, but it would do the job. Their relationship had no future, because she had no future. Bruno's affiliation with her could shatter his family by exposing them to government scrutiny. She should have accepted all this earlier. The secret of A was always going to come out eventually. It just hurt that the end with Bruno had to come so quickly, in an unplanned, impersonal phone call, a sucker punch to a boy who'd given her the best clue so far—*Carbajal*—and who'd only called to spend more time with her.

"Liv—"

She swallowed a typhoon of hot tears.

"You're too much," she said. "You're too clingy. I'm not into it."

"Wait, what?"

"We'll talk later," and even this lie was rancid: They might never talk again, not if this night played out as it probably would. By morning, her photo, more salacious for being drawn from BHS yearbooks, might be splashed all over the news, and not just local media, but national, international. The whole world would know. No college, no future. She'd felt sick a lot over the past month, but this was different: Her innards melted into lava, and her head dunked under it. She slapped a hand to the door and powered down the window so that rain would pelt her.

"Liv, don't hang up. Talk to me. If there's anything—"

"Don't call me back," she pleaded. *"Don't call me back."*

The tears she wouldn't let her eyes leak came running from her pores. The phone, slick now, began to slip from her palm, and she jabbed at the screen's red button, three or four times, until Bruno's name winked out, and then a truck horn was blaring, and she was way over the center line, and she wrenched the wheel, and cars behind her laid on their horns, too, and her heart burst through the hot sludge of her chest, but she was alive, still alive, or something close to it.

22.

FIFTY YARDS FROM HER HOUSE, LIV rolled past a single red car parked on the Custer Road shoulder, just visible in the rainy twilight. A soft glow meant that the person was killing time on their phone. Given the patchy distribution of Doug's invite through what Liv imagined were emails and texts, confusion could be expected, and this person was ninety minutes early. Another would arrive soon, then another. But she still had time: She'd put the whole thing off, nail boards over the shed door, whatever it took. She just had to grab a couple of things, then get out to the shed and get to work.

But her return to the house was met with a surprise as unpleasant as any invading army of skinners: her mother thumping a knife against a cutting board while two pans sizzled on the stovetop. The place was a fog of rich smells that, to Liv at this moment, smelled worse than blood. Mom was not supposed to be here. She could not be here.

"Mom," Liv said, and continued in her head: *You have to leave right now.*

"I took the night off, baby. Going to make us a special dinner."

Her mother grinned gaily, once again the young woman Liv had seen in the photographs she'd shoved in A's face. It felt like a knife was sliding in and out of Liv's gut. Aggie Fleming was trying to work past the destruction of her family, trying to turn around the mess of their lives. It was the most worthwhile of ambitions—but why did it have to be tonight?

Liv smiled or nodded, she didn't remember, and floated toward the living room window.

She stared from between curtains, heart racing. Everything was about to explode. In the kitchen, her mother was starting to plate food. Out front, kids would keep arriving. If Aggie didn't hear them congregate, she'd see them once they began amassing at the shed, and then Aggie would go back there, she'd have to, and she'd make Liv unlock the door, and Liv couldn't take that. And then there was Doug, the night's wild card. Liv checked her phone every thirty seconds for a return call, but the last notification was still Bruno, its paltry three-minute-and-forty-six-second length belying the call's blunt force. She fumbled out her phone, started to text Doug, *MOM HOME PLEASE STOP*, but only got one word into it before Mom was tapping her on the shoulder.

"Food's up," her mom sang. "A twenty percent tip will be added to the bill."

Liv let the curtain fall and moved, dreamlike, into the kitchen, her brain bruised and whirling. She could see no way out—every door seemed blocked by trays of food. Liv sat at the table, her vision doubling until there were not two place settings but four, as if her father might yet amble in from the bathroom, only to be joined by Doug, the old Doug, who'd regale the table with how his latest corn maze design best applied his patented Trick.

The special dinner Aggie had promised was just that: beautiful baby spinach salads with sherry-sautéed Bosc pears, glistening bits of bacon, pecans candied with sugar and cayenne pepper, a balsamic-and-olive-oil dressing, and a sprinkling of parmesan, with two side plates of homemade rolls, homemade herb butter, and fanned slices of Gruyère cheese. Liv didn't think she could feel anything but dread at this point, but she was wrong. Heartbreak cracked her in half. Aggie Fleming could cook. She could do lots of things. She'd once been a person with skills and aspirations, not a broken-down cash gatherer whose life, already falling apart, was just about to be smashed flat.

Aggie smiled, lifted her glass of water in a toast.

Water, not wine—and like that, Liv knew how to remove her mother from the pain of what was about to come. It was worse than what she'd done to Bruno. Save for the harm she'd inflicted upon A, it was the worst thing, she felt certain, she would ever do to anyone. She drew her water glass back, withholding the toast. Her lips trembled as she forced out the hideous, betraying words.

"We need to have wine with this," she said.

Aggie's forehead tightened. "Oh, honey."

Liv's fake smile felt like flesh peeling from her face.

"Come on," she teased. "If there's one meal to have wine with, it's this one."

It was clear that Aggie wanted to object. Liv banked on her mom's insecurity, fully aware of the cruelty of it. He mother, understandably, might think she and Liv had drifted too far apart to have comfortable conversation. A little wine might smooth the edges, set her mind and stomach at ease, and so Aggie shrugged, capitulating to the easier path. She climbed the kitchen stool to reach the cabinet where she'd banished the bottles.

"Chardonnay." Her voice tried for camaraderie. "Good for salads. We'll have to add ice."

She poured a small glass for Liv and a full one for herself. An ugly yellow color: A's terrified urine, the pus of split tumors. These were the liquids Liv deserved, and she completed the toast and drank, and over the rim watched her mother do the same.

"I know we missed Thanksgiving last year," Aggie said. "Should we say what we're thankful for?"

"That's okay," Liv said, because there was nothing to say.

Liv pushed food around. Her mother ate. When Aggie went to the bathroom, Liv took the last Vicodin she had, ground it between spoons, and stirred it into Aggie's glass. When her mom returned, she took bigger gulps than before. Liv refilled her mother's glass and checked her phone and glanced at the front window, wondering if more people had arrived early, and when she turned back around, her mother's glass was half-empty and Liv refilled it again. Instead of a dinner it was euthanasia, with Liv the loyal nurse feeding toxins to her beloved, but terminal, patient.

By the end of dinner, Aggie was sloppy, her mouth over-wet, her eyelids heavy, her gestures large and erratic.

"Tricia told me," she said. "You know Tricia. Amber's mom. Tricia told me you were going around with a different boy now. Not Doug at all. Is that true? Or is Tricia a liar? My daughter the man killer, I said."

"It's not true," Liv said. And it wasn't, not anymore.

Aggie knocked over her glass, but it was empty. She tried to focus her eyes upon the tabletop droplets, but it was too much work.

"Sorry, Mom," Liv whispered.

With only minutes to go before eight o'clock, Liv went to her mother's side and helped her stand. Aggie's body felt as if it belonged to a different creature. Believing this made it easier on Liv. This wasn't her mother. It was another captured, injured beast. Liv hurried the beast down the hall and into the bedroom, and let the beast curl into a ball atop the mattress. The beast made moist murmurs, but Liv had to hurry. She shut the door, threw on her raincoat, and sprinted into the backyard, quick as a deer, admitting that tonight she was a beast, too. The time of humans had passed.

No time, no time. Quick, quick, improvise. An idea hit her, a crazy one, her only chance. She snatched the tools she needed and evaded her old friend, whose car she heard rattle into the driveway, and she reached the shed minutes before anyone would make it to the backyard. She knew by the din of laughter that the assembled teens were waiting under umbrellas for Doug Monk, their grand marshal, to parade them to the show. The sound of so many people so close to A was terrifying, but Liv did what she had to do before a line of twenty-some teenagers snaked around the side of the house.

Liv crouched in the rain at the edge of the woods to wait, watch, and listen. She therefore wasn't present for the show—she could only hear the loudest noises near the end—and yet, shivering against the wet bark of a tree and wrapped in a white sheet of her own breath, she believed she could picture every single thing that happened.

It goes like this. Doug reaches the shed door and whirls around with enough dash that you can imagine a magician's cape joining his ensemble of jacket and shorts. He welcomes one and all, as if instead of trudging across a soggy lawn, they have arrived at an exclusive club. He ignores the tittering at his cordiality, pretends he doesn't see the flasks of liquor passed about. There are people here who lampoon Doug at school, and that should bother him, but it doesn't. He's too proud of the attendance—strong for having had only one day to pull it together.

Liv knows how Doug can monologue, but to these kids, his ability to harness so many words is an amusing surprise. They laugh and applaud, and Doug, as always, is deaf to their derision. He gets serious now. He motions them to be quiet. He cautions that they shouldn't be scared by what they're about to see, nothing's going to hurt them, and this gets some in the crowd cheering louder, even while those with keener survival instincts feel their first twinges of concern.

When Doug switches the subject to Lee Fleming, the frivolity ebbs. What does Liv's missing, basket-case father have to do with this? And where, come to think of it, is Liv? Doug's off script now, ranting about how Lee Fleming tried to warn the whole ungrateful town, but no one listened. Even the most belligerent audience members feel a cold, eely slither in their stomachs.

Doug unlocks the padlock and flings open the shed door. Everyone has been to a Halloween haunted house before, and girls squeal and burrow into their boys, and everyone laughs. There's a nervousness to the sound. Liv pictures the whole group waffling, but no one backs down. This is Doug Monk. You think anyone wants to admit being spooked by Doug Monk? Some guy goes first, and the rest crowd in after.

The fluorescents dump light like white paint. The contents of the shed are revealed. Those things all over the walls, holy shit. Are they weapons? A couple years back there'd been rumors, but everyone assumed the reality was a few handmade knives, not dozens of terrifying tools mounted like antlers in a lodge. Those nearest the walls try to edge back, but they're packed too tight. Kids who live on farms recognize the hot claustrophobia of livestock shoved to the killing floor.

Doug is the room's deadliest weapon. He's standing with his back to them, looking at the floor. A sound catches their divided attentions. It is a soft, high-pitched sound. Those in the back have trouble isolating the source, but those in the front see it plain as day. At Doug's feet is a wrinkled blue tarp. It bulges in the middle. It is covering something. Whatever it is keeps moving. Whatever it is whimpers. Everyone stares. No one breathes.

Doug stares, too. He looks as if he might have lost his nerve, and in some ways, this is the most frightening thing of all, because the crowded kids have no choice but to hope Doug Monk knows what he's doing. Screens, though, are a way of establishing control, and out come the gadgets, glowing wands to ward off the fear, to reduce it to a harmless video file that will serve as proof of their survival.

Recording video means that Doug can't stop now, even if he wants to, and Liv knows he wants to, because by now he can tell something's not right. When has A ever been covered by a tarp? Doug doesn't kneel down beside it as planned. Instead he reaches for the tarp as one might reach into a fireplace to extract a valuable. He pinches it with thumb and forefinger and lifts it away.

Under the tarp is a dog. A sheepdog mix with mud-spatter spots, whiskered with age, whining because it has been leashed for ten minutes in the cold. For a moment, the possibility of horror lingers, and the crowd holds its breath. But there's something funny about this dog. It's wearing a Chicago Bears football helmet. After the dog blinks at all the people, it recognizes Doug, and its lips stretch into a goofball grin. It stands, and without the tarp pressing down, the football helmet falls off, and when the dog begins dancing from the excitement of so many humans, it's inevitable that somebody laughs.

You know how it goes. One laugh breeds a second. The girl who laughs second has a goofy-sounding laugh, and it provokes a third. The absurdity of the situation breaks over everyone. What a relief it is to crack up! Everyone guffaws, howls, roars. If Doug had intended this as comedy, it would be a smashing success, but he's too shocked to play it off like a joke.

Some of the cameras have lights. Doug has to squint. He looks unsteady. There are two whole days before classes resume. Forget the Jackson Stegmaier video; this footage will trump all others. He'll be the biggest joke in town. Except, perhaps, Lee Fleming, whose madness, in the form of a shed full of lunatic weapons, will be fully exposed at last. Everyone in Bloughton will see that Lee had been dangerous after all, and they are lucky to be rid of him. In other words, the opposite result of what Doug intended.

Get out, Doug says. *Leave*, he says. But it's warm in the shed, and a rollicking good time, and no one listens. A girl squats down to scratch John's ears, and Doug grabs the dog by the collar and yanks it away. He does it too hard; the dog yelps. People object, call him names. *Get out*, he repeats, but invectives have started to fly. Doug's not just a creep, he's a psycho, mean to animals, and the cameras catch it all. Doug flails his big arms and screams for them to get the fuck out, and get the fuck out they do, because the night has been crazy, this kid is crazy, and those crazy weapons look like they could really hurt someone.

23.

"I NEVER SHOULD'VE GIVEN YOU A KEY."

Doug hadn't moved from the exact center of the shed. He drew long, shuddering breaths through his nostrils, his mountain shoulders rising, then dropping, all those tons of granite. Liv stood just inside the door, rain drizzling down her raincoat, back aching from too much time shivering in the woods. John licked her palm, the only spot of warmth in the world.

"It's over," she said.

"Where is it?"

"Where's A, you mean."

"Fine, A. But it's an *it*, Liv."

"Safe. A's safe."

Doug mashed the heels of his hands into his eye sockets, as if grinding away the vision of those mocking classmates, their gleeful mouths, their glowing cameras. His cheek bulged with the fierce throb of his jaw.

Be the tallest you can, Liv told herself as her ice-block heart battered against icicle ribs. Doug's whole body was shaking. She thought she could feel his vibration through the floor. She inched away and John followed, sniffing skinner all over her. Liv's fear was that Doug could smell it, too.

"We need to turn A over to the police," she said.

"No."

"You were about to show A to every idiot in school. That's ten times worse! Everyone saying who knows what? A million rumors! Turning A in to the police, it's so much easier."

"We just turn it in, we lose control of the narrative. We lose control of everything."

"This isn't a contest. We don't have a choice anymore."

Doug barked laughter from behind his hands.

"What is this *we* shit? Since when is there a *we*?"

"I don't know. Since forever? Since we were little? We're friends, Doug."

His flung his fists from his face. His eyes bloomed with blood vessels scratched open by his own knuckles, the scarlet streaks magnified by thick tears.

"Would a friend do this to me? They were laughing at me, Liv!"

She shrank against the wall. A serrated blade from her dad's version of a Russian pioneer sword nibbled at her spine.

"Everything got out of hand," she said. "Nothing ended up how we planned."

Doug laughed again, a splattery sound that ejected snot, and wheeled away from Liv as if afraid of what he'd do if he looked at her a second longer. He paced right, hit a wall, paced left, hit another.

The room was too small to offer escape from the jeering echoes. He planted his hands flat against a wall, nudging aside a ceremonial Egyptian ax and a Renaissance-era hunting cleaver. Liv could see muscles tighten beneath his jacket.

"They call that 'mission creep,'" he said. "Objectives shift. Happens in any war." He exhaled, and it narrowed into a high, tinkling whine that made John's ears perk. "Your own *dad*, Liv. I tried to save his name tonight. And you ruined it. How could you do that? How are you suddenly okay with A? Did you forget who owned that compass you're wearing?"

"Go home, okay? Get some sleep. And then in the morning, let's take A to the police. Let's do it together. Tell them everything we know. They will help, Doug."

"Those Bloughton fucks who never gave a shit about Lee? Who never hardly even searched for him?"

"There are other things we can do for my dad. Car, bow, hole—it's a name, Doug. Carbajal. You and me can investigate that. We can do it together."

"Oh, did your Mexican boyfriend translate for you?"

Liv drew a breath and held it. "What?"

"You think I don't know? I know everything, Liv. It's not hard. All I have to do is pay attention. To my *friend*. That's what you said we are, right?"

"Bruno doesn't have anything to do with this."

"He doesn't? That's pretty hard to believe, Liv. We find A, and for a couple weeks we're good. And then suddenly you're hanging out with this new guy no one knows, and you change your tune?" He switched to a shrill tone. "'Don't use my dog to scare it.' 'Where'd you get my Bears helmet?'" Doug's knuckles were bone white against the wall. "It's just a coincidence this guy shows up and you start acting this way? Like you prefer A to your own dad? Do I have everything exactly right?"

Liv pressed her skull between her hands. Doug wasn't going to listen. She'd have to proceed alone with the police. He was humiliated and enraged; if she gave him the night to get his head together, maybe he would see the sense of it. She slapped her thigh to get John's attention.

"C'mere, Johnny. Let's go, boy."

The dog stood. Liv took a single stride toward the door, halving the distance. When Doug spoke, his wry, sly tone was so unexpected it stopped her as solidly as would a piercing scream.

"You think I care what you do with Bruno? I don't. Kind of makes me wonder, though. What would A do with sexual stimuli? I mean, we've done so many experiments, right? Seems like a missed opportunity not to test that, too. Maybe I should go over to the Pink Lady and, you know, rent a dancer for the night. Dress A up in Lee's clothes and a hat so she thinks he's a normal guy, and then have her wiggle around. See what happens. Take notes in my book. Worthy of study, don't you think? Dancers are expensive, though. Maybe if we pooled our cash. Since we're partners and everything. Since we're *friends*."

Liv stared in disbelief at his hunched form.

"Jesus, Doug," she said.

Doug's backbone hitched. Laughter and tears, all mixed.

The shrill mimicking returned. "'Jesus, Doug.'" His arms shook. "Jesus, Doug." His legs shook. "*Jesus*, Doug." His whole body shook. "*Jesus, Doug!*"

Lee's weapons had slept in shadows for so long that Liv had stopped seeing them, but this, she realized too late, had never been the case for Doug. In a single, smooth motion of breathtaking coordination, Doug's left arm lashed up into the northeast corner of the shed—no, it was the Armory, forever the Armory—and snatched the battered handle of his old companion, the Aztec club Maquahuitl, swiping it from its hooks, and though he was older and stronger now, the wood was still thick and the thirteen sharpened stones still heavy, and it dipped low and lethal like a bladed pendulum, at which point Doug's other hand joined the first, and now he had control, and the arc continued, missing the ground by inches and swooping back upward to smash into the southern wall.

"*JESUS, DOUG!*" he cried.

Weapons fractured upon impact. Wooden spears fired off their stone spearheads, flint arrowheads exploded into shrapnel. Liv hit the floor on instinct, covering her head, feeling nothing strike her but hearing a whole battlefield clatter across the concrete. She saw a gray blur—John scurrying aside—and taking the cue, she pistoned her legs away from the noise. Her spine hit a wall and she looked up, expecting to see Doug's face a purple mask, Maquahuitl's whole weight coming at her.

Instead, he was cradling the club like it was a broken arm.

"You ever think of me, Liv? Of *me*? At least if those kids were out there talking about what they saw here, it'd be something real, right? Something for *me*? It's like all that stuff we used to do as kids. Visiting that monster made of animal parts. Trying to get into the grave robber's apartment. Going to see the meteor in the fire station. I could be one of those things, Liv! Maybe it sounds like shit to you, because you'll have college and jobs and husbands and kids. But that's my future. That's all I've got. People would come to see me. And not for fireworks. I could be *proud.*"

"You're better than that," she said, but it was a rasp.

"Stop lying to me," he said. "If I lose A . . . I've got nothing left, Liv. Nothing."

Doug Monk had never looked so lonely. The only sounds in the shed were the factory chugs of their inhales and exhales, John's desolate whimper, and the skeleton rustle of the first crop of dead leaves mincing across the yard.

Concrete rumbled. It was Doug, dragging Maquahuitl along the floor, toward the door. Liv pushed herself to a sitting position. She watched Doug pass John, who sat with neck lowered, ears flattened, and eyes rolled up to Doug, his buddy since puppyhood. *Pet him,* Liv prayed. One pat on John's head and she would believe that Doug might still be okay. Instead, she had a horrific vision that seemed every bit as plausible. Doug's arm shooting out. Maquahuitl descending in an overhead crescent with the force of a dropped anvil. The stone blades passing through John so swiftly that his head took its time to fall from his body.

Doug did neither. He plodded through the destroyed shed, shoes sploshing through rain that twenty-some kids had tracked in. He paused at the threshold and looked about, as if considering trying to find A before being demoralized by the thickness of trees and shades of night. Just outside the door, Liv's brutal vision came to life. Doug lifted Maquahuitl over his head and, with three shattering, shuddering blows, smashed the knob, the padlock, and all the connecting wood. Nothing would be kept safe inside the Armory ever again.

24.

FOR THE NEXT HALF HOUR, LIV BECAME acquainted with the pulsing torture of paranoia. If this is how her father felt following his escape from abduction, no wonder he'd created the Armory, no wonder he'd built the traps. Liv stayed crouched in the shed long after she heard Doug drive off, her head tilted toward Custer Road for the gravel snap of his return. The rain dwindled, and she began to trust her hearing.

She couldn't wait all night. A was out there where she'd left it, naked, coated with rain, and it was unseasonably cold. She pulled herself to a standing position, scooted John out the door, and gathered the blue tarp. Before she exited, she stepped over to the far wall and removed Mist—her old ally, the double-bladed antelope horns—from its hook. She felt better having it in her hand, hidden beneath the tarp.

There was no big secret to where she'd stashed A. Thirty feet off the path toward Amputator, she'd tucked the alien under a wild hedge. Carrying A had been no more difficult than a schoolbag. It'd been shivering then; now, ninety minutes later, it wasn't shivering at all and dread flowed up Liv's throat. She passed her hands over A's body. It was shockingly cold. It was too dark to see much, so she wrapped A in the tarp, both for warmth and so that no one could see it—her mother, for instance, roused from a boozy bed—and lifted it once more.

Liv charged straight through the backyard, right through the swing-set tangle, straight up the back steps, where John waited. Before she could maneuver her hand from under the tarp, she paused to marvel at the soft, peach-hued kitchen light spilling from the back-door window. Never had she seen A under anything but the harshest of lights. A looked smaller, sadder.

Mist made opening the door difficult. Abruptly, then, Liv was indoors, a landscape as foreign to A as the alien ship would have been to Lee. Liv found herself experiencing it as a skinner might. The baffling variety of stovetop, table lamp, and laptop-charger lights. The druid drone of the refrigerator. The blunt odor of air freshener. The taste of still air, like paint. Liv lived here, this was her home, but it was only through muscle memory that she was able to carry A down the hall, past the closed door behind which her mom snored, and into her own bedroom. John followed and settled on the floor, looking worried.

The bedsprings didn't react to A's weight. Liv dropped Mist and gingerly began to unwrap the tarp. A's flesh emerged, stripe by pallid stripe. The skinner had never looked as freakish as it did here, beneath the Midwestern tableau of pennants and posters. Liv had the bewildering sensation that she was seeing herself on the bed, and this was simply what she'd always looked like just under the surface.

Using a sweatshirt, she dried A off. It was freezing cold, still. She grabbed the far end of the blanket and folded it over A, then folded over the other end as well. A moved then, at last, a series of epileptic convulsions, and Liv panicked, folding up the sheet, then the mattress cover, as much material as possible, snugging it around the alien and tucking it tight. It wasn't enough; the tremors continued. A was going to shiver itself to death, right here in her bed, if she didn't do something.

So instead of setting up her computer and finally getting down to the business of Carbajal, she crawled into the bed. She didn't know what made her do it. Stories she'd read, maybe, of stranded mountain climbers surviving with body heat. Liv parted the layers of blankets and slid beside A, pressing close. It was nothing like it had been with Bruno in the costume room, where each part of her had found a natural opposite. Nothing fit. A's round head rolled off her cheek like a ball she couldn't balance. Its shoulder bone jabbed her sternum. Its backward-bent legs pressed painfully against her shins.

None of it mattered. She curled her arms around A's cool, fragile body and held tight. It shivered. Was it because of bodily chill or her aberrant human touch? She placed her lips against its earholes and shushed like she used to shush John when he was agitated by thunder, except in these shushes she hid words: *I'm sorry, I'm sorry, I'm sorry*. She stroked A, too, hoping to generate warmth, her fingertips still surprised by the terrain of webbed membranes, bony extrusions, and shriveled tumors. She closed her eyes and told herself that this was Bruno. Or her mother, or her father, anyone at all overdue for embrace.

Soon she didn't know the difference between A's extremities and her own. The skinner's heart recovered a stable tempo, and Liv's breathing, in response, leveled off. From under her own ribs radiated an unexpected feeling. It wasn't happiness—there was too much to fear—but it was, she thought, a type of contentment, maybe brought on by exhaustion, maybe not. The police could wait until morning. Right now, A needed warmth and sleep before suffering renewed trials.

Liv closed her eyes, cupped A's head, and tucked it beneath her chin. There, it fit after all. *Tomorrow*, she told herself. Her confession to police, the fallout, the taking away of A—all sorts of hell could be confronted tomorrow. Tonight she was tired. It seemed as if her bed was a box of fine sand, and she sank into it until she was covered. She fell asleep and had a dream that felt very real: A's thick, three-fingered hands moving clumsily across her body as it tried to pull bits of bedsheet over the scrapes she'd suffered in the shed, bandaging Liv as she, for so long, had bandaged it.

25.

SUNDAY. IT HAD TO BE SUNDAY. LIV
would tell herself later that, given her slumberous fog, she could be
forgiven for mistaking the day as one from the past two years: the
knocking sounds (Doug rapping at the window), rustling sounds
(Doug collecting John's feces in a bag), and thumping sounds (Doug
raiding the kitchen for Pop-Tarts). Liv threw an arm over her eyes,
prepared her usual reply of *Can't you be late for once?*

What was different now was that Doug was inside her room. He
was touching her. She must have slept too deeply, and he'd decided
to jostle her awake. She swatted at him, then a complete recollection
of A landed all at once. The precise space the skinner took on the
mattress, its weight in her arms, the reedy sound of its breathing. She
knew all of this despite A's absence. She heard Doug's grunt of effort,
too quiet to be trusted.

The show. The crowd. The rage. It was Saturday, not Sunday. She squinted. Doug was stepping away from the bed. What was happening? He balanced A upright while he wound the tarp around it. He lifted its wrapped body into both arms, and it seemed by accident that he caught Liv's eye as he turned to leave.

She blinked up at him, confused, dimly alarmed, and feeling a great ache in her empty arms. Doug, in reply, did the least expected thing. He didn't snarl in disgust of how she'd slept alongside it. He didn't whip Maquahuitl from behind his back. What he did was smile, a smile as gentle as the hands he'd used to remove A.

"A's light." He chuckled softly. "Light as a ghost."

Liv wiped a clump of tangled hair from what felt like a puffy face. She hoisted herself to an elbow. She looked around. The September dawn produced a paltry, sea-green silt that made her room look as if it had been transplanted to the woods out back. Her survey ended on the murky, conjoined form of Doug and A. She'd hoped a night of meditation would calm Doug, and it seemed to have done that.

She scanned the floor and found Mist swaddled in a sweater. The weapon was too far to reach—and what would she do with it if she had it? Perhaps it was some enzyme that had seeped from A's flesh, but she was so, so, so tired. Last night, all she'd wanted was to turn over A to the authorities. This morning, though, she felt in her exhaustion a relinquishing of those ideals, all so burdensome.

"You said it wasn't justice," she whispered. "To . . ."

"To kill it," he finished.

"But maybe . . ." She swallowed, her throat tight and feverish, and those prophetic words of her father wheezed out one last time: "You know what to do."

"Don't worry," Doug whispered. "I'll take care of it."

Liv's body doubled in weight: guilt, grief, acceptance. Last night Doug had confessed that A was the only thing of value he had left, but now he seemed willing to let that thing go. And in doing so, he would save Liv's life—her potential, her future, everything for which her mom had worked so hard for so long. All Liv had to do to accept this gift was to give in to the weariness, just this once. Not move. Not dispute. Not do anything.

Doug picked his way across the messy floor. Liv opened her mouth but didn't make a sound. Her mother would hear. Or Liv herself would hear, and the sound would coerce her into making a second sound, then a third, and wasn't all of it, here at the end, pointless self-destruction? There was a great, unanticipated relief in seeing A slip from her responsibility, a relief she'd felt once before, when her father jumped an electric fence. Letting things go hurt. Keeping them around could hurt even more.

Doug paused at the door and glanced over the top of A's head.

"I'll see you soon," he whispered. "I promise."

Liv was nodding. She knew it by the taste of salt; her nodding had shaken free tears, hopefully the last she'd taste for a while. Doug disintegrated into the hallway without Liv having said a single word to A, not even the simple shushes she'd made hours earlier: *I'm sorry, I'm sorry, I'm sorry.*

She lay down and pressed a pillow over her face, still ripe with

A's odor, and told herself, over and over, that this was the only way all of this could ever realistically end. Anything else—rescuing her father's name, discovering the significance of Carbajal—had been a fantasy of heroism that she, no hero, had no hope of pulling off. If she couldn't be the steadfast soldier her father had trained her to be, then it was a lucky thing that Doug could.

FOURTH STANZA:

THE HEART'S CELLARDARK

26.

LIV BRAVED THE SHED LATE THAT AFTER-
noon, and before she could reach the first bulb, she could see that all
messes had been cleaned. There were no signs that A had ever existed,
and Liv wondered if, over time, she might convince herself that that
was true. The only task left was to dismantle and destroy Amputator,
Hangman's Noose, Crusher, Hard Passage, Neckbreaker, and Abyss.
Difficult tasks, but ones for which she'd waited a very long time.

What she didn't expect, upon yanking the light string, was that
the shed wasn't only cleaned, but cleared. And *shed* was the right
word now, not *Armory*: Doug, in completist fervor, had taken every
last one of Lee Fleming's weapons from their pegs and hooks. All
that remained were twenty-some chalk outlines and several dangling
chains.

Liv's sense of loss throbbed like a toothache. The weapons, though
born of crazed obsession, had been tangible proof of her father's life.

But she'd relinquished *Resurrection Update* to Doug without a fight, and he would have considered the weapons part of the same deal: He was Lee's rightful heir, not her. She found herself staring at the wrist compass, the only artifact she had left. She watched the nervous wobble of the needle, how it pointed north no matter what. Maybe it could still lead her in the right direction.

She plucked Mist from her bedroom floor and placed the weapon in the back seat of the station wagon, safekeeping until the next time she passed an unobserved dumpster.

Liv walked into Bloughton High's halls two days later feeling untethered and shaky, and that fragile openness, in contrast to the guarded clench and evasive ducking of the past weeks, must have shown. People's looks lingered, as if she were crying, and they couldn't ignore the urge to comfort. For some, shame at having attended Doug's "show" might have had a part. Maybe they'd been sympathetic to her all along, and she'd just been unwilling to see it.

Krista was standing right next to Liv's locker when Liv reached it. Krista hadn't planned it; she'd been held up by the calculus teacher. But the teacher scuttled off and there they were, the two of them planted in front of each other like gunslingers. Liv stared, emptied of artifice, as vulnerable as a creature zip-tied in front of someone who hated it.

Krista formed a child's deep frown, an exaggeration to lighten the sadness.

"Oh, Liv," she said weepily.

Liv shrugged vaguely, not knowing what to say, but needing her friend back badly, so badly. Krista did not disappoint. Her arms lifted, and Liv found that she still knew how this worked. She tilted into Krista's embrace, and her arms, acquainted with holding Bruno in passion and A in sorrow, tightened around Krista in regret.

"I'm sorry," Liv whispered.

"Don't be," Krista said into her ear.

They unlocked but held on to each other's forearms. Liv didn't want to be so far from her friends ever again; it took all her willpower not to pull Krista back against her body.

"None of us went to that thing of Doug's," Krista said. "I want you to know that. We knew it wasn't right. How is he?"

"I don't know," Liv said, and she didn't.

Krista nodded. "Okay. Well, you better sit with us at lunch, all right?"

Liv felt a flutter of panic. But social panic was a gift after the life-and-death burdens that had controlled her emotions for weeks.

"I can't," Liv said. "I'm too embarrassed."

Krista frowned sternly. "Stop it. We miss you."

"Even Monica?"

Krista laughed. "She's actually human. She just doesn't like anyone to know it."

She squeezed Liv's arm and departed. Liv opened her locker and hid her face inside it for half a minute, flushing so hot that she felt as if she were lying on a warm beach towel surrounded by her circle of friends and laughing so loudly she could barely hear the distant tide: *Car. Bow. Hole.*

Doug wasn't at school. Liv hadn't expected him to be. He was off doing—no, she wouldn't let herself think about it. She had to focus on her future. That meant, for now, presenting a cold front to Bruno.

Liv hoped there might be a time when it was safe to resume some kind of relationship with him, if he would accept it. But she'd been too impulsive with too many things. She needed to see Doug one more time and ensure that all danger had passed. For Doug and Liv, yes, but also for anyone Liv might like, or even love.

She didn't spot Bruno until lunch, and not before she was tucked between Darla and Amber, and Monica was monologuing about how she'd fended off some creep at the movie theater. Bruno stood in the aisle, giving Liv an imploring look. Liv met his eyes once, then looked back to Monica, bolting on a smile that felt like iron and insisting to herself this was the only way forward.

When Liv got home, Aggie was there, in that gap between vet clinic and steakhouse, and she'd changed into clothes suitable for scrubbing crud beneath stovetop burners. The rest of the kitchen was sparkling, and Liv's head swam in the chemical cloud as she watched her mom scour with a strange zeal, like she was hoping to polish away all evidence of their drunken dinner.

"Hi, Mom," Liv offered.

Aggie didn't turn from her task. "Look in the trash."

Liv stepped on the foot lever. Inside were a dozen bottles of alcohol, all emptied.

"That's everything in the house," Aggie said.

Liv had a lot of people to whom she owed apologies, and what had been so surprising at school was how, with every one, she'd felt lighter. If not for Bruno, she might float up into the clouds.

The words were easy, really, once you had practice: "Mom, I'm sorry."

"You will not be like me," Aggie said, still scrubbing. "I won't allow it. If there are problems, we'll deal with them. No more drinking for me. For you, no more dodging around with Doug or whoever. You've got someone you like, you march them straight up to the front door. We're going to be honest with each other from here on out. It's the only way we're going to survive, Liv. We only have a few months left together, after all. Agreed?"

She sounded sad, but it wasn't a bad thing; the sadness was clear-eyed, aware of its origins. Liv gazed at her mother, hunched uncomfortably over the stove, the back-and-forth jerk of her cleaning arm, her slight frame that, though dented, the world had yet to fell. The rhythmic scratch of the cleaning brush could be the beating of Aggie's heart, or Liv's, or both of them, synchronized at last.

"Agreed," Liv said, discovering she was on tiptoe, already that much closer to clouds.

Doug didn't show up to school on Tuesday, either. Liv couldn't help it; she added up his absences. It was an exercise she'd been doing for years so Doug didn't set off a chain reaction of his father being tracked down and Doug being put into protective custody. He was already veering too close to trouble. If he failed out of the semester due to it, she knew the book would close on Doug Monk for good, and though that might be what he wanted, it stung Liv to imagine. No matter what he'd done, if his hand suddenly appeared, she'd still pull on it, still try to lift him from peril.

Bruno was also absent. She didn't know what to make of it; surely he was too healthy to ever submit to illness. Liv accepted the possibility it was her coldness that had driven him away. She told herself to accept it. He'd be back soon enough, probably tomorrow, and looking at him would be hard all over again.

Her final class of the day was English. Today it was being held in the library, the same place Doug had once printed out all four hundred pages of the *Army Field Manual 2-22.3*. The librarian was going over how to access information databases, something they'd need to master for college. Liv was barely listening. Two hours ago, she'd had a surprise encounter with Coach Carney, who'd suggested Liv stop by after school to talk about spring soccer. Liv focused on that: spring, an inconceivable, magical season; sweating for good reasons again; colliding with other bodies in the way that garnered applause.

The database in front of Liv was billed by the librarian as the standard for accessing news content, anything from yesterday's headlines to Civil War–era circulars. The librarian expressed envy at the students having such a tool at their disposal, but Liv saw Hank, sitting to her left, open a browser to check sports scores. He winked at her, and she smiled.

"Give it a try," the librarian said. "Search anything you'd like."

Liv stared at the empty search bar. And the word just sliced into her brain:

Carbajal.

She had every reason not to type it. It was breathtaking how much happier she'd been in the three days since Doug had carried A out of her life. Three days, though . . . that was too long for him to be gone, wasn't it? Far longer than it would take him to humanely snuff the life from an injured creature, something he'd done time and again after a squirrel got caught in a trap. An idea that had fluttered just out of her consciousness for days landed home. Doug was not necessarily doing what she thought he was doing.

She killed the thought, cursored over a browser app. She should emulate Hank, load up something frivolous. All she had to do was waste forty minutes, and then she'd be meeting with Coach Carney—and why stop there? Swing over to Principal Gamble's office just to let him know she was okay, and then drop by the auditorium to make a real apology to Baldwin. No more loose ends, her life fully back on track.

Her fingers, those ten traitors, typed the eight letters and hit enter.

Once started, she couldn't stop. Every click felt to Liv like Maquahuitl plowing into the shed's concrete. The database had an intuitive interface; either that, or she was driven by a detective's gusto, modifying her search within geographical limits, narrowing it to results including terms like *alien* or *strange* or *mysterious*, filtering out magazines and wire feeds in favor of newspapers, and clicking on abstracts to scan the content for anything that might trip an alarm.

After an unknown amount of time, something did.

Liv leaned into the screen until she could see individual pixels. On the screen was a feature article dated six years ago, translated from a Spanish-language Des Moines weekly, an interview with a Charles Grimwig. But the highlighted search result offered this: *Grimwig was born under the name Carlos Carbajal, but he adopted the pseudonym when . . .*

Liv brought up the full-text version and swallowed a held breath. Carbajal, the piece explained, had adopted Grimwig when getting started in journalism, wary of institutionalized racism that might keep his résumé unselected. After getting a staff job at the *Monroe-ville Courier*, he was stuck with the moniker, though now he went out of his way to do interviews like this one, to make sure positive Latino role models were visible in Iowa.

The bell rang. Students were standing, erupting with the relief only the day's final bell induced. Hank whistled for Liv's attention, but she only shook her head, unhappy to pull her eyes from the screen for even that long. Hank frowned before leaving, and Liv knew she had just made a step backward in regaining her status. That would be followed by another: She was going to miss her meeting with Coach Carney, and there would be no apologies to Gamble or Baldwin, not today. She couldn't leave this computer; the plastic of the mouse felt fused to her fingers.

A search for *Charles Grimwig* brought an explosion of results.

"Glad you're finding this useful," the librarian said.

He had no idea. Liv discovered that Carlos Carbajal, writing as Charles Grimwig, had been filing stories for the *Monroeville Courier* as far back as twelve years ago. His bylines, however, quit four years back; the most recent hit Liv found was from the *Courier*'s competitor, the *Post*, which ran a four-paragraph story describing local journalist Charles Grimwig's firing from the *Courier*, an event shrouded in mystery.

The *Post* writer laid out the facts as she knew them. Longtime local reporter Grimwig had been investigating misconduct in an unspecified federal project and had been arrested outside Bloughton, Iowa, for falsifying credentials and trespassing on restricted property. The tone of the article was dry, but Liv could sense the reporter's exasperation at Carbajal's refusal to be quoted. Liv felt crushed inside powerful paws. A had given her the name of a journalist? Then Carbajal had to be spoken to, and right away—because her hunch that Doug was out there doing something he shouldn't was hardening.

There were no follow-up stories, either from the *Courier* or *Post*, but Liv didn't need them. She closed out the database and opened a browser. Anyone her age was a master at digging up personal information, especially for people too old to know how to effectively hide it. Five minutes, she figured, were all she would need to find out where Carlos Carbajal lived. She did it in two.

27.

THE TALLEST BUILDINGS IN BLOUGHTON were churches, cheating with bell towers and spires. There wasn't a four-story business or residence in the whole town, which gave the nine-story apartment complex in front of Liv the feel of a citadel. Monroeville was four times Bloughton's size, habitual destroyers of Bloughton sports squads. Liv knew she was in enemy territory, but hadn't expected this level of dislocation. Even Bloughton's worst homes—the Monk house, for instance—had a sense of ownership lacking from this street. Half the windows were boarded up. The gutters were gluts of soggy litter. Black wires from defunct cable services dangled down apartment buildings like worms left to roast in the sun.

Liv looked again at the directory of handwritten names, each paired with an aged plastic doorbell. The button to unit 302 looked dusty and rarely pushed, and though the name beside it had faded from sunlight, it was legible enough: Carbajal. Liv took a steadying breath, too aware of the lob of her heart, and pressed the button. She flinched, expecting, for some reason, to hear one of A's chirps. But there was no sound at all. She waited, listening for doorbell-hating dogs.

The lobby door abruptly shot open, socking Liv in the shoulder. She stumbled back as a woman in a baggy blouse with an unlit cigarette in her mouth backed out, arms wrapped around a plastic hamper of laundry. The woman glared, tightening what looked like toothless lips around the cigarette. Before Liv could count the reasons not to do it, she stuck her foot in the door.

She slipped through the gap and hurried past a bank of silver mailboxes and into a mildewed, carpeted stairwell blotched with stains. It took one stair before Liv, cross-country runner, gasped for air. She regretted not bringing Mist, which still rested in the back seat of her car. She should do something to protect herself. Send an email to Krista with the building address. Find a store that sold pepper spray. But these offered too many opportunities for her to chicken out. She was here. She would carry this through.

Liv reached the third floor. The peeling wallpaper was a green-and-silver jungle print. The iron-gray carpet was balding, and two of the three lamps had burned out. It smelled like cabbage, and, from a distant apartment, Liv heard the lonely warble of a Roy Orbison song. She took out her key ring and slotted keys through the fingers of her left hand. Of all the wild weapons she'd handled in her life, this was the best she could do.

She knocked on unit 302.

"*Ohhhhhhhh!*" Instantly, a man's incensed moan.

Liv took a step back, wanting Mist, wanting it now.

"*You want to kick me out? See me pick food from your trash cans next week? You want to live with that? I'm a disabled American, you son of a bitch! You kick a disabled American to the curb and your ass is going to end up in hell!"*

Liv's mind spun. This man believed her to be some vindictive landlord. She adjusted her perspiring palm around the keys.

"Mr. Carbajal, it's not—I'm just . . ."

She trailed off, uncertain how to describe herself or her mission. From behind the door, she heard the clang of a utensil being dropped on a plate. The creak of a chair, the groans of floorboards, a hoarse exhale. Twenty seconds later, the man spoke again, much softer, but so close to Liv that she gasped. He was right behind the door.

"Just what?" he prompted. His voice was a mushy drawl, as if spoken behind food.

"A girl." It sounded both massively inadequate and disparagingly true.

A bolt lock was shifted, a chain lock thrown. The door flew open six inches. The room was unlit, almost black despite it being the middle of the day, and Liv could discern only the outlines of the man's rumpled bathrobe, crooked glasses, and unkempt hair. He stood motionless for several seconds. His breathing was louder than the Roy Orbison, a husky wheeze with fluting undertones.

"Planning to take my eyes out with those keys?"

Liv flushed, thrust the key ring into the pocket of her coat.

"I wanted to ask you about . . . why you got fired." She swallowed; her throat burned with anxious acid. "I've . . . seen things."

For a time the man stared. Then he chuckled, the distant rumble of coming thunder.

"I thought you'd never get here."

He turned and shuffled into the dark apartment, leaving the door open behind him.

"Shit," Liv muttered. She raised her voice. "Can we talk somewhere else? A coffee shop or something?"

He disappeared around a corner. Liv cursed again, confirmed the locations of her keys and phone, and stepped inside. She paused to let her pupils widen. The place felt like a junk shop, though she couldn't make out specifics. Objects darker than the general dark threatened from all sides, shelves and piles teetering with jutting, irregular shapes. The spice of decaying books shot into her sinuses.

"The door," he snapped. "Landlord son of a bitch wants my money."

Liv closed the door against her better judgment and continued inside, navigating by fugitive slivers of sunlight. She turned a corner, undefinable granules crunching underfoot, and saw the man lower himself into a chair at a small table. Behind the table, the window shades were drawn, and, more alarming, sealed to the frames with thick black tape. Light eked from a dozen fissures, flecking dots of sun across books, clothes, and uncleared plates. There was one other chair, at the man's right elbow. Liv touched it, felt a layer of crumbs, and brushed them off before sitting.

Carlos Carbajal stared straight ahead at the wall, and Liv could see him only in profile: tangled hair, sloping forehead, brushy mustache. She investigated the right side of his face. His brown skin was shades darker from beard growth, and wrinkles cascaded from his eyes like Monk family fireworks. With his right hand, he picked an object off the plate before him. Liv expected a cigarette lighter, maybe something harder, but it was a container of Tic Tacs. Carbajal thumbed it open, tossed white pellets into his mouth.

"Don't tell me your name," he said. "I don't want to know."

Here was a man farther off the grid than Lee Fleming had ever been, one who, if the nonfunctional doorbell was an indication, barely interfaced with the outer world. What did she have to lose by divulging the outrageous truth? If he responded like she was crazy, she could say thank you and get the hell out of there.

"We caught one," she said. "My friend and I. In a hunting trap."

She watched his bushy right eyebrow lift. Still he did not turn her way.

"I don't know what you mean." His tone was artificially flat.

"You do. I know you do."

"You'll have to be more specific."

"A thing. Like a person, but . . . not."

Carbajal looked down at his table of rubble.

"What'd you do with it?" he asked softly.

"We . . . kept it."

"You still *have* it?"

She thought of Doug and A, their uncertain fates. "Sort of."

"Holy shit. Holy fucking shit, girl."

Carbajal chuckled, then coughed. His chest resounded with phlegm. He choked on it, his face going dark purple, thick strands of spit glossy in the sunspots. He panted, hocked, and spat on the floor. He wiped his mouth.

"Lung cancer," he gasped. "On my last goddamn leg here. The mints help."

Two days of apologies and she was still going: "I'm sorry."

He flapped an irritable hand. "Look at this place. I'm dead and buried."

"It . . . the thing we caught . . . it said your name."

"Is that so? I suppose that's flattering. Probably overheard someone talk about me. Thought I could help, offer protection. Wrong about that, though."

"So you saw one of them, too?"

"One? Little girl, I saw a whole group."

"Then why didn't you say something? Why haven't you told anyone?"

He slammed the Tic Tac container to the table. "Don't you judge me. Don't you dare judge me, little bitch."

Liv tensed. *Little bitch* was not *little girl*. The apartment layout raced through her mind. Estimates on how quickly she might leap from the chair, how many steps it would take to reach the door.

"They wiped me *out*," he seethed. "Persona non grata. The good old US of A. But you think they shut me up? You think they shut up Carlos Carbajal? I've got a computer, girl. And I know how to use it. I've got software and plug-ins that block prying eyes. I'm still out there. People call them conspiracy sites, like that's a disparaging word. But conspiracy's the *right* word. That's the word you use when there are multiple entities—right?—colluding to enact a secret policy. Log in to any of the top sites. Mr. Brown—that's what I go by now. Mr. Brown has thousands of followers. Go ahead and check. Thousands."

All of this was delivered straight to the wall. *Mr. Brown* rang a shivery bell. Hadn't Doug, on his birthday night, included that username among those he'd been following on Internet forums? Liv held her breath and waited to see if the flood of words would persist. Instead, he twirled his hand impatiently for a response.

"I'm sorry," she said. "I'm sorry they did that to you."

Carbajal blasted derisive air from his mouth. Apologies, it seemed, were repellent, a long-lost language of sensitivity of which he wished not to be reminded. He shook the Tic Tacs in a fist; the sound leaped at Liv like a rattlesnake.

"Vulnerable little doe like you. How old are you anyway? You were my daughter, I'd ground you till you were seventy, walking into a dark apartment like this. On the other hand, what do I know? Never had any kids. I'm sterile as a stick."

"I'm . . . sorry?"

"So what's the story, then? You a Mr. Brown fanatic, or you got some other game? Forget that—if you really caught one in a trap, why didn't *you* tell the police? Why haven't you taken twenty million photos and spread them all over the Net?"

It was a question so sensible that even a man of debatable sense knew to ask it. Liv looked from Carbajal's suspicious right eye into her lap. She'd never said it out loud. Saying it out loud was the end, she'd always known it, but it was also, in ways that mattered, the beginning.

"We . . ." Her neck ached from how it hung. "We hurt it."

"Define hurt."

"We beat it." Each word a hook into her flesh. "We . . . tortured it."

"Because you were scared?"

Liv nodded, but it only agitated the lie into a more toxic form. "No. That's not true. We were mad. We *wanted* to hurt it."

Carbajal tapped mints into his mouth. He sucked, his jaw circling.

"Now why," he said in a voice nearly pleasant, "would you want to do that?"

"Because." The word cracked, as loud and wet as Carbajal's cough. "It took my dad, and we had to do something, didn't we?" Absolution, that's all she wanted, one adult to say that what she'd done was forgivable. "The alien took my dad, and we had to punish it."

Carbajal almost deigned to look at her, rotating his head an inch from its stubborn profile view. He did it because he was startled—Liv could see it in the fall of his brow, the slackening of his frowning lips. She believed she had broken through; she watched for the apologetic drop of his shoulders.

Instead, he tipped his head so far back that Liv thought it might tumble off his shoulders. He laughed. Not another scornful chuckle but a booming, full-throated howl that shot to the ceiling and exploded around the room. Tic Tacs fired from his mouth, hard white projectiles. Spit, too, slopped down the front of his bathrobe. He pounded his fist against the table; his old chair squealed. He laughed harder and harder, and when the laughs were joined by coughs, it all got mixed up—gleeful sickness, painful glee, there was no telling.

Slowly Carbajal gained control. He leaned over the table, his back hitching with the last, mocking spates of laughter.

"I'm sorry," he wheezed. "But, little girl? That thing you caught isn't an 'alien.' Aliens don't exist. That thing you and your friend have been torturing is a man."

28.

LIV FELT NEITHER THE CHAIR AT HER back nor the floor at her feet. Stupor slopped over her like thick paste, slowing the race of questions. Several managed to crawl across her brain like wounded animals, but only one made it all the way: Had what she and Doug done been worse than she'd even imagined?

"Long as you're sitting down with your mouth shut," Carbajal said, "let me tell you a story. It's a story I tried to file four years ago before some very persuasive people made sure no one printed a word. Some shithole Iowa newspaper, you think they've got the stones to fight that kind of pressure? Fuck no, not when there's high school football to write about. You'd know this story already if you read the forums."

Liv inched her fingertips across the tabletop. Chipped, scratched, but real. This was all real, every bit of it was happening.

"They teach you about Anatoli Bugorski in school? Of course they don't. Our kiddies shouldn't dream about anything but sugarplum fairies. Anatoli Bugorski was a Russian researcher who got an accidental proton beam to the noggin in 1978. Five hundred rads is enough to kill you dead, and this guy took three hundred thousand. Dead meat, right? Except the guy doesn't die. His face puffs up and he has the odd seizure, but he's alive. He's still alive today. Now there's no more Soviet Union. The gulags are empty. The guy is *talking*. He says there's others like him, a whole platoon of proton warriors. 'I am being tested,' he said. 'The human capacity for survival is being tested.'"

"This is . . ." Liv heard her own voice as if through a wall. "Some kind of test?"

"You didn't find your way to shithole number 302 without putting in some miles on the World Wide Web. You ever come across something called the Biatalik Program?"

If anyone had followed the wild forum postings of Mr. Brown, it would have been Doug. Yet this particular detail, this single one, was Liv's to claim. It was Carbajal's pronunciation, she thought, that subtle trace of a Spanish accent, the strokelike slowness of his speech, that made her recognize it, and instantly. She *had* heard of the Biatalik Program, though she hadn't known it at the time. It was her second crucial misunderstanding; Liv began to wonder if her brain, in self-preservation, had fought all truths from the beginning.

Biatalik Program, *Bee-ah-tall-lick Pro-gram*. Or was it, misheard under radio tunes and party chatter, *Be the tallest you can*?

Major Dawkins had spoken these words in confidence to Lee Fleming at the major's last birthday cookout. The memory was vivid, as are all memories of crying parents: her father's face against the major's Hawaiian shirt, his skinny back convulsing, while Liv, hunting for a reason to hope, had instilled the major's gibberish phrase with false inspiration. The instinct of a little girl, she thought, the very thing Carbajal kept calling her.

"Major Dawkins," she whispered.

"Good girl," Carbajal said. "He was part of it. Think nuclear missile silos. Where does the government hide those? Bumfuck, North Dakota. Nowheresville, Missouri. Motherfucking *Iowa*. Places where no one's looking. Biatalik Program, same deal. They needed an isolated place where they could explore the human form. Bugorski times a hundred. Chernobyl in a test tube. Don't think America's any better. Anytime the good old US of A tests a bomb, we chain up a few hundred beagles in the blast zone with Geiger counters clipped to their ears. Check the forums, girl. But animals only get you so far. You said your dad saw one, too?"

"And he disappeared," she whispered.

"Biatalik was what they call 'born classified,' TS/SCI—top secret/sensitive compartmented information. Stuff even the Oval Office doesn't need to know. Done without a dust mote of ethical oversight. One of the test subjects must have gotten out. Your dad saw him, and it put messed-up ideas in his head about UFOs, that'd be my guess. There would have been people plenty unhappy about what he saw. Your dad was a reporter?"

The words hurt to say: "A teacher."

Carbajal tsked. "Even worse. People trust teachers. If he started talking—well, shit. I don't want to say this. I'm not a cruel person. But Major Dawkins, any of those Biatalik fucks . . ."

"The major was a friend! He loved my dad! He wouldn't have tried to trick him!"

"Did I say he wasn't a friend? He probably did love him. And thought that this was his only shot to live." Carbajal sighed. "Doesn't matter. Your dad's dead now. They would have killed him. Sorry, but that's how it is."

Liv had never believed anything different, despite Doug's enticements that, by spreading the skinner's blood, they might prompt some sort of exchange. No one, though, had ever pronounced his death aloud. It hit her like a slap. She saw black spots. Strangely, though, she was grateful. This stranger had planted a gravestone where the rest of them should have long ago.

"None of it was super-villain shit," Carbajal continued. "It never starts that way. People always think they're doing the right thing. Two doctors headed it up, Faddon and Nance. The best and brightest. I'm sure Mengele was the best and brightest, too. Please tell me your school teaches you about Mengele? This Faddon and Nance, their plan was to rid the world of degenerative disease. Who's going to argue with that? Move the pancreas over here so it's easier for doctors to access. Thicken a bone plate over there to protect vital organs. Accelerated eugenics, that's all it was. I'm sure they had a nice word for it. Me, I'd call it mutation. The one you saw, what did he look like?"

He—the pronoun punctured her. A human. A man. A sick, struggling patient that, instead of helping, they'd ground through the gears of a second hell.

"Eyes," she sputtered. "Big eyes."

"That's easy: superior vision."

"A second knee. It bent back."

"Like an animal. Land speed would be off the charts."

"Ribs. On the outside."

"Organic body armor. You see where this is headed?"

Liv tried to nod, but instead her head only shook, back and forth.

"Military applications," Carbajal drawled. "They got a way of creeping in. It's fucking Faustian. At least your teachers taught you Faust, didn't they? Dr. Nance got cold feet. She was young, idealistic, way over her head. She sought me out. It was some Deep Throat shit. Notes left on my car. Coded phone messages. She tells me they're using prisoners. Lifers. Giving them get-out-of-jail-free cards in exchange for a year or two of experiments. I'm not going to lie, little girl. It was exciting. I'm a pissant reporter in dull-as-a-board Iowa—right?—and here's this nuclear bomb placed in my lap. I'm seeing Pulitzers. I'm seeing Nobel Prizes. So I went in alone. Had my camera, my recorder. God, I was stupid. So, so, so, so stupid."

He stared at his hand for a while, as if craving the mints he held but unable to spur his arm into action. When he spoke again, his quaggy voice was further jelled by emotion.

"Sorry, but here's the truth, and you deserve to know it. You and your friend are no better than Faddon and Nance. You really convinced yourself you were doing good by doing bad? That's the oldest self-deception in the book. You're going to find out what that kind of deception does to you when you get older. When it's just you and your nightmares, night after night after night."

Liv thought of her comfortable, rumpled bed, of holding A, and wondered if she would ever sleep so well again.

"Biatalik fell apart," Carbajal sighed. "Of course it did. The prisoners, their bodies all rearranged—most of them weren't going to live. And the ones who did? Those walking petri dishes? You can't push men like that back into society. You'll end up with a whole slew of Anatoli Bugorskis, out there telling the truth. Far as I know, the compound was sealed up, and the whole program brushed under the rug."

"The survivors," Liv whispered.

"What happened to them? What do you think? Who's going to bemoan losing a few rapists and murderers? On the other hand, there's you. You have one of them in custody. He escaped. Hid out somewhere. My god, the life he must have lived. The world—right?—it never fails to astound."

"And the doctors?" Liv managed.

Carbajal shrugged. "A job like that, you sign away constitutional rights. Best-case scenario, they dropped into the shadows, same as me. You want to know the truth? Mr. Brown's thousands of followers don't mean shit. End of the day, I'm still here in my hidey-hole, no better off than those prisoners. I keep hoping one day I'll get a private message on the forums, and it'll be Dr. Faddon or Dr. Nance. Wouldn't that be poetic? To find out we all ended up alone in dark little rooms?"

Liv's eyes had fully adjusted to the murk. This only made the evidence of Carbajal's life more oppressive. An assortment of liquor bottles to put Aggie's old collection to shame. A garbage can overflowing with TV dinner trays. An empty aquarium lined with scum, a listless stab at companionship. A fedora, the dapper accent of the roving reporter, relegated to a dusty top shelf, never to be worn again.

"You satisfied?" Carbajal clacked the Tic Tacs to the table. "You get what you came for?"

Had she come to be ruined? That's what she'd got. The world outside, so bright and of such depth, seemed unreal to her now, the idea of returning to it revolting. How could she go back to Bloughton and smile at her mother, joke with her friends, and stand in front of teachers, all while knowing what she'd done? The only way to convince herself she didn't belong in this crypt was to reject all of it.

"I don't believe it," she said from clenched teeth. "There's no proof."

Carbajal's right eyebrow rose.

"The girl wants proof? Here's proof: Your father got one glimpse and ended up dead. Here's proof: Faddon and Nance, verifiable geniuses, wiped off the face of the earth. Here's proof: Fourteen months ago in Florida, Major Dawkins blew his head off with a military sidearm."

A picture of the major popped inside Liv's mind, his bullish forehead, his block chin, his mustache so neat and silver it might have been made of steel, followed by a second picture, all those straight, hale lines scrambled into wet, red meat. Liv gasped to refute the whole idea but was silenced by Carbajal's shout.

"You want more proof? Do you?"

He swung upward from his chair with unforeseen agility. In the same fluid motion, he ducked his face in front of Liv while thumbing the switch on a table-side lamp. The click was soft, and the bulb lit up a wan, orange wash, but it was enough to overpower the blacked-out windows.

The left half of Carbajal's face, shrouded in gloom until that instant, was a glossy, mealy cluster of fatty extrusions and thick patches of stiff hair. It held a roughly human shape, like a manne-quin head melted and stirred with a stick, but the ballooned left eye and deep canal of the left cheek defied all rationalities of muscle and bone. The jump from the chair made Carbajal pant, and Liv watched a sheer lamina of skin pulse where the left half of his mouth should have been.

"A souvenir from my visit to their lab," he said. "They weren't overly thrilled by my proposed exposé."

Liv recoiled and toppled off the side of her chair. The carpet was dank and crusty, and she bounded up, her spine striking metal shelv-ing. Carbajal lurched to the side to match her distance, his face mer-cifully sliding from lamplight.

"The good looks are just the start, really," he said. "The teeth on that side are soft as chalk. Once a week I have to flush my left ear of yellow gunk so rancid it stains the sink. I throw up half my food. You know how I said I was sterile? Truth is, I'm as impotent as a sock, not that anyone's interested. And the lung cancer? Little girl, I haven't smoked a day in my life."

Liv wanted to run. She could be in the hall in seconds. But she had no place in the world until she could make things right, or as close as possible. She held her ground even as Carbajal halved the distance, capering close enough that she could again see his knobby, gouged face. He held both hands upward as if to get her opinion of a new outfit. His left hand looked like a hoof, a thick, wedge-shaped club.

"Wh-where was it?" she stammered.

"Oh, no, you can't go there. It's not safe. You know what might be in the soil there? In the water? Strontium 90, plutonium 239/240, all sorts of bad shit. You think I'd send a defenseless doe anywhere like that?"

She lifted the wrist compass. "It—he—he had this; it was my dad's."

Carbajal choked and sneered. "You think you know what's best, do you?"

"If my dad was there, if there's any record of him, I have to—"

Carbajal pressed in, his face inches from Liv's. She squeezed her eyes shut but could feel the swampy billow from his half mouth and smell the spoil of his row of rotted teeth.

"*This* is your record. This *face* is your record."

Liv forced open her eyes. His face was all that she should see; it occluded the whole world. She straightened her back and bit down, imagining her own teeth grinding to powder. She widened her eyes as much as she could and took it all in, because she'd seen worse, participated in worse, was worse. Though Major Dawkins had never actually said it, that didn't mean it wasn't good advice: Liv had to be the tallest she could, for just a little bit longer.

"Tell me where it was." This time she said it gently.

The anger vibrating through Carbajal, some due to her, she knew, but much of it due to the unstoppable slippages of an unfair world, shook out through his extremities: the long, gray whips of his hair, his hand and hoof, the broken, once-proud shoulders. He seemed to sink a foot into the floor. His breathing, once slowed, sounded as if it came from a mouth that was whole. He looked at her, his huge, directionless left eye as sky blue as A's, the other a sober, weary, saddened brown.

"If you *were* my daughter," he said, "goddamn, I would be so proud."

29.

WITH TWITCHY FINGERS SHE TYPED
Carbajal's directions into her phone. They were absurdly simple,
involving none of the sorcery of Lee Fleming's blind plunges into the
forest. Take this county road to that state highway, turn right at that
crossroads, hang a left down this dirt road. She didn't wait to make
the trip. She couldn't. She'd inferred from Doug that he'd intended
to euthanize A, but when she thought back on what he'd said while
carrying A away, she couldn't recall one solid piece of evidence. She'd
only wanted it to be true. If she could find physical evidence of
Carbajal's story, she could find Doug and shove it in his face. He
wouldn't torture a human being, no matter how far gone he was.

Liv couldn't forget that, in addition to A, Doug had nearly every
weapon in Lee's armory.

She steered as if through wet cement. Every car in her rearview
mirror was a plainclothes cop ready to arrest her for what she knew

and what she'd done. Every pedestrian in her peripheral vision pointed an accusatory finger. Her station wagon exhaust pipe leaked blood, and the engine emitted not asthmatic thwacks but A's high-pitched, pleading cheeps.

It was only because she arrived at the site from a new direction that Liv didn't recognize it sooner. She parked the station wagon in the dirt driveway, a cloud of road dust erasing the real world behind her. Here was where the Biatalik Program had been centered. Of course it was. How could it have been anywhere else? She exited the car and stared up at the house.

It was like any century-old two-story country abode except that the roof was scraped of shingle and sagging, the windows broken, the paint peeled from wood. No one had lived here in ages, but it wasn't the house that was important. Liv drifted to the left, beneath the cracking knuckles of a leafless oak, and traced fossilized wheelbarrow ruts as they wound past stooped barns, weed-strangled grain bins, a collapsed chicken house, and twin rusted silos. Beyond all that, rippling along the horizon, were the thunderbird wings of Black Glade.

This was the farm where her father had forced her to take *Resurrection Update* before hopping the electric fence with Lizardpoint. Before running, he'd glanced at the sky and said to her, *Anything can happen under a sky like this.* He'd been right: She had returned to the last place she'd ever wanted to see again, not creeping from the woods this time but pulling up like she wasn't afraid of anything. Sweat began dripping down her face. She'd never been more scared in her life.

Liv opened the car's rear door and took out Mist.

This is where Carbajal's instructions got specific. Liv wobbled across lumpy terrain. Weeds swayed as critters dashed. She passed a pen that might have once housed slobbering cows but was now a mud pit cordoned off by slouching wire. She passed an outhouse in the process of being sucked into the earth. Above the outhouse, the skies darkened. Black Glade snagged hold of the sun like Hangman's Noose. *Turn back*, she begged herself. *Drive away.*

The silos were behemoths as inscrutable as Giza pyramids. Liv felt woozy and had to look down; she walked to the base of the second silo as Carbajal had directed. A treacherous ladder clotted by vines was bolted onto the exterior, and just thinking of such a suicidal climb sickened Liv. But she wasn't headed up. She ducked beneath some sort of chute and skirted the concrete base until she found a small access hatch. It was fringed in yellow decay, its handle so corroded Liv thought it might crumble in her hand.

The hatch stuck when she tried to open it. *Good*, she thought. *Get out of here.* Instead, she decided to kick it open, then changed her mind. All that noise in these swaths of silence? It might rip the screams from her tensed body. She propped a running shoe up against the silo. With leverage now, she pulled the handle. Metal squealed, the sound of her fraying nerves. On the fourth tug, the hatch popped. Liv dodged clear of it. It was as if she'd cut a neat rectangle through reality. Beyond the hatch, nothing, an absolute void.

Liv climbed through it, straight into unknowable horror. Inside, the hot air was stiff straw against her exposed skin. There was a light source ninety feet straight up, gray daylight pinholing through ventilation slats. Light smeared down the inside of the silo like drool.

Liv stared back at the ground, where Carbajal had told her to look. The fear of blundering into a bladed farm instrument limited her to small steps, but she stomped those steps, listening for a hollow thud, praying not to hear one. But there *was* a sound. She cocked her head. The hatch squeaked in the breeze. Wind rattled the siding of melting sheds. Liv reached out, pulled the hatch shut. It was darker now, but quieter. She closed her eyes, held her breath.

Music: It hummed from a hidden place.

Her first thought was a car radio, someone who'd followed her, maybe Carbajal, so he could murder her where no one would see.

Except this music came from inside the silo. On this scar of a property, nothing could be more unexpected. Liv crouched, her knees knocking, both to hear it better and to prevent her own collapse. She shuffled on all fours, pushing Mist along the ground, scattering mouse droppings, feeling the sharp, ancient corn on her palms. The music continued. It was tremulous but had a rhythm, a sleepy swing like a slowly plucked guitar.

There, she felt it. A seam in the concrete. She dug her fingers into it, then slid those fingers until the seam made a right-angle bend. Another hatch, just as Carbajal had promised, and she felt for a notch, a knob, a lever. Near her knees she found a heavy ring. She slid her body clear of the hatch and took the ring in both hands. And there she paused, her head bowed in prayer posture, hair dangling in dirt, the lackadaisical lope of the song vibrating her bones. Her fright approached paralysis. There was no closing this hatch once it was opened.

Hinges yowled like a cat. From below came a different variety of light, electric sources of varied wattage, bulbs, and shades. Silhouetted was the shape of a ladder, six rungs, and before Liv could arrange her body to take the first step, a new verse of the song began, and now she could hear it, the nodding pace of the guitar, the mournful twang of the singer. *Country-western*, Liv thought. *Dolly Parton?* Liv remembered a drive with her family, this same song coming on the radio, Dad wanting to change the dial, Mom deflecting his hand so she could sing along.

Liv picked up Mist, the weapon profane alongside this gush of warm memories. She dropped one foot on the ladder with a dull clang. Then the other: *clang*. She climbed down, her trembling legs brightening with orange light, the music growing louder, perhaps the safest, softest sounds that could have possibly greeted her in this underworld. Her heart pounded regardless, big fleshy smacks against her lungs. Her body would give out any second now, any second.

The first thing she saw was a needlepoint. She blinked, and shivered, and wanted to climb away. Its cheer was ghastly, unspeakable. *God Bless Our Home*, it read, in the aslant lettering of either a novice or someone too old to guide a needle. The phrase was bordered by crude likenesses of flowers. In the center was a clumsy depiction of a house with a peaked roof and red chimney, the Xs of the stitches so loose it was nearly abstract. It could be the house on this property, Liv thought, and the idea was appalling. There were no peaked roofs or brick chimneys, not down here.

She followed both light and music around a drywall elbow and like that, she was no longer alone. To her left was a living room. To her right, a kitchen. The rooms began abruptly, like one of her father's theater sets viewed from a backstage wing. The living room was carpeted with incongruous strips, some colorful and shaggy, others drab and crewcut. There were two chairs, both of them wood, though augmented with misshapen, home-sewn cushions. A low, chipped wooden table was between the chairs. On it, a checkerboard, red destroying black.

Both chairs were occupied. Liv choked down her gasp. The chair backs prohibited her from getting a full view of the checkers players, but they had turned in their seats and were getting a full look at her. The closer pair of eyes looked normal, though the head in which they were set was oddly noduled, as if the skull were burled with bone. The second pair of eyes wasn't normal. One rolled like a marble like A's eyes; the other was focused but so bloodshot Liv expected actual blood to dribble. There were floor lamps, but they were dead, leaving the room to be lit by a single source of flickering blue light. Television light, Liv recognized, though when she edged closer, what she saw instead was a wooden crate from which a rectangle had been sawed. Sitting inside, a wad of blinking blue Christmas lights.

It was a fake TV.

All of it was fake, a flimsy copy of a dimly remembered domestic world. A fake living room. A fake carpet. The cross-stitch had a fake picture frame made of masking tape. Liv stared at the checkers players, unable to breathe. No one else breathed, either. No one moved. Slowly, as if on a swivel, Liv turned to face the kitchen.

It was brighter, four mismatched table lamps and a bulb over the sink. From where she stood, Liv had a partial view of a shelf, upon which rested the kind of knickknacks found in any rustic Midwestern kitchen. Each item was just wrong enough to be repugnant. The porcelain child holding a teddy bear had been broken, then glued back together, its face an abomination. A wooden rooster had been exactingly repainted, but by someone whose eyes didn't work; the tail feathers were army green, the breast neon orange, the comb black. There was a jolly gnome, too, but only the top half of it, grafted to the tail of a rubber shark. Liv didn't feel that any of it was meant to disturb, which only made it more disturbing.

On the counter was a record player. Propped beside it was an album cover, Dolly Parton stretching inside a tight red sweater alongside the words *Greatest Hits*. Dolly was still singing, the record still turning.

Another step toward the kitchen and Liv found the worst thing: more people. One man had been washing dishes; only the ripple of sudsy water proved he wasn't a cardboard cutout. Two others sat at a folding table, each holding a hand of cards, the cribbage board between them forgotten. Slowly the man with his back to her lowered his face until his cards covered it like a hand fan. He was ashamed, Liv realized. The overalls he wore did little to hide the soft blisters that covered his long arms and gorilla back like Bubble Wrap. His cribbage opponent had no opportunity to hide. He was dressed in an old dress shirt tucked into baggy, belted slacks, and wore a broken watch. So humdrum was his attire that Liv had to force herself to accept the shape of his head. It was oblong and curved with doughy bulges at the chin and forehead. He set down his cards, and a strange shiver ran through his sleeves, as if there weren't two arms inside but rather two braids of tentacles.

Liv's whole body quaked. Why was she here? She could not recall.

Right, yes, to find evidence to force Doug to stop, but this was so much more than she'd expected, and she was so much less—a single girl, down here all alone.

The man at the sink suddenly shielded his face and ran off into darker areas. Liv couldn't see lower than his waist, but his footsteps sounded like a team of horses, a manifold clopping that made her wonder how many legs he had. Liv's dry, blinkless eyes trailed back to the sink. Over the soapy dishes was a half-open window bedecked with summery yellow curtains. It looked out directly onto a cement wall.

A door creaked, same as any door in any house. Liv peered into the farthest reaches. Distant light gleamed off a floor. Bathroom tile, she thought. These men, whatever had happened to them, had to eat, hence the dishes. They had to use a toilet, hence a bathroom. She took a step forward and saw a man's shape, unlike the others as straight and sharp as a razor. Behind the slim man huddled others, jostling for his protection, and only then did Liv notice that the two TV watchers had snuck away, their checkers forgotten, their disfigurements remembered.

From across the bunker, the slim man looked right at Liv. A sob emitted from her throat. The slim man straightened his sleeves. Liv shook her head, wishing him away. He began to approach. He did not move like the others; there was no fugitive scurry, no abnormal lope. He strode past a potted fern (plastic), past a bowl of fresh fruit (ceramic), past a rotary telephone (connected to nothing). This dwelling, Liv thought through a fearful haze, had everything necessary to make one feel right at home. No, that wasn't right. She had yet to see a single mirror.

She'd wielded Mist a hundred times but never used it. Now it rose, sliding up her hip, behind her back, slippery in her spasming hand. The slim man wore dark clothes that made his face look paper white. When he was ten feet away, Liv recognized that his face *was* white—he wore a mask. She whimpered. The mask was a novelty from a dollar-store Halloween aisle, molded plastic and an elastic strap. At some point, it had been covered in white paint, and detailed with black-dot eyes and a smiley-face mouth.

Smiley Face stopped at handshake distance. Liv felt the sting of scared tears.

"You've come," he stated simply, "to set them free."

Liv drew a cold, quaking breath. Hearing intelligible English down here was this nightmare's wildest detail. Though muffled behind plastic, the man's voice had a musical quality. Liv regripped Mist and moved her head, intending to indicate that, no, he was wrong. But she felt the skin of her neck crimp: She was nodding. Despite the stifling fear, she'd try to get every one of them up the ladder no matter how many legs they had, through the silo hatch no matter the sensitivity of their strange eyeballs. To make up for how little she'd done to help A, she'd try.

"I can't think of any other reason you would find us," Smiley Face said. "And I thank you for the thought. Can I fix you a cup of tea?"

Liv wiped sweat from her eyes and stared into the indifferent black dots of the mask's eyes. Did tea mean sitting down? In this ghoulish farce of a kitchen? She shook her head, and that shook her shoulder, which shook her arm, and she felt one of Mist's points jab her in the backside. The pain emboldened her, and she spoke, her voice breaking over Dolly Parton.

"You're keeping them down here," she rasped. "You can't do that."

He gestured with long, delicate fingers.

"I don't lock doors," he said. "You saw yourself."

"Then they don't know," Liv said. "They're confused. They're scared."

Smiley Face folded his hands in front of him.

"Are you sure," he asked gently, "it's not you who's confused and scared?"

He drifted to the right, under the kitchen light. Liv hissed at the motion and revealed Mist as a warning. Smiley Face either didn't see the weapon through the mask or didn't care; he stepped over helixes of warped linoleum and settled a hand upon the giant's bubbled neck. He stroked, each blister fattening under the pressure of his hand before rimpling back into place. Smiley Face wore dark blue hospital scrubs with short sleeves. His bare arms, from what Liv could see, were normal.

"You've made an easy mistake. Freedom—it's not to be found up there. Have *you* ever felt free?" He leaned onto the back of the vacated chair opposite the giant. "Think of all the things you ever wished you could say."

Liv credited the masked man's sedate tone for being able to understand his instruction. She thought of the things she could have been brave enough to tell her mother, about her drinking, about Doug, about A. Liv hadn't needed to go through all of this alone, if only she could have made herself open her mouth.

"Think of all the things," Smiley Face continued, "you ever wished you could do."

This list was even longer. Helping her father in a way that might have prevented all of this. Trying to understand A instead of being afraid to relinquish her rage. Being there for Doug in the years he'd needed her most.

"Down here, true freedom is possible," Smiley Face said. "I know that's not the reason this program was founded. But you can't control life's gorgeous, ungainly sprawl. You can't curtail evolution. I believe this, what you see, is what Biatalik was destined to be. Everyone here is a truly unique being, one of a kind—I've seen to it. Isn't that what everyone up there fights so hard to be? One of a kind?"

Liv thought of her dad, his dogged campaign to get incurious teenagers to care about poetry. She thought of Doug, striving to formulate corn mazes of legend. She scanned this cellar world and did, for an instant, feel a startling current of dozy warmth. All the struggles of the bright, noisy, overcrowded overground, what was the point of any of it?

"My orphans," Smiley Face sighed. "I love them so much."

Carbajal had said the Biatalik subjects were life-sentence prisoners, but under the wing of this masked man, they displayed no antisocial tendencies. They behaved, in fact, like model citizens, like her own dad during off-hours, relaxing on cushioned furniture to while away time with television and games.

"Who are you?" Liv whispered.

Smiley Face touched his white mask with the same delicacy as he'd touched the giant's blisters.

"It's been so long since we've had a visitor. There was a man, a military man, he used to come and leave crates of food in the silo. I don't know if it was under orders or if he just wished to help. Fourteen months ago, he stopped coming. I don't know why. Since then, it has been difficult. Our supplies are getting low. We've had to begin rationing. We could use a new friend. Perhaps that friend could be you? What do you think, Olivia?"

Hearing her name spoken aloud delivered no particular blow. Instead it burned like a sliver starting to fester with infection. Her shock peeled back just enough to recognize that everything about this situation felt inevitable. From the day she'd seen this farm from behind an electric fence, she'd never really left it.

"I'm Dr. Faddon." He gestured at the wrist compass Liv wore. "And you're Olivia Fleming. I've heard so much about you."

His next gesture was at the knickknack shelf, and Liv sidestepped onto gummy linoleum so that she could see the rest of it. On the far left was an object she recognized, an object that, for two years, she'd only known by its chalk outline. It was Lizardpoint, the turn-of-the-century Ghanaian fighting pick, its barbed point, hyena-hide fitting, and lizard-skin grip transformed, via its placement, into something as innocent as a figurine.

"We've been so worried about him," Faddon said.

Liv's eyes sandpapered against tender sockets.

"He's the only one of my orphans to ever leave," Faddon continued. "Not long ago, off he ran. We, of course, had no means to go after him. That compass you're wearing, he never took it off. It reminded him of his family, he said. While he could still talk, that is."

Liv thought of A, clutching her dad's compass.

Her veins went cold even as her body melted.

"No," Liv said. "No, no. No, no, no, no."

There was no hope of pushing the truth away, not anymore, not ever again. The being known as A hadn't kidnapped or killed her father.

The being known as A *was* her father.

30.

HER SILLY FIRST THOUGHT: *THAT'S WHY*
John wouldn't attack him.

Liv pushed off of a refrigerator covered with crayon drawings, her sweaty palms squeaking. Fear of death strangled her, but so did fear of living, and she needed to help the people down here as much as she needed to know the awful truth. She stumbled, twirled, and was beyond the kitchen and into the living room, oriented toward the deeper compound rather than the ladder offering escape into the civilized world, or the world she'd always considered civilized until this instant of understanding the atrocities she, Liv Fleming, had committed.

God, the things she and Doug had done to him.

Liv floundered forward, Mist clipping the plastic fern and tossing it, her elbow knocking arts-and-crafts projects from the wall, each item catching the blink of the holiday-light television before darkness ate it. She had to enter that darkness, sink into its tar pit. She dove into it. Doors appeared on either side. Her breath screeched through a pinholed throat. The first door was open, and it was, indeed, a bathroom, inside which three sets of eyes shone from the dark next to the toilet, though who could say it was three people? It could be one man with six eyes, couldn't it? She felt thin, gray. The scant "biologic evidence" her dad had ranted about in the town square oozed from everything down here, just as it oozed in Liv's backyard shed.

"Olivia? Olivia?" Faddon was in pursuit.

Other doors were open, too. In a room on the right, she discerned the outlines of what looked like bunk beds with shapes shivering beneath covers, as if she were the dreadful one, the cold-blooded invader. The last door on the right was shut, but a sound came from behind it that struck Liv as especially chilling. It was a throttled wheeze coming in the pattern of inhale, exhale.

A lone door waited at the end of the hall. Liv kicked it open. Her hand flew to the wall for a light switch. Light flooded from the ceiling, a bank of fluorescents ten times brighter than anything in the bunker, and that made sense, for this was the operating room, where it all happened.

A surgical table with wrist and ankle harnesses held the room's center, while cabinets and shelves gleamed with instruments more threatening than the Armory's weapons: scalpels, forceps, syringes, hemostats, scissors, tweezers, needles, suction tubing. Liv's heart skipped, skipped. There was a low hum, and Liv turned to see a refrigerated cabinet, inside which rested, in painstaking rows, bottles of solutions in a vivid array of colors.

"He was sick."

Faddon's voice, right behind her. Liv whirled to face him, swiping Mist through the bluish light, missing Faddon's tunic by inches. She backpedaled into the operating table. Faddon's white mask was blinding in so much light. He held out two hands in an appeal for calm.

"Lymphoma," Faddon said. "Stage four. You may have noticed unusual behavior in him at home. An inability to sleep or eat? Spells of inattention? Bursts of uncharacteristic emotion? He wasn't going to live, Olivia. Lymphoma spreads rapidly. He had one year at the outside. But he had a friend. A friend who knew of the Biatalik Program, what we were doing down here, what we were *capable* of doing."

The bullet-caved face of Major Dawkins again raced through Liv's mind, and she mourned its gored tatters.

"This was practically Lee's home," Faddon said affectionately, surveying the room through his mask. "He received more treatment than most. I saw to it. We'd barely begun, of course, when he first ran away—without clothing, I might add. He was in a terrible state. He wouldn't have remembered a thing. As I said, we were not equipped to go after him. But I was happy when he returned. The cancer had spread so terribly by then."

Liv thought of how sick her father was that last year, how, during the final hunt in Black Glade, he'd had to pull himself along with tree trunks.

"But let me tell you something, Olivia. We did beat that cancer. It was everywhere, in every organ, and we erased it. Other changes occurred, of course, but change is good. Change is progress. Dr. Nance didn't see it that way, but she lost faith. She's the one who brought the reporter here. Is he how you found us? It's a pity, the only great failure of Biatalik. Dr. Nance betrayed every man down here, your father included. While all I did was try to make him a better Lee Fleming than ever."

Liv couldn't help but follow Faddon's wandering gaze. Gripping the railing of the operating table, she shared the same view her father had had all those times he'd lain prone atop it, and suddenly, with an almost audible snap, everything came together, each piece of legend he'd doled out to students. Lee's tall tales had been remarkably accurate, only confused by the formulas Faddon and Nance had pumped into him.

The Floating Pumpkin wasn't some mystical alien globe, radiating anesthetic before retracting into the ceiling. It was the adjustable surgical lamp that hovered over the table. The skinners didn't shed their blue skins, they shed their blue scrubs, and the reason Lee had insisted they didn't have mouths was because they'd worn surgical masks during operations. The two giant tubes Lee had said suctioned him into the skinner spacecraft were, of course, the twin silos. And the Green Man? That towering, silent, omnipresent loomer? It was an old-fashioned movie poster tacked to the wall, *Frankenstein* with a lime-colored Boris Karloff shambling toward the viewer. It was an incongruous detail that would have leaped out at any man secured to this table.

"A gift from Dr. Nance." Faddon's hands were clasped at his chest. "Her little joke. She called me Dr. Frankenstein. I keep it there in remembrance of happier times."

"You turned my dad into a monster," Liv gasped, even as she knew that what had happened in her shed was just as foul as what had happened here.

"Your father achieved a higher state. To release one's grip on one's physical form—it's what I've been saying: It's freedom. Think of it. Wars, terrorism, radicalization, all of it would disappear if every human being was their own individual race, if there was no more this group versus that. The men down here have become the very *idea* and *spirit* of humanity. The divine spark itself. The closest to angels the world has ever known."

Faddon smoothed a crease in the poster.

"I only wish I could join them. But someone has to mix the solutions. Operate the instruments. It's why I wear the mask. So they aren't discouraged by the unexceptionality of my face. The orphans are my children, and any good father sacrifices for his children. You know that more than anyone, don't you?"

She did, and it would haunt her for as long as she was cursed to live, but instead of shrinking back against the cold steel of the table, Liv took advantage of Faddon's distraction and plunged forward, slashing with Mist to make sure he kept away. What he'd said struck her like a spear. Children, a father. The Biatalik prisoners had a mother, too, didn't they? The woman who'd given Faddon the *Frankenstein* poster: Dr. Nance. Liv ought to flee, get out of here before being turned into one of these things, yet the final uncoded detail from Lee Fleming's ravings teased her.

The Whistler.

Liv rushed from the room into the hall and threw open the

first door, the one from behind which she'd heard the wheeze. The room was very dark, and there was no light switch she could feel. She entered anyway, sensing beneath her feet dirt, not concrete. She bumbled forward, blindly swinging Mist, until her shoe struck a hard object. She looked down. It was stone. She knelt. A stone block, and carved into it were figures the darkness didn't permit her to read, though her fingers identified them as letters.

It was a grave marker. This was a cemetery. Liv stood and staggered, and her eyes, still adjusting, found another marker, then another, then, popping like mushrooms, a dozen more spread across the dirt. Not all of Biatalik's subjects had survived, and here was where they were buried, here was where Lee Fleming, if he'd been luckier, would have ended up.

It wasn't as silent as a cemetery should be. The whistle was there, clearer now, a sibilant gasp followed by a flapping exhale like air spluttering from a balloon. It was the sort of squeaking, repetitive noise, she thought, that would have penetrated the brain of anyone on the operating table. Liv took another step, tripped past another stone. Something smelled bad. Like sweat, like urine. She noticed that her own body blocked the light from the open door behind her. She stepped to the side to let the light reach the back wall.

Liv never got a good look. The light was never bright enough, her eyes never acclimatized. But she got a glimpse, and for that she'd forever be sorry. Little was left of Dr. Nance that could be considered human. The outline of her body, visible against the wall, had the contour of a beached seal, a shapeless blob lacking observable limbs. What Liv could see of her skin suggested a rhinoceros texture speckled with scabs from continual injections. The Nance-thing rippled as she shuddered with wretched life. Embedded in the fatty tissue, like raisins into dough, were the scattered vestiges of obsolete parts: a pinkie finger, an eye, a nipple, a sprinkle of teeth, and there, in some random spot, a mouth, a gash that puffed labored breaths with a birdlike whistle.

Faddon's shadow moved in front of the light source, blotting out Nance. He'd insisted his orphans were angels, but here in the cemetery, his shadow only shrugged.

"Dr. Nance still plays a vital role. She's the alpha tester of every serum I make. Yes, she's being punished, but honestly, I couldn't do this work without her."

Liv ran. She booted a grave marker, and the pain in her toe was explosive, but she didn't stop, shoving Faddon, taking no ownership of Mist as one of its blades sank into the doctor's shoulder. Faddon yelped and fell against a wall, taking Mist with him. He grappled for Liv as he fell, but she ripped away, snapping the cord on the smiley face mask. For a second, she saw Faddon's face, a soft, revoltingly ordinary face, and then he was twisting in pain, clamping a hand to a wound that had begun to well blood.

Liv turned and shouted. "Run! All of you! He's hurt! Get out! Get out now! Go!"

She leaped to the next room, heart at triple time, and kicked the door.

"Get out! Get out!"

At the next room she shook the post of a bunk bed.

"Go! Go! Go!"

Room to room she ran, shouting until her voice broke. Most men remained in place. But a few, steeled criminals not fully bent into subservient beings, took heed. Liv felt the motion of warm bodies like circulating blood. She flapped her arms, herding them, and heard the scrunch of their bodies colliding near the kitchen, the moans from their gnarled palates, the uncertain thuds of legs no longer built to scale the rungs of a ladder.

"Olivia?"

Liv turned, and in the backlight of the operating room saw Faddon, his smiley face askew, coming down the hall, trailing blood. Liv, her nerves on fire, suffered seconds of struggle. Should she help him? No, he was a surgeon, Dr. Frankenstein, and would sew himself back together. A more critical thought: Should she go back and help Dr. Nance the only way she knew how, by finding Mist and driving its blade into the boneless lard of her body, over and over, until she was finally dead? The decision was made for her: After what Faddon said next, she ran and didn't look back.

"Bring back your father?" he begged. "I miss him so much. And you can join us, too, Olivia. You can be one of us, too!"

31.

THE SKY WAS MOLTEN METAL THAT DUSK was cooling to embers. Still, it was real light from a real sun, and Liv found herself blinded upon passing through the silo's hatch. Her knee rammed the metal lip, and she fell to the dirt, her broken toe shooting pain up her calf, her palms skidding across gravel. She rolled onto her back and held her hands above her. They bled, but they were *hands*, human hands, with smooth skin and five fingers, and she wanted to kiss them and taste the clean, untainted blood.

She gripped a rung on the outside of the silo and hauled herself up. She thought she heard a buzzing from below, and her heart punched. What if Faddon had hit a fail-safe button that would rouse the military to belatedly mop up the mess of the Biatalik Program? *Hurry*, she told herself. She took a step. Her foot flared in agony. She gasped and sobbed. She thought of the cross-country meets, the long jogs up to the Dawkins place, the endless miles she'd run for no good reason when now, *right now*, was the only run that ever mattered. *Run*, she ordered herself. *Run!*

She did. The pain came in rapid, hot blasts, like the bang-snaps Doug tossed in for free with firework orders. She pushed herself across the lawn and into the front yard, where she collapsed against the car's still-warm hood. From there, gasping, she saw lonely, lumbering forms, just three of them, visible against the vast cavity of Black Glade. These were the only three brave enough to escape Biatalik, beings who'd known flat floors for so long they pitched and heaved on outdoor surfaces. One moved in a sideways skitter. Was he the one with multiple legs? One pulled himself along, branch to branch, with gibbon arms. Did he have any legs at all? Still another crawled on his belly, his serpentine spine cresting from and diving into dead grasses.

She felt nauseated, grappled at the station wagon door, and dropped down inside. What if Faddon had been right? The Biatalik prisoners seemed to have deduced their only real option, the same one taken by Frankenstein's monster: dissolve into the woods and become Black Glade myth that would plague generations of children to come.

Carbajal's jeer crackled from the dead car radio.

You think you know what's best, do you?

Carbajal was correct, and with the subtlety of a swinging scythe. She *hadn't* risked everything to save A when A was just some creature from a distant place. She was no better than any other torturer who followed Doug's *Army Field Manual 2-22.3*, people who chose, with self-serving brutality, who deserved to be treated with humanity and who didn't.

Liv cranked the ignition to cover the journalist's cackle and shifted to reverse. She might have had trouble getting here, but she knew just how to get to Doug's house; the whole world tipped that way— you only had to let the decline pull you. Dragons of dust spread their wings behind her. Fifteen minutes later, she was seeing the landmarks that hadn't changed over the three years since she'd been there. The empty, baleful piggery building. The abandoned church over which graduating classes spray-painted their years. The dirt strip that led to Doug's home.

Trees here were a dying species, weeds their conquerors. Even in the early twilight she could see the oily black half acre into which Doug had said he'd shot a flare before having to call the fire department. The damage was worse than he'd suggested. His damage usually was. She pulled into his driveway and stood there in the stillness.

The fireworks garage had fallen prey to an explosives malfunction Doug had never mentioned. The roof was an improvised patchwork of plywood. Doug's car was gone, which meant there was no point in going inside. There would be no Doug, no A, nothing. The only proof he'd been here over the previous months was half of a Ping-Pong table that he'd set up against the wall to play by himself. Rain had softened and scrunched the table into an arachnid fist of metal.

Liv got back into the station wagon and sat there, engine idling, watching new dragons grow in the taillight crimson. She thought of the Biatalik runaways. If they were found, they'd be shoved into cells, the same kind that Doug had wanted to create for Subject A, Subject B, and so on, sketched alongside Lee's *Resurrection Update* margin notes. When Liv recalled those sketches now, she connected them to stickler eraser burns and revision lines of Doug's corn maze designs. She might have even thought of it herself, the secret of where Doug was hiding, if her phone hadn't vibrated right then.

It was Doug.

Ready for you at the Monk Block.

Liv stomped the gas and shouted to the pain of her broken toe.

Many years had passed since she'd been to the Monk Block. Prior to Mr. Monk's renting the fifteen acres to farmers, he'd occasionally truck the two kids there to play amid the expanse of cool, green, uninterrupted grass. The memories were crackling live wires, severed like their friendship but popping and hot. Liv followed the soot smell, the station wagon's steering wheel nudging her into every correct turn, the headlights switching on by themselves as darkness fell. These supernaturalities had to be real; she had no more control of her body.

She turned onto a measly dirt path. Corn encroached from fields on either side, long, dry leaf tongues lapping the car windows. Thirty yards down, a padlocked gate bolted to two posts impeded further progress. The gate hadn't been there when Liv and Doug were kids. Had gates even existed back then, before so many of the world's dangers had thickened? Liv's throbbing foot held the brake to the floor. She could hit the gas, try to bust through. She could put the station wagon into reverse, creep out of there, get on with her life.

Instead, she turned off the engine, turned on the red hazard lights, and took out her phone. There were so many people she could call for help: Mom, the police, Principal Gamble, anyone. What she saw, however, was a message from Bruno from earlier, a patient red dot waiting to be noticed. Yes, it was Bruno she wanted to speak to, no one else. She didn't listen to his message; she tapped his number. His voice mail picked up.

"It's me." Her voice was brittle in the quiet car. "I . . . I wanted to tell someone . . . to tell you that I'm . . . I've gone to find Doug. There's this farm, this land his dad owns, and I think he's . . . I have to leave the car. I don't want to do it alone, but . . . Bruno, I don't know what's going to happen. After this, I mean. Maybe nothing. Maybe I'll be there tomorrow. If I am, I want to talk to you. I want to kiss you. But if I'm not . . . I just want . . . The time I had with you . . . I'll miss you. I guess that's what I want to say. If things go . . . if you don't get to talk to me again . . . I'll miss you."

She gasped, the sound startling her, and stabbed at the phone until the call ended and she could snuff the screen's hopeful light inside her coat pocket. Bruno, her mom, her own future—none of it could be allowed to matter right now. Her father's suffering was all she could allow herself to think about.

Getting out of the car was like slipping into cold water. With the headlights killed, velvet blackness met the blinking red lights, and she had to stand with her hands on the gate until her night eyes awoke. Liv peered over the gate, listening for the pulse of her own heart like her father listened for the pulse of an electric fence.

"Doug?" she called. "It's Dad! It's Lee! A is Lee! Doug?"

Nothing. She limped along the path for a minute before seeing, rising through the mud of night, a long-held vision turned real: the Monk Block Corn Maze. Whereas the corn glowed with a coat of moonlight, the maze entry dove to black. Liv squinted and made out the first left turn. Her stomach cooked in its acids. The opening left turn had always been a part of Doug's Trick. To kick off the labyrinth with compulsory turns was to make clear to walkers that they were being *led*, and had, in fact, little choice in how their journey would end.

Liv stood on her toes, the injured one flaring, and stretched her neck. There was no telling how far Doug had gone. He'd had four whole days, enough time to do all the things he'd long talked about doing, provided he could scrounge up the money: scan his best design into a web program, acquire a GPS device, rent a zero-turn mower. Liv felt a wave of awe, followed by a shiver of doubt about everything she believed. Lee Fleming had encouraged Doug's creativity, lauded his designs when everyone else had scoffed. Doug had finally paid back that confidence. Was it one life saved for one lost?

"Doug?" Her throat was a clogged rasp. She cleared it. *"Doug."*

She stepped close enough to the maze entrance that a corn leaf lazed outward and traced her throat, sharp as a knife. She didn't want to enter. She looked about, hoping for a reason to delay, and found one. Twenty yards to her left stood a modest aluminum outbuilding, probably erected by a farmer to house gear he didn't want pinched. Call it whatever the farmer liked; it was a shed, and Liv wondered if it might be that simple, that Doug had transferred her father from one shed to another.

She worked her way around the outbuilding's side, found the door, and noted both its lack of lock and the dented jamb that suggested the lock had been clobbered. The door squeaked open. The contents were pedestrian. A wheelbarrow piled with work gloves, hand cultivators, and seed bags. A tractor tire cradling a carton of dust masks. A twiggy tangle of hoes, rakes, shovels, spades, and picks. There was no space for hiding anything. Liv was both crestfallen and relieved; she felt cornered and wanted out.

One step backward was as far as she got. There *was* something in here: a scent. She inhaled. Under the peaty odor of dirt and the sneezy tickle of pesticide squirmed sourer smells. Doug's unwashed hair, sweaty clothes, stale gorp. Much stronger, A's smell. Liv took her phone from her pocket and turned on the flashlight.

Liv swung the light from side to side. Shadows lurched, and details particularized. Over the wheelbarrow ran a shelf stretching wall to wall. Like the shelf in Faddon's kitchen, this too was covered with small items. It was the neatness of these items that leaped out. Jars and bottles, clean and free of dust, each placed an equal space from the last like teeth in a jaw.

Liv came closer. The white light gleamed from glass too brightly for her to see anything, so she moved it to a more oblique angle. With a trembling hand, she picked up a mason jar. She brought it close, rotating it for the best angle. The contents looked limp and soft. For a moment she held out hope that the jars contained nothing worse than canned foods.

It was an eyeball. A's eyeball, her dad's eyeball. It was bloated, double its usual size. Liv recalled the eye's perpetual nervous twitch, the strongest sign of Lee Fleming's stubborn life. More than revulsion, Liv felt a bruising grief. The bottom of the eyeball was flat, having conformed to the jar's shape. The sky-blue iris had gone a coin gray. It stared at nothing.

Somehow Liv put it back without dropping it. She swung the light over the shelf, and now that she knew the morbid context, a glance was all that was required to identify other artifacts. A bottle containing one of her father's fingers in some kind of oil. A section of plywood upon which had been tacked dozens of multicolored tumors. A padded case that had once held an engraved pen but now held Lee's short, bony tail.

The other jars, who knew? It all blacked out as Liv staggered away. Like Lee Fleming's Armory, this was no mere shed. This was a sideshow to the main attraction, an in-progress museum waiting for description cards. Even after degradation in front of classmates, Doug still insisted on being a showman. Ages ago he'd angered her by saying that if she didn't want to work the maze, she could run the adjacent barn. Usually owners sold cider and corndogs, he'd said.

Sometimes they turned it into a haunted house, he'd said.

From outside the building came a roar, loud as a passing jet. The world lit up. Liv threw herself against a wall, cowering, suddenly knowing that, one way or the other, this was the end, the end of all of it. She opened her eyes a slit and found that she'd collapsed into the cluster of farm tools. She took hold of the pointiest thing she saw—a pitchfork—and exited, grimacing against deafening concussion blasts and squinting into blinding starbursts of lights.

32.

ONCE UPON A TIME, LIV KNEW WHICH
names went with which fireworks. Chrysanthemums, peonies, girandolas, willows, flying fish. All she knew about this one was that it was
the size of a planet, exploding into dozens of whistling pink streaks.
The cornfield went purple, an alien landscape, and Liv wished for
it to be true, that she'd been abducted to the place her father had
believed he'd gone, and from there watched the distant earth, that
tight fist of misery, finally detonate.

Before the wiggling trails dissipated, a fresh round of crackling
began, and sparks plumed from a spot maybe fifty yards into the
maze. It thickened into a fountain of liquid fire, higher and higher, as
green and red gusts of smoke billowed. This one was easy, a Roman
candle, or more likely, a ream of Roman candles. *I'm here*, it said in
its bang language. *Come and find me.* She angled toward the mouth
of the maze, tripping and catching herself three times, unable to take

her eyes from the soaring, sparkling spout. The corn was as dry as kindling. There would be a fire. The whole field would go up. What was Doug thinking?

Liv hesitated at the maze's opening. Mazes had brought her here. The improbable twists of her long relationship with Doug, the inconceivable turns of rogue science. The corn on either side of the entrance bloomed with phosphorescent color. She trembled; the pitchfork slipped inches in her grip. Not once had she been able to successfully trace her finger through Doug's Trick.

She forced herself to think of the Biatalik giant paused at the fringe of Black Glade. He'd had more to fear than she did. Liv looked down, saw Roman candle sparks reflected in the glass of her father's wrist compass. Captured there, the sparks were so small. All her fears, she told herself, could be that small. His compass told her what it had always told him: The quickest way between two points was a straight line.

Liv charged down the mown path, and when she hit the left turn she did not turn. This was corn, not electrified fencing. She hurtled through a patch before bursting into a mown junction that she also ignored, keeping a compass trajectory toward the towering sparks. The maze seemed to come alive at her rejection of its rules. Thatches of ragweed cinched around her ankles. Corn leaves sliced thin cuts into her hands, neck, and forehead. With the pitchfork she batted away the worst of the stalks, which popped like her father's bones when hit with a baton.

"It's Dad!" she cried, though it was lost in the fireworks' crackle. "It's Dad, it's Dad, it's Dad!"

The size of the central clearing was so big that Liv, expecting more corn soldiers, careened ten feet into it before falling. Keeping both hands on the pitchfork, she hit the dirt hard, her shoulder bursting with pain. She rolled, bringing herself to an elbow, and there he was, Doug Monk, facing away from her, squatting in his army-green shorts, holding a butane lighter to the end of a long wick. It took, and Doug scuttled back to watch it burn. Liv squinted in the strobing light. It looked as if this batch of Roman candles was wired to another, then another, a chain of fireworks intended to keep going for thirty minutes, an hour, even longer.

Doug jumped back from the new flume, his feet knocking over his school backpack. He looked feral, his clothes filthy, his face smudged in mud, shreds of corn caught in his hair. But he looked happy, Liv thought, content at what he'd built and orchestrated. His smiling face oscillated to watch hundreds of sparks fall harmlessly to the dirt he'd cleared, and that's how he caught a glimpse of the one element he hadn't planned for, at least not this soon.

He turned so fast that he tripped. Gorp spilled from his pocket.

"What are you doing here?" he demanded.

Next to the candle's percussive reports and the ringing of Liv's ears, he sounded distant and muted. His face squashed into bewilderment, or rage, and this time he belted it.

"What are you doing *there*?"

Liv tried to push herself upward, but her shoulder, her palms, her toe, everything hurt, and she fell flat. Doug showed no sign of concern. He shook his head, his greasy hair twisted like more wicks ready to be lit. He was gesturing wildly.

"Didn't you see the entrance? I set it up so you wouldn't miss it! I lit the fireworks to guide you!"

"Where is he?" Liv panted.

Doug looked aggrieved. "A? I told you I'd take care of it."

"That shed over there. I saw what you did."

"What *I* did?" Doug rubbed his weary-looking face with both hands, his sweat turning dirt into mud. "You started it. The first night, remember? I'm just finishing because you don't have the balls. You literally don't have them." He studied the stalks she'd broken, turquoise now in the fireworks' light. "I'm going to have to repair all that. Do you know how long this took me?"

"Doug, listen to me." Liv struggled to her knees. "Did you hear what I was yelling?"

"We can repair it together. I'm sorry I yelled."

"*Doug!* You need to *listen*!"

He frowned, pooching his bottom lip like a grouchy toddler. His eyes crept off across black dirt, reaching the second bundle of Roman candles as the nucleus flickered to life. He smiled, watching the sparks chisel through gathered smoke, but the smile faltered. When he spoke, Liv could barely hear over the erupting booms.

"I've been thinking it over, the whole thing. Building this stuff was harder than I thought. All the turns, the circles—the Trick? It's easy to get lost in it. Real easy. You can make yourself think you're going one way when really you're going the other. Last night, I got lost inside it all night. Felt like a month. Felt like my whole life."

He *had* been lost, for a long, long time, and Liv might have been able to show him a shortcut out if only she, too, hadn't been lost for so long beside him. None of this should have been her responsibility. There should have been someone else to help. She thought of her stop at the Monk house. Mr. Monk was no father of the year, but Liv couldn't believe he'd let the property slide as far into ruin as it had. Especially the collapsed roof of the fireworks garage atop the most valuable goods the family owned. That collapse seemed to symbolize so much.

The Roman candles sputtered, dunking Doug's face into shadow. Liv, still clutching the pitchfork, used her thighs, still strong from years of training, to piston herself to a standing position. The wick on the third cluster of Roman candles crackled and glared like a cigarette, and when the first shots fired, dousing the clearing in yellow light, Doug smiled again, until he turned to find Liv upright, wielding the pitchfork. His smile dropped like the sparks.

"You're not right," Liv said. "You're all screwed up. Now listen to me."

Doug's head grew too heavy for his neck; he stared at the ground. It was the same pose Liv had seen him adopt all of his life when facing those who only saw in him the deviant he seemed fated to become. He made a vague, rolling gesture, a sad amalgam of nod and shrug. Then, a single chuckle—a firecracker pop of self-loathing.

"Guess it's no big surprise," he said. "Guards at military prisons get mixed up all the time. Turn as extreme as the extremists. Then they ship home and everyone calls them psychos. But it's not their fault, you know? They got caught in the Trick, too, and can't remember the way out. It's all there in those files you never read."

Liv didn't dare feel sympathy, not this late. "Tell me where he is. I'll tear this whole field apart, Doug—I swear I will."

Doug's eyes shone. "We're all the alien to someone. That's all I mean."

"That's what I keep saying! Why won't you listen? A's not an alien!" Liv moaned. "He's my dad. He's Lee. Doug, *A is Lee*."

Doug lifted his face until it was again spangled by bursting color. "What?" he asked softly.

Liv panted, her face wild and open, begging him to understand. Colors radiated over his frozen face. Liv noted his spilled backpack, recognized the book jutting from it, and hurried to it. Tucking the pitchfork under her arm, she snatched up the book. The pages were bloated and stained, the cover snarled and smutched, but she almost sobbed, because it felt like her dad, the wrinkled cover the texture of his skin, the rain-softened pages one of his trademark cardigans.

Over two years since Lee had tried to make her accept his copy of *Resurrection Update*, she accepted it. The lighting was wild, kaleidoscopic, but intensely bright. She riffled through stiffened pages, squinting past Doug's marginalia to focus on Lee's annotations, written during his sickest period. Unlike his mind, Lee's handwriting was focused, the same block letters he'd used to pen encouragements on English papers. This, Liv thought, was why her dad had wanted her to have the book. The clarity of these poems had cut through his muddled mind, and only here, in these pages, had he been sane.

This wasn't a book by James Galvin. It was a diary by Lee Fleming.

He'd explained all of this to Liv years ago. *Poetry*, he'd insisted, *is full of secrets*. And here were his.

Page 20: "The sky was an occasion / I would never rise to. I had my doubts," Galvin wrote, to which Lee had added, *Doubting my* memory—doubting the sky—was it a ship? Was it really? Page 42: "This is for the night your body was neither here nor there," footnote, *I fear I've been here all along. What if it's all a mistake?* Page 209: "Dogs howled in pain from a lethal frequency," footnote, *There were other abductees. Other patients?* Page 255: "I saw / a drop of blood at the center of everything," footnote, *YES: blood, there were needles, was I in some sort of hospital?* Page 252: "The little people behind the scenes are getting ugly," footnote, *Doctors—they were doctors— WAS I REALLY ABDUCTED???* Page 242: "A broken window hangs around my neck," footnote, *Cancer? Do I have cancer? Is that why I was there?* Page 101: "I wanted to tell you, the girl," footnote, *How can I make this right to Aggie?* Page 123: "You were a perfect stranger, Father," footnote, *How can I make this right to Olivia?* Page 150: "Real events don't have endings, / Only the stories about them do," footnote, *FIND THE PLACE, GO BACK, DO IT FOR THEM.*

The italics, in other words, were his. All the things Liv had learned from Carbajal and Faddon, Lee had already figured out, until he closed the book and the truth got jumbled again, though not jumbled enough that he couldn't lead his hunt right back to Biatalik's front door. His parting words to Liv ached with an apology he'd only half understood: *You have to let me go. I have unfinished business.* So he'd gone back, to save his loved ones the grief of his slow demise, or, just maybe, be cured by Faddon's miracles.

These events, laid bare, sickened Liv. This father she'd adored had made what could only be viewed as a series of horrible choices. He'd taken Major Dawkins's earnest invitation to reverse his cancer with an experimental procedure out of his family's view, but the hole he'd left in Liv and Aggie's life had been worse than cancer—the tumors of losing him had practically killed them. And then, after all that, Lee had crawled back home? Exposing Biatalik might have been his noble cause, but Liv would never know. She'd never, ever know, and knowing *that* felt like being staked to the ground, forever caught.

Liv let the book fall shut. She looked up at Doug. The fuse was between batches of Roman candles, but she could see his fluttering hair.

"That's impossible," he said. "Stop lying!"

The firework erupted, gushing into the sky. It felt as though it had fired inside her; she shot upward, the book tumbling away, the pitchfork rising, the pink and blue smoke seeming to rise from the brain cooking inside her skull. There was no time for debate. She lurched with such speed that Doug stumbled back. Liv plunged through smoke and shouted at the shrinking stalks.

"*A! A!*" That was wrong, sick, irresponsible. "*DAD! DAD! WHERE ARE YOU?*"

There came a response, a rustling like corn leaves, but larger. Liv rushed past Doug, ducking as individual sparks cavorted along the pitchfork's tines. A nebulous shape rested twenty feet away, in the center of the single mown path to the clearing. It was the size of a person, and as she barreled closer, Liv recognized the blue tarp, that fucking blue tarp, bound around a body with loops of duct tape.

"It was supposed to be the end of the Trick!" Doug's voice cried from a forgotten world. "If you'd done the maze right, it would've been your reward!"

Liv reached the bound body and stared down in paralyzed horror.

The tape was tight, but her father was alive under there, bucking to get out, a fish tossed to dry land. The tarp had started to tear, and Liv could see a dagger of pale flesh, some part of him that Doug had yet to harvest and catalogue in his jars.

Liv's knees tremored, ready to drop to a kneel so she could start ripping the tarp, but she locked those knees back into place. There was no sense to any of it. Unwrap him, and then what? Look upon his dying body while his surviving eye took in the sight of the daughter who'd turned against him? Convince herself that doctors could save him? She knew him too well to think he'd want any of that. The true mercy here was to do what Doug hadn't and release him from everything. It was a mercy he'd been owed since A's advent, and the dreadful burden of it gathered over Liv like wet cement.

Do it now, before losing the nerve, before Doug intervened. She throttled the pitchfork and lifted it with both hands. She couldn't breathe. She couldn't cry. But she groaned, a eulogy for the kind of person she'd never be again, not after this. She felt a spark land on her back, sharp as a cutlass pushing her toward plank's end.

"No!" Doug cried. "You're wrong! Don't do it!"

"I'm sorry, Daddy," Liv gasped. "I'm so sorry."

She drove down the pitchfork. A split second, but it felt like a long journey of winding turns, endless, minuscule decisions of angle and force. None of it worked well. The pitchfork was poorly directed, and the thrust hiccuped with hesitation. But it was four sharp points versus a thin sheet of plastic and soft flesh. It was enough, and she felt in her shoulders the quake of metal against bone, the spasm of shocked muscles tightening around invading spikes. Liv let go of the handle, and the pitchfork stood upright until the body jerked and the tool toppled to the dirt.

Doug's voice was hoarse.

"You weren't supposed to do that! What did you do?"

The body convulsed once more, then was still. Liv took a step away. Then another. Another. She glimpsed Doug clutching his head between his hands, still shouting, the main attraction of his future sideshow gone for good. Liv's hands were numb, making it difficult to take out her phone. She toggled to the dial. Her wobbly finger, though, could not manage 911. She took a breath, swiped to Recents, and brought her thumb down on Bruno's name. This was easier. She would tell him exactly where she was. He'd call the cops, the hospital, the fire department. He, not Doug, would take care of everything.

She heard Bruno's phone ring through her speaker.

She also heard his ring tone right there in the clearing, a few feet away.

Liv's eyes rolled upward.

Beneath the translucent blue tarp, a soft glow. A phone receiving her call.

"Oh," she said. "Oh no."

33.

THE CALL ENDED, WENT TO VOICE MAIL.
Liv's finger slipped down the touchscreen, ended the call, then slipped more, and Bruno's message, time-stamped yesterday, began to play. *It's Bruno*, he said, without his usual verve, though his voice, as ever, was a dozen nuances of tone and spirit. *I know you don't want to talk, and that's fine, but maybe you'll listen. I just ran into Doug. Well, he hasn't seen me yet, but I'm looking right him. He's at Wilson Hardware. I heard about his thing at your place, and that must be why . . . why you're feeling however you're feeling. So I'm going to talk to him. If you're not going to tell me what's up, maybe he will. I just wanted you to know I'm doing this. I'm not trying to be sneaky or anything. I just miss you.*

Somehow she had arrived back at the tarp. She was staring straight down at it. Blood oozed from four equidistant punctures. This time she surrendered to tremoring knees, dropped down, took hold of the edge of the tarp, and pulled. The tape held firm. She picked up the pitchfork, feeling a slop of warm blood, and used a tine to pick at the tape. It ripped, and a section of tarp peeled free, and there he was, her beautiful boy.

All the facts from their first-day-of-school get-to-know-you floated back to Liv like petals. Bruno Mayorga, age seventeen, from Nuevo León, into drama, chorus, and tennis, brother to Mia, Elena, and Bianca, so kind and sexy and happy.

"He's the reason you left me," Doug said, but it sounded questioning, as if his original motive had broken its zip ties and dragged itself away.

Liv's eyes crawled down the side of Bruno's face, across tilled dirt, up the muddied hair of Doug's legs.

"I made this—" Doug stopped short, then blundered ahead. "Because I love you. Lee, too. I love both of you. So much, Liv, so much. I didn't mean for Bruno to be—he just came up to me and I—I convinced him to come out—but Liv, just look *around*. There's so much *land* here. No one has to know. Half of this is yours. I'm *giving* it to you. Why don't you run it with me? Can't you even consider it? Can't you take just one minute and consider it?"

Liv felt his warm hands settle onto her shaking shoulders. Some dumb thing he'd probably seen in a movie, a virile man comforting an emotional woman. Liv's brain whirled back to their conversation under the stars, all that shit he'd said about pretending to be girlfriend-boyfriend. Perhaps the arrangement had been real for him all this time.

Rage poured from Liv, out of her mouth, nose, eyes, pores. She took the pitchfork in both hands, twisted around, and leaped.

The handle struck Doug on the nose, and he fell back, hands clutching his face. Liv dashed through the dirt like a released hound and threw herself on top of him, thrusting the handle. Doug raised both hands to stop it, and Liv saw blood spurt from a gash in his lip and wash over his teeth, turning them pink. It was nothing at all compared to what they'd done to her dad, and she shoved her weight behind the handle, pounding it against his mouth a second time.

It was the least advantageous method of attack she could have attempted. Her body on top of his was no heavier than Jackson Stegmaier's on the first day of school, and Doug, his arm muscles ballooning, bench-pressed her just as easily. The pitchfork handle rammed her ribs, and she felt herself being lifted. She fought back with her legs, but it was no good; Doug flipped her onto her back and she rolled, her broken toe and bruised shoulder electric with pain, and when she opened her eyes, she saw a rain of sparks coming straight at her. She was too close to the Roman candles and tried to push herself away, but Doug fell over her like a tree, blocking out the fireworks, the pitchfork his now and shoved into her chest.

Tears dripped from Doug's red eyes into her own. Veins puffed from his forehead as he pushed the handle harder. Liv gripped it, too, but her arms had no leverage, and the handle pressed against her throat. Doug clenched his bloody teeth and screamed as rockets of colored smoke churned above him.

"I LOVE YOU! I LOVE YOU! I LOVE YOU!"

The vibrant fireworks were engulfed by black bursts of oblivion. Doug's sobbing face went dim. Liv's hands slipped from the pitchfork, and the handle sank like a rolling pin into dough, and she felt bisected, her throat collapsed, and she was dead, she was sure of it, a kernel lost in the corn.

The pressure was relieved. Moments had gone missing. Her torso was torqued, her nose flat to the dirt, her back heaving with needling inhales. She gasped and vomited. Her throat seared with acid blood. She remembered Doug, his weight and heat. Liv turned to her side, her neck throttled with asphyxiating agony. Blotches of red obscured her vision, but there was Doug, a few feet away, still holding the pitchfork, brilliant purple sparks caroming off his shoulders.

He was gaping up at a figure standing beside him.

There came the blur of a swung arm. A thick gray object connected with the side of Doug's head. Liv saw a lattice of blood spurt from Doug's ear, made orange by the fireworks. He cried out and capsized, then writhed his body toward the corn. Liv made an inadvertent noise that filled her mouth with blood, and she spat, and choked, and kicked herself farther away to get a better look.

Looming over Doug were the ravaged remains of Lee Fleming, a demon dragged from hell and fire-lit with red smoke. Never had Liv seen him, in skinner form, manage a single step unaided, but now he moved of his own power, scuffling after the crawling Doug. The initial wound from Amputator had never healed, and the bone showing through frayed ankle skin was bowed, either from a torment of Doug's or from the simple stress of walking, as he'd apparently done, through the maze until he'd won out over the Trick.

The biggest alteration to Lee was not the missing tail, or the missing right eye, or anything else she'd witnessed in the outbuilding's display. It was the missing half of his left arm, and this time it hadn't been Doug who'd done the severing. Part of a zip tie was caught on the splintered bone, draped with strings of lacerated flesh. To escape from wherever Doug had tied him, perhaps spurred by the cries of his daughter, he must have chewed his arm off, like animals caught in the backyard traps had so often tried to do.

In his right hand Lee carried a weapon. Not Lizardpoint—it was on a tchotchke shelf in Faddon's kitchen. Not Mist—it was last seen stabbed into Faddon's shoulder. What dangled from Lee's hand, cutting a trench through the dirt, was Maquahuitl.

Lee pursued Doug with tightrope caution. Doug, clutching his pulverized ear, stopped trying to outpace him. Lee's three-toed feet came to rest next to Doug, nearly stomping his beloved copy of *Resurrection Update*. Lee's left eye bulged from its socket, skittering over the long-lost treasure. Doug, too, blinked at the book before staring up at Lee in defenseless awe.

Tears ran down Doug's cheeks. "Lee . . . is that really . . ."

Lee rocked back, Maquahuitl building momentum in larger arcs. Lee's ankle bone popped with the trauma of so radical a motion, and his dry underarm webbing, once a glistening film, ripped down the center. Lee, though, seemed to be beyond pain. Maquahuitl swooped, a playground swing at its highest crescent. All he had to do was step sideways to deliver a killing blow to the boy he'd caught strangling his girl. Just as likely, all Doug had to do was lean his head into Maquahuitl's path to erase all guilt and shame.

"I didn't know," Doug sobbed. "Oh, Lee. You told us, you *said*, you said if something happened to you, we'd have to . . . What did I do? What did I . . . oh god, Lee, *I didn't know!*"

Doug chose a third option, if choice was a thing over which he had any more control. He burst from his crouched position so fast that he accidentally struck Lee with his shoulder. Doug rebounded and tore off in a mindless rightward curve. He ran like the blood from his ear had flowed into his eyes, and Liv saw, before it happened, that he was headed for the active cluster of Roman candles. He legs struck first, and he bent in half, his upper body dipping into the inferno. He wailed and twirled out the other side, his shabby jacket blooming with fire. He flapped and kicked, tipping the bundle of fireworks, which began pouring hot sparks directly into the corn. The conflagration was instant: Twenty feet of dead crop combusted with a sound like torn fabric.

The destruction dug a second path from the clearing, and Doug, as if beguiled by this radical method of maze making, wandered into it, a human fireball, another flare shot into the field. Liv wondered if his thoughts, in these crazed seconds, mirrored hers: When wounds of sadness, loneliness, and anger healed poorly, any atrocity was possible. Liv's last sight of her oldest friend was his white-hot shape gazing in wonder at the apocalypse he'd created before he stepped out of view, trailblazing his final path, their conspiracy broken at last.

Liv shielded her eyes. The fireworks were finished now, but the fire was only starting. She looked for her father, identified his shape where he'd fallen. She tried to stand, but her throat was swollen, she could barely breathe so she crawled on all fours, slowly. The thirty seconds it took to reach him exhausted her; she collapsed next to him, draping her arms over his body the same as she'd done in her bed.

Maquahuitl had driven several ribs into his heart. His every smallest muscle twitched. His single eye rotated, sheening with firelight, until it settled, jittery no longer, upon Liv. She curled her arms around his skinny chest and nestled her head into his frail neck. Daddy, this was Daddy, and *she* was the biologic evidence that he had existed.

She kissed his damp, sticky head and cried, her tears slicing clean lines through his dirty skin. He trembled, and one of his thick fingers grazed the wrist compass. His tongueless mouth gummed but made no sound. Because he couldn't speak, Liv felt she must, but had no words worthy of the moment. She made herself recall the last thing he'd said to her, his favorite Galvin quote, and now, since she was the one saying goodbye, she repeated it.

"'Perhaps you didn't realize / Anything can happen under a sky like this.'"

In the middle of the state he loved, next to the book he adored, alongside the child he would have done anything not to hurt, Lee Fleming died. His body, every infinitesimal flutter, quit at once, and there was a slight sinking like a sedative had taken effect. It was a surprise to Liv how swiftly his body, even in proximity to such a fire, grew colder.

She thought she might stay by his side all night. That's what she wanted, but a twinkle of rationality survived in her skull—flames would soon surround her. Achingly slow, with a body halfway broken, Liv brought herself to her feet, took her father by the thin wrist, and dragged him toward the whipping flames until the exhalations of heat grew too intense. She knew what to do next. Get down on her stomach. Use her feet to push the body into the first row of smoldering stalks. Her father would catch fire and incinerate, and from his ashes people of science would learn nothing at all.

But she didn't. She stood there, staring into the storm of swirling ash. Doug had made this clearing plenty wide, and dirt didn't burn. The Biatalik prisoners, if they were careful, might evade eyes in the Black Glade's caliginous thickness, but Lee's body should be found when authorities came to clean up the mess. It would serve as testimony, against her and Doug, yes, but also against everyone who'd thought they could do whatever they wanted, no matter how awful, without moral rebuke.

The Mayorgas, though, deserved none of the poison they'd absorb from Bruno's involvement. Liv's throat had loosened enough to claim sufficient, if agonizing, gulps of air. Recoiling from hot gusts, she crossed the clearing and hunkered next to Bruno's body. His face was still perfect, carrying the same slight smile he'd had when they'd lain together in the costume room. Even his hair, his pride and joy, wasn't too badly mussed. Liv took out her phone for the third time that night. Her hands were slick with sweat, and the phone slipped to the ground. That was good; the ground held it steadier than she'd be able to. She extended a finger and touched the digits *9, 1, 1,* each press pushing the phone farther into the dirt.

She heard a tinny voice answer, no doubt asking after the nature of her emergency, but Liv didn't pick it up. She was busy picking up Bruno. With one arm under his neck and another under his knees, she lifted. Her legs shook with effort. She didn't think she could do it. But bravery, she realized, existed all around her. She only had to open her eyes against the stinging firelight to see it. The bravery of the Biatalik mutants, leaving their prison. The bravery of Carbajal, sacrificing everything to the truth. The bravery of her mother, despite her frailties, working to right the sinking ship of their life. And her dad's bravery, most of all, in the final moments of a life marked by unimaginable terror.

Liv shouted at the phone the pertinent details of the Monk Block, though she had no idea if the operator could hear. Leaving behind the operator's pipsqueak pleas, she tromped into the corn, over the same stalks she'd bashed down when arriving. The fire hadn't gotten there yet, and the paths Doug had mowed were forcing the blaze to find creative ways to leap the gulfs. Liv pictured her compass and walked, Bruno not so heavy after all, and this time the ragweed didn't snatch, the corn didn't slash. Instead the plants seemed to part before her, bowing in deference.

She emerged from the maze entrance. The outbuilding, she noted, sat on dry, yellow grass and already the blaze was curling in that direction, as if sentient enough to go after evidence. There was nothing Liv could do; Lee's corpse, she had to believe, would survive. She hitched up Bruno and directed her wobbling body to be the tallest it could and keep going. She collided with the grille of the station wagon, which sprang whole from its hiding spot in the smoke. She opened the driver's door and managed to turn on the headlights, until the calculus of getting Bruno's body inside the car became too much. Her legs trembled, her spine wavered, and she lost her footing in the dirt. When she fell, right behind the car, she made sure that it was her knees and elbows that took the damage.

The hazard lights turned everything red. The alien planet—she could imagine she'd reached it after all. On this planet, the air was red and smoky, and death was only a dream. She pulled at the tarp, yanking, even biting, and after a time made progress, peeling it like the skinner skin of Lee Fleming's flawed memory. Bruno was unbound, and she ran her hands over his red clothes and red skin and red blood. It was like he was made of wounds, but wasn't everyone? Maybe here, on this backward red planet, wounds only made you stronger.

Liv took her coat off and then her shirt, which she knotted around Bruno's wounds as tightly as she could. Then she rubbed her hands over his skin, trying to warm him, and when her arms couldn't move anymore, she used her entire body for the same purpose. The fire's roar made it difficult to hear, but she believed she detected sirens, and believed they were getting closer, though on this planet, there was no gauging distance, or time, or purpose, or intent. She ducked her head through red snow and pressed her lips to Bruno's red ear and whispered a word over and over, the only word she knew in this alien language, but a magical one, one given to her by her father, the only word she'd ever need.

"Live," she said.

"Live," she said.

"Live," she said.

Was it an echo or a gasp?

"Liv."

AUTHOR'S NOTE

On January 19, 2017, federal judges declassified excerpts from the Senate Intelligence Committee's 6,700-page report on the CIA's torture program. These excerpts described the recurrent use of such "enhanced" interrogation techniques as sleep deprivation, pharmaceutical injection, confinement in small boxes, and waterboarding, which, in the case of Abu Zubaydah, was inflicted eighty-three times in one month. The report concluded that these torture regimens did not elicit useful information and that some of the psychologists who designed them showed "blatant disregard for the ethics shared by almost all of their colleagues."

On June 2, 2017, the Trump administration ordered federal agencies to return all copies of the report to the Senate, making it highly unlikely that these copies would be made public and introducing the possibility that they would be destroyed.

ACKNOWLEDGMENTS

———

Thanks to Richard Abate, Adam Hickey, Amanda Kraus, Craig Ouellette, and Christian Trimmer.